When his head ducked  eyes deepen, darken.
Felt the sudden trembi
then his mouth dived .... on hers.

She tasted like warm, dark chocolate. Rich. Soft.
Meltable.

Nothing in the universe tasted exactly like chocolate.
Not good chocolate. Not really exquisite chocolate.

But she did. And no, it wasn't the Bliss she'd been
indulging in that put that "exquisite taste" idea in
his mind. It was her. Her mouth. Her taste. Her lips
molded under his, melted under his. She went still,
on the inside, on the outside.

And damn it. So did he.

JENNIFER GREENE

Blame
It on
Chocolate

HQN™

ISBN 0-373-77145-2

BLAME IT ON CHOCOLATE

Copyright © 2006 by Alison Hart

Recent books by Jennifer Greene

Lucky
Hot to the Touch
Wild in the Moment
Wild in the Moonlight
Wild in the Field

To incurable chocoholics everywhere.
Of all the vices worth enjoying, this one seems
awfully close to number one.

I gained ten pounds researching this book for you.
Taste-testing the best truffles on the planet
was hard work! But worth it.
Trust me on this....

Blame
It on
Chocolate

CHAPTER ONE

WHEN THE ALARM CLOCK BUZZED on Monday morning, Lucy Fitzhenry leaped out of bed. It was hell waiting for that alarm. She hated wasting time on sleep when her life was so brimming full. She wasn't just jazzed to start the day; she was kite-high and dancing-ready.

She made it three feet across the room before the nausea hit. One second she was fine, the next she was beyond miserable. Thankfully she made it into the bathroom before a major upchuck.

Afterward, she knelt on the cold tile with her elbow crooked on the toilet seat, too weak to get up—at least for another couple seconds—feeling infuriated in general.

She knew she was getting an ulcer. This was the third time in the last two weeks her stomach had done the revolt thing, and healthy twenty-eight-year-old women with cast-iron stomachs didn't hurl for no reason, so that had to be it. An ulcer. An ulcer caused by stress.

It was tough for a fussy perfectionist who'd always been big on responsibility and doing the right thing and making everyone happy to suddenly take on wickedness. She was trying. She was putting her whole heart into it. But it definitely wasn't coming naturally, so she had to struggle at it, and changing one's personality was unavoidably stressful.

Her stomach rolled one more time, but the ghastly part of the nausea seemed to have passed. She hoped. Slowly she pushed to her feet, opened the glass doors to the shower, and flicked on the faucets.

She'd had the clear glass shower doors put in last week. That, and her sleeping naked, were two visible signs that she was gaining on her wickedness goal. Another concrete measure of progress were the purple satin sheets on her bed. Temporarily she didn't have a guy to vent all this new wildness on, but one thing at a time. Her stomach needed to recover from all these personality upheavals before she gave it any more stress.

By the time she climbed out of the shower, she was not only feeling fine again, but picking up speed. She ran naked into the kitchen to pop a bagel in the toaster, then charged back to the bedroom to raid her closet. Since ninety percent of her wardrobe consisted of either designer Gap or designer Old Navy, the day's clothes decision was hardly tricky. She opted for Gap today. T-shirt. Sweatshirt. Jeans—not her favorite pair; they bagged a little in the butt, but she should have known better than to buy a size seven without trying them on; they were always a little big.

Back in the bathroom, she poked in her contacts, smacked on lip gloss, and ran a brush through her chin-length blond hair—her hair was so fine it was already nearly dry. Then she claimed the bagel and streaked for the front door…taking ecstatic, if hurried, pleasure in galloping over the white carpet. White. WHITE. White, thick, plush and totally impractical. The print over the fireplace of the eagle flying over silvery-green waters was another splurge—she fiercely, fiercely loved that picture. But both the print and the carpet were further proof that she was mastering the indulgent, impractical, wicked thing.

Of course, the carpet wasn't paid for. And neither was most everything else. But as of two months ago, she was no longer renting. The duplex had a mighty mortgage, but it was still hers-all hers. Possibly she was the latest bloomer of all late bloomers at twenty-eight, but what the hey. She'd had to fight harder than most for true independence, and for darn sure, she was grabbing life with both fists now.

At the front door, she yanked on the jacket her parents had given her for Christmas—a white Patagonia number that was crazily impractical considering her work, but unbeatably warm. And on the first of March in Minnesota, there was still a solid, crusty foot of snow on the ground, the temperature cold enough to make her eyes sting. She locked the door, still pulling on her white cap with the yellow yarn daisies. She'd have hat hair all day, but who cared? She'd look like a train wreck after the first hour of work anyway.

With the hot bagel crunched between her teeth, she slid into the driver's seat of her old red Civic, turned the key and begged it to start—which it did. The baby just liked to be coaxed on cold mornings. Praying for the Civic had become a second religion. The Civ had more than 200,000 miles on her. Lucy's newest theory was that if she gave the car enough wash-and-waxes and changed its oil long before it asked and vacuumed it twice a week, it'd be too happy to die. At least until she got the living room carpet and couch paid for.

In Rochester, where she'd grown up, people knew what rush hour was. Not here. Eagle Lake probably put up traffic lights out of pride, although some cars did show up to keep her company once she reached the highway. Originally she'd chosen Eagle because it was a nice, long drive from her parents—and also because there was already a solid nest of singles and other young couples in the area—but it was a good half-hour commute to her job. She finished the bagel, tuned the radio up for a kick-ass beat and was singing hell-bent for leather when her stomach suddenly produced an unladylike belch.

Not AGAIN. Yet the nausea came on like a battle-ship, heavy and ugly and overwhelming. Her skin turned damp and hot so fast she barely had time to pull over to the shoulder and brake. Hands shaking, flushed and hot, she leaned over the passenger side, argued with the door, thank God got it open, arched her head out...and then nothing.

The bagel stayed in. The bite of freezing wind on her cheeks seemed to help. Eventually she sank back against the headrest, feeling weak and yucky, cars speeding past her. The practical voice in her head ordered her to quit messing around and call the doctor, enough was enough with this nausea thing.

But her emotional side kept trying to figure out what she'd done to deserve this. Yeah, she was trying to be more wicked, but basically the sins on her conscience wouldn't fill a list. She'd skipped school once in kindergarten. She'd thought evil, evil thoughts about Aunt Miranda—but then, so did everyone else in the family. She'd gone to a party one time without underpants. She'd let Eugene hang on too long. She'd borrowed her sister Ginger's blue cashmere sweater in high school and got a spot on it and never 'fessed up. And yeah, there was that one other occasion.

She'd come to call that one other occasion the Night of the Chocolate.

But as quickly as that memory surfaced, she shuffled it, fast, into the part of her brain labeled Denial.

God—if there was a God, and she thought there was—just couldn't be paying her back for that one. She'd already suffered enough.

When it came down to it, she'd lived like a saint 99.99 percent of her life. She dusted under the refrigerator, never took a penny that wasn't hers, always flossed. Her family relentlessly teased her for becoming a fussy old lady before she was thirty—which really hurt her feelings.

The point, though, was that this stomach upset thing wasn't a sign that her life was about to spin completely out of control. It was just an ulcer or something like that. A something that a visit to the doctor—however inconvenient and annoying—would resolve once and for all.

And just like that, she felt better. Her hands stopped trembling and the weak feeling almost completely disappeared. Cautiously she restarted the car and pulled out on the road. She didn't turn the radio up and sing like her usual maniac self the rest of the way—why tempt fate? Sometimes it paid to be superstitious.

Twenty minutes later, she was still okay. In fact, not just okay, but feeling totally fine when she spotted the thousand-acre fenced-in estate. She turned at the tasteful, elegant sign for BERNARD'S.

The sign didn't bother spelling out Bernard Chocolates. It didn't have to. Anyone on four continents—at least anyone who appreciated fine chocolate—would easily recognize the name.

Even though it was Lucy's second home, getting through the property every morning was more complicated than joining the CIA. Still, she was used to it. At the front gate, she simply popped in ID to make the electricity security fence open.

The driveway immediately forked in three directions. The road to the right led to the plant. The middle road meandered up to the Bernard mansion. Humming now, Lucy took the familiar third road that curled and swirled a half mile, bordered by lush pines and landscaped gardens.

A moment later she reached another electric fence—this one fifteen feet tall, with a gate that was both locked and manned 24/7. Instead of waving her through, Gordon hiked outside when he spotted her crusty Honda. "Hell, Miss Fitzhenry, I was about to call the cops. You're seven minutes late. I was afraid you must be in an accident."

Sheesh. Was she that predictable? "I'm fine, honest. Did you have a nice weekend?"

"Oh, yes. Me and the missus saw a good movie, had the grandkids over. In the meantime—both Mr. Bernards are up at the house. Asked me to tell you to stop by around ten this morning if you could."

"Thanks. And you have a great morning," Lucy said as she rolled up her window, but her pulse suddenly bucked like a nervous colt's. Her pulse, not her stomach, thank heavens. The nausea seemed to be totally gone—but she still couldn't stop the sudden bolt of nerves.

The nerves were foolish, really. Any day now, she'd known the Bernards would summon her for a serious meeting. Her last experiments had been beyond successful—so successful that they affected the entire future of the company. That was great news, not bad.

It was just that she normally met with Orson Bernard, not his grandson. On paper she reported to the senior Bernard, and God knew, she adored the older man, loved being with him and working with him both. Still, Orson was well over seventy and long retired. Everyone knew who really signed the paychecks these days.

It wasn't as if Lucy didn't like Raul Nicholas Bernard. She did. Orson's grandson was too darned adorable and charming and sexy not to like. Everyone liked Nick.

She just always got rattled around him. He knew it. She knew it. Probably the birds in the trees knew it—which made her reaction to him all the more embarrassing. Realizing she was chewing on a thumbnail—a habit she'd broken at least ten years ago—Lucy firmly blocked that tangled thought train.

Behind her, the fence clanged shut. She caught Gordon's wave from her rearview mirror and had to smile. Physically Gordon resembled a sublet Santa, but his background included intensive years as an army ranger.

It regularly tickled her funny bone that she could conceivably work in a place that required such expensive and extensive security. Funnier yet was that she actually had power over the security staff. Her. Lucy Fitzhenry. A woman who couldn't control her own flyaway hair, couldn't drink champagne without a fit of the giggles, and required a daily milkshake to maintain 110 pounds.

Her mood turned serious as she took the last curve. A huge structure loomed in sight—her building. Her baby. From the front, the architecture resembled any other high-tech contemporary office structure. Sleek, lots of windows, clean lines. Past the office was the giant lab that everyone shared, then the spiderweb of individual labs, and far back—not in sight from any road—came the network of greenhouses.

She parked in the front row and hustled inside. This early in the morning, the core staff were holed up in their offices, trying to shovel through paperwork chores before they could move into the real meat of the day. Reiko, who must have had her hair scalped on Saturday, yelled out, "Hi, what happened to you?"

Lucy had to ask about Reiko's squirt-aged son—who she'd love to marry, if he wasn't a mere four—then sprinted on. Or tried to. Fritz and Fred had offices next. They'd both graduated from MSU last spring, although Lucy secretly thought that they weren't men but druids. They were never tucked or brushed. Ever. Not even once, by accident. Their brains were sharper than lobster traps, but their humor was primordial and they were so dorky that she'd be amazed if they'd ever had a date. She was even more amazed how much she loved them. Still, like drone twins, they both showed up in their doorways at the same time to yell out, "Hey, Lucy, were you sick? Did someone die? Will the world survive your being late?"

"Would you cut it out, you guys? You act like I've never been late, for Pete's sake."

Actually, she hadn't, but she was still offended that everybody labeled her so anal. You'd think she always colored inside the lines.

Which she did. Almost always. Except for that one serious time—but cripes, why did that have to keep popping into her mind today?

The instant she reached her office, she hung her jacket on the rack and switched on the computer. Her office was the size of a minute, but the walls were painted a pale peach and had a wily mile of ivy winding this way and that around the window and file cabinet. A stuffed Garfield supervised a corner of her desk. The only bare wall had floor-to-ceiling old posters of ads—Fry's Cocoa, Bensdorp's Cacao, Xocolata Amatller, Caley and Berne. No French labels.

French chocolate wasn't brought up at Bernard's.

Such was considered on a par with yelling the F word in church.

Her favorite poster came from some trade show promotion that she didn't remember—but the picture was of a woman wearing a dress made out of chocolate. Lucy only had to look at that dress to salivate.

She thumbed through the incoming mail and e-mail messages accumulated over the weekend, then grabbed a mug of tea from the break room and took off for her real work.

The central lab was quiet. It wasn't the kind of lab that had beakers and Bunsen burners. The lighting was fabulous, the white floor clean enough to serve dinner from, and the work counters looked like someone's designer kitchen—which, in a sense it was. This morning, though, the melangeur and conching machine and tempering kettles gleamed in the silence. Even with nothing going on, the smell of cacao haunted the room…a sexier smell than Chanel No. 5 any day, Lucy thought.

Past the labs came the greenhouses. She passed by Reiko's projects, then Fred's. The third greenhouse was her personal emotional Tiffany's—or that's how she thought of her work, as bringing her something worth more than any diamonds a lover could buy. She clicked in her security code, then entered.

Instantly, she was in another world, and so deeply immersed she forgot the time, the day and everything else. In a standard greenhouse, plants were organized in precise, tidy rows. Lucy's setup was more a complex undercover garden of cacao plants, with youngsters mixed with mature and older growths. What a stranger might think was exotic and wild was actually a carefully planned environment.

She checked temperature, moisture levels, scents.

Back when she was seventeen, she'd entered college to become anything but a doctor. A degree in botany had seemed distant enough from medicine, but still, she'd never expected working with anything like this. It was a dreamer's paradise.

Mentally she thought of cacaos as plants, even though she knew darn well they were trees. The history was part of the fun, or she'd always thought so. The original mama of all the cacao plants showed up somewhere around 15,000 years ago and was named Theobroma Cacao. Of course, Theo's offspring had hugely evolved since those first wild, straggly trees in the Amazon basin of Brazil.

It didn't smell like the Amazon here. It should have. The best cacao didn't have to come from the Amazon, but ten thousand years hadn't changed certain facts about chocolate—good cacao only grew in rain-forest conditions. Period. No exceptions. All attempts to coax chocolate from any other growing environment had failed.

Lucy knew the lore as well as her own heartbeat and she'd fought as fiercely as any mama lion for the survival of her personal babies. Bending down to study one of her oldest plants, she lifted one of the oblong, wrinkled leaves to study the football-shaped criollo pad. This one was heavily pregnant and close to bursting—which, in principle, couldn't possibly happen.

The soil here had none of the "required" fecund, decaying matter of a rain forest but was plain old Minnesota topsoil, give or take certain nutrients. The temperature was cool, rather than equator-tropical. And the shade and mist absolutely required for cacao plants to thrive was the opposite here. Her babies loved slightly dry soil and adored sunlight.

All these experiments could have failed. There should have been no possibility of growing cacao under these conditions—at least not good chocolate. For damn sure, not unforgettably outstanding chocolate.

Sometimes the impossible came true, though. Sometimes a girl had to take a chance that no one else would take, if only to find out what she was made of.

A woman had priorities, as far as Lucy was concerned. Growing up, she'd heard a zillion times about how civilization was destroying the rain forests. She'd listened. She'd cared. But come on. Maybe the greenhouse effect was destroying rain forests, risking natural cures for cancer, risking changes in the climate across the globe, risking the future of the planet and all that yadda yadda. Lucy had bought the bumper stickers, for Pete's sake. But it's not like she had the power to save the earth. Cripes, she couldn't even control her own hair.

But realizing that losing the rain forests would mean losing chocolate for all time had changed her perspective, because it made the problem personal. A world without chocolate was unthinkable.

The problem was enough to make even a quiet wallflower type suddenly turn power-hungry. The first day she'd taken this job, she'd sunk her teeth into the work with ardent, uninhibited, unbridled passion.

Reiko's gentle voice suddenly came through the intercom. "Hey, Lucy. You got a call from the big house. Nick and Mr. Bernard figured you got your hands in mud and forgot the time—obviously they know you, cookie—but it's after ten."

Damn. It couldn't be. She just got here. But when she glanced at her Swiss Army watch, it was twelve minutes after ten already.

Good thing her stomach problem had cleared up because she streaked the building at a breakneck pace. Even though she did have that tiny tendency to get lost in her work, she was never late and positively never late for a meeting with the Bernards.

It was faster to run cross-country than to drive. Seven minutes later, out of breath, her work boots damp and her hair flying, she charged into the mansion through the kitchen door—it had been well over a year since she'd wasted time bothering to use the formal front door.

Although her parents were a long way from poor, the Bernard wealth was something else again. For the first six months, she'd been lost just trying to find a bathroom in the place. The mansion was built like a castle, three stories, with turrets and mullioned windows and porticos. There were rooms for this and rooms for that and rooms probably no one had been in for the last century—which was about how old the house was.

As she pushed off her boots and whisked off her jacket, she heard the housekeeper singing down in the laundry room and the sound of a vacuum upstairs. Didn't matter. She knew where she was going. There were meeting places all over the mansion, but for small gatherings Orson always choose the sunroom—a six-sided room built of waist-high stone and then glass walls climbing to a hexagonal peak.

She loved it almost as much as he did, and as expected, she found him ambling from window to window, enjoying every view. Orson was tall and lean, his face a rectangle of expressive wrinkles, his head balder than a pool cue. Never mind his age, he was still more full of hell than any ten men in her own age bracket.

"Lucy!" His face lit up when he spotted her, and ignoring the employer-employee relationship entirely, wrapped an arm around her shoulders in an affectionate hug.

"I'm sorry I was late. I don't even have an excuse. Gordon told me you wanted me here at ten. I just got busy in the greenhouse." She hugged back before stepping away, thinking that he always made her feel more like a co-conspirator than a minor underling of a major business magnate. He was shrewd and warm and as stubborn as an old goat. Possibly he'd been a bear to work for in his younger days, but Orson was using his retirement to go for dreams he'd never had a chance to when he was younger. And she *was* one of his happiest co-conspirers.

"I guess we'll forgive her, eh, Nick? Get yourself some coffee or tea from the table. The three of us need to have a powwow."

She swallowed quick before turning to greet Nick. Then wanted to swallow a second time.

Nick had suit days and working-clothes days. Today he was in serious navy-blue, and he wore a suit the way a young Cary Grant used to, all careless grace and elegance. Usually she could handle him in a suit, because there was so much natural distance between her dirt-under-the-fingernails and his classiness that they might as well speak different languages. When he was wearing a black T-shirt and jeans, though, she had to admit he made her heart thump.

This morning, the sharp white shirt and formal

navy-blue didn't seem to do the distance-job. Her throat still went dry. Her pulse soared like a leaf in a high wind. He had his grandfather's long rectangular face, the strong jaw, the strong cheekbones, the startling blue eyes. His hair was a thick dark brown, and no matter how ruthlessly he brushed it, it never lay quite straight. It wasn't curly or wild exactly, more like it had an irrepressible rebellious streak. Just like him.

Near anyone else, she didn't worry about her appearance—between messing with dirt and chocolate, she just didn't have a job requiring haute couture. Around him, though, she felt hopelessly conscious of her kid-like jeans and flat figure. She could put forty-seven style products on her hair and it'd still be fine and flyaway. She always chewed off her lipstick. If she could afford to shop on Rodeo Drive, Lucy had the sneaky suspicious she'd still end up looking like an all-American kid sister. Glamour just wasn't her. And that was okay. With everyone else.

"Nick," she said warmly, "How's your Monday going?"

She'd fantasized about him all her life. Maybe technically she hadn't met him until she hired on at Bernard Chocolates, but that was neither here nor there. He made her feel hot and achy the way she always dreamed a guy would make her feel. Every cell in her body, every pore, came alive when he was in the same room. His smile gave meaning to the word *yearning*. His eyes gave in-depth potential to the whole concept of lust.

It was so tiresome.

"So far, the Monday's been a little wild. How's yours going, Luce?" He handed her a mug, peach tea, a scoop of sugar, without having to ask. It wasn't the first meeting they'd had together.

It wasn't the first time he'd been quietly considerate with her, either.

Unfortunately, his being nice never stopped her heart from thundering, her eyes from looking, her pulse from hiccupping every time she was around him. She took her mug and settled on a chair next to Orson, hoping that she'd get a grip before she had to kick herself.

In the beginning, she'd found her reaction to him kind of kicky. She hadn't had a crush in years; it was kind of fun—and God knew, he was a sexy hunk, so why not enjoy it? But time passed. She was serious about her work, and both wanted and needed to be taken seriously—which he did. The crush thing just stopped being cute. It shamed her to respond in such an immature way to a guy who'd always been good to her—in a big-brother, thoughtful-employer kind of way. Nick Bernard may only be in his early thirties, but they might as well have been a century apart in experience and lifestyles.

When she and Orson settled in the thick, soft upholstered chairs, Nick pulled over an ottoman and hunkered down, then motioned for his grandfather to start the dialogue.

"Lucy…you know we've got our miracle. The quality of those experimental plants is beyond anything we've ever dreamed. But now it's time to do something about it."

"Yes, sir." This was exactly the subject she was expecting and she couldn't agree more.

"It's not time to stake the company on it, or to put all our bets in one basket yet."

"Of course not, sir."

"But it is time to make a move. If this develops the way we hope, we'll be buying land and creating an extensive cacao forest in several locations. But for now, we have ample space to put up five or six more greenhouses—enough expansion to play with some products and real production. Obviously we'll want to stagger the plantings, so we'll have varied ages and varied crops coming into production at different times."

"Of course, sir."

"I'm unwilling to take this off-property where there's such a huge security issue. As I know you understand, word of what we're doing could have an explosive effect on the Coffee and Sugar Exchange. We're talking an immediate effect of millions, if not billions. But that's potential. All we know right now is that we've got a taste of something that looks like gold. It hasn't been completely tested."

She put down her tea. Somehow she couldn't finish a hot drink to save her life this morning, but for darn sure, she was too excited to drink it now. "I know, I know. And I just totally agree with everything you're saying."

"Well, good. Because this is really your brainchild, Lucy."

"Oh, no. Not really. I mean, I think of it as my baby—but you both know I only hired on after the whole experiment had been started. It wasn't originally my experiment—"

"Yes, but you're the one who took it on. Who brought it to fruition."

"Only because Ludwig was such an incredible teacher." She hadn't forgotten the old man—Orson's horticulturalist—who'd brought her into the fold, made mincemeat of her botany degree, and then taken the time to give her the intensive, practical education that mattered.

"This is no time to be modest, Lucy. I know what Ludwig did. But I also know what you accomplished on your own in the last few years. More important yet, we know that we can completely trust you, right, Nick?"

Lucy glanced at Nick, only to feel uneasiness stir. Whatever was on Orson's mind, Nick clearly didn't agree with his grandfather. His handsome face went still, his expression cool. "Yes. We trust you, Lucy."

He didn't say *but,* but she mentally heard it. Orson continued on.

"When we take all this public—several years down the road—I don't know what kind of management setup we'll need. Or what part you'll want to play in it. But right now, we want to expand and yet stay private. Put serious money into more extensive experiments and yet not take untoward financial risks." Orson leaned back and crossed his leg over a knee the same way his grandson did. "Lucy, I wonder how much you feel you could handle."

"Me?"

"I'd like you to manage the project. Handle the labor to get the additional greenhouses up and running. Plan the planting program. All of it."

"Me?" she echoed.

"I don't know why you're sounding surprised. The staff already thinks you're a terrific boss."

"But I'm not exactly a boss," she objected. "I never thought of myself that way. Once Ludwig left…well, we all function as a team. Reiko's older than I am. And Fritz and Fred…well, they're more like puppies than employees. I mean, I've never actually given anyone orders to do anything—"

Orson smiled affectionately. "Actually, you do, Lucy—but in a way that everyone appreciates. And I have total faith you can handle the promotion. In fact, there is absolutely no one else I want to do it."

When he mentioned the salary that went with the

promotion, she almost fell off the chair. She wanted to. Actually, she wanted to leap on the couch whooping and screaming, but of course she didn't.

"Mr. Bernard, I'd love a chance at this. I can't tell you how hard I'll work and try to deserve your trust in me." She tried to sound her subdued best, but her head was still yelling ohmygodohmygodohmygod. New car, here we come! Hell's bells, she might even move up to an Accord.

Here she'd been so sure this day was doomed for a nosedive because of that ugly bout of stomach trouble. Had she ever been wrong. And really, she should have known. She'd worked hard and long to make a life plan come together. Her life wasn't going so perfectly by accident, but because she'd fought so hard. Darn it, she deserved it.

But just then, she glanced at Nick again.

CHAPTER TWO

NICK STARED out the sunroom window, jingling the change in his pocket, watching Lucy charge across the lawn back to the greenhouse. The dogs had found her—no surprise. The only shock was that they hadn't found her before this.

Baby was a full-blooded Great Dane, where Boo Boo—well, Boo Boo's name was self-explanatory. Baby had been bred with a ribbon-winning sire and dutifully stood for him, but the minute she'd been brought home, she took off and found her own choice of lovers. Boo Boo was the result. The dog's coloring and size were pure Great Dane, but the ears drooped and the tail was wrong and his expression was downright dopey.

Either way, both dogs were bigger than Lucy. The faster she ran, the more they appeared to be chasing her, but that wasn't really true. They simply bounded and leaped around her, thrilled to have their favorite female visit. They adored her. When Boo Boo latched on to her wrist, he never left a mark. When they lavished kisses on her face—and she screamed—they just wagged their tails, understanding that she wasn't remotely annoyed.

Nick wanted to shake his head.

Lucy—whose creative horticultural talents could potentially bring in a multiple seven-figure windfall for Bernard Chocolates—had a red nose, a dog-licked chin, a silly flower hat that had fallen in the snow, and jeans with a hole in the knee.

"She's too young," Nick said to his grandfather.

Orson stepped behind him, carrying a fresh mug of coffee. "I know she looks young. But she's just under thirty. You were running the manufacturing operations at that age."

"But that was only because I had to. Because Mom and Dad died. Because you were ill. And because Clint couldn't tell a balance sheet from a bowling ball."

"Your brother is just as smart as you are. He could have taken the ball if he'd just had the interest, the ambition. Once he got that young woman pregnant, everything went downhill for him. The point being, when your parents died, you were both too young to run a company. Technically. But you grabbed hold of the challenge and made it happen."

Nick had heard the refrain of this story too many times before. It was Orson's gospel. Gramps would have forgiven his grandsons all kinds of goofs—car wrecks, losing a few million, run-ins with alcohol or drugs, probably even a bank robbery—but he was ancient-old-school as far as women. A man didn't get a woman pregnant and leave her. Period. Unfortunately, Clint had made exactly that mistake. Orson had never forgiven him, no matter what Clint had said or done since.

Every once in a while, Nick tried playing go-between. It always worked the same way. Trying to intercede always resulted in his head getting kicked from both directions. But right now, his older brother's problems weren't on the table. The situation with Lucy was.

"Lucy isn't me. It's not the same thing."

"No, it isn't, but we're not asking her to run an international manufacturing operation, either."

Nick heard the stubborn note in his grandfather's tone and knew the old man was spoiling for a fight. Orson loved to fight and most of the time Nick gave in. The Bernard Experimental Station was one of Orson's wild-haired follies, which in itself didn't bother him. Orson, after all, had turned Bernard Chocolates into the multimillion-dollar operation it was. If he wanted to fritter away some money, God knew, he was entitled. This situation, though, was different.

"Lucy knows that new breed of cacao is potentially worth a fortune. She's not used to pressure. She's not trained for it. It's not a fair thing to put on her shoulders."

When Orson didn't immediately argue, Nick focused again on the view below.

She was almost out of sight now, but not completely. A copse of tall blue spruce formed a privacy barrier between the house and experimental station. She had almost reached the woods.

Her hair looked more silver than blond, especially in sunlight, and was finer than filament. She wore it chin-length and simple, but it whished around her face every time she moved.

He knew she wasn't as young as she looked—it had to be challenging to look mature for someone who barely reached five-three and had that baby-fine hair. He'd never seen her wear makeup. Maybe she troweled on five pounds of face paint when she went out, but he only saw her at work. Makeup made no sense in the damp, warm environment of the greenhouses. Her skin was so damned gorgeous, he thought she'd be silly to goop it up anyway.

The eyes, though. God. A guy could look into those hazel eyes, get lost and never find his way out. They were dark gold and mesmerizing, framed with a thick fringe of short lashes. Sometimes, talking to her, he could look and look and look in those eyes. Forget who he was, forget how different they were, forget how young she was.

"She doesn't have the background to take on this kind of responsibility," Nick said firmly.

"Oh? What kind of background is that?" Orson's

tone was wry. "She took Ludwig's experiments and turned them completely around. On her own. Alone. She's creative, bright, intuitive. She works harder than any three men. She's responsible to the nth degree."

"I know all that," Nick said testily.

But Orson wasn't through singing her praises. "Everybody loves her. She may not think of herself as a leader, but everyone else does. She's always at the head of the pack, making the work fun for everyone else, bringing fresh ideas and spirit and excitement to every project she's involved with."

"Gramps, I *know* all that. And I like her, too. It's just…" Nick wasn't used to fumbling, but it was hard to find the right word to phrase his objections. Saying everyone liked Lucy was like saying the sky was blue. Of course they liked her. She was like a fresh breeze on a dark day, always upbeat, always finding the right thing to say. And she listened. She tilted her head just so, listening to whoever was speaking intently. She heard people. She didn't just talk. She really heard people.

Like him.

One time—God knew how she'd gotten him talking—Lucy had definitely heard *him.*

Orson was still musing on the nature of the project. "Obviously there are areas we'd have to take on ourselves. I don't know how many extra employees we'll need to hire. And security is a critical concern—but you can take that on, can't you, Nick?

She'd be in charge of the growing, the plantings, the direct work. But you could oversee that, as well."

"You don't think I have enough to do?"

His grandfather regarded him patiently. "I think you'll find time for this because you're as excited about the idea as I am."

"Maybe."

"You thought it was an old man's foolishness. That I was throwing away money on these experiments. That there wasn't a chance any of them could possibly work."

"Don't rub it in."

"But you were as thrilled as I was when the results came through. That chocolate was better quality than any we've ever produced. Better than any we've ever tasted from any company. Anywhere on the globe."

"All right. All right. So I'm as excited as hell," Nick said irritably.

Orson smiled, but then he turned serious. "It's not just that I feel Lucy has earned the promotion and opportunity. I do think that. But also there are few people in this life that I completely trust. That girl has integrity. She wouldn't pick up a dime on the street that wasn't hers."

"That's partly why I think she's too young. She's naive. *That* kind of young. Still idealistic. All that shit."

"So am I," Orson said mildly.

Nick shot him a grin. "Yeah, but you're hopeless. Besides, you're my grandfather, so I can find a way to protect you whether you want me to or not."

Orson smiled back, but then he simply looked thoughtfully at his grandson. "Do you have some personal reason you're not comfortable with Lucy?"

"Of course not." Nick easily and immediately put that question to bed, but he thought *damn right he had a reason.*

She was attracted to him. It was an embarrassment for her—a problem that cropped up the minute he showed up, that other people noticed, that made it hard for her to work with him. He didn't want her hurt, and didn't want to put her in any situation where he knew she could be hurt.

But explaining that to his grandfather would only make it more awkward for Lucy—and himself. The answer was simply to stay as far away from her as possible.

"Look, Gramps, put her in charge, if you want. Give her the promotion. But we've got a dozen irons in the fire over the next few months. I've got to be in Europe part of that time. So let me think on it, see if I can find someone else who can watch over her and the project."

"Someone besides you."

"Exactly."

"We both know this is something that could revolutionize the chocolate industry. We just can't put it in the hands of a stranger," Orson said.

"I know. I agree." It was a worry in itself that Lucy had been the one to come through with the miracle. If Nick had ever believed it could happen, he'd have hired massive, unprecedented security for the project from the get-go. But that was like fretting over spilled milk. "I'll find the right person."

"As long as it isn't you," Orson repeated again.

"It won't be me," Nick expressed with absolute certainty, then glanced at his watch. "I've got to get rolling. Madris going to drive you to the doctor's this afternoon?"

"Between you and Madris, someone's hounding me nonstop. I'm sick of it."

Nick turned away from the window completely, ready to concentrate completely on Orson now.

She was out of sight.

FOR A MONDAY that started out darn worrisome, it sure turned out fabulous. The instant Lucy got home, she dropped her jacket…on the floor. Peeled off her boots. Then, as an afterthought, chucked the rest of her clothes down to her underpants.

Yes. With the word *promotion* singing through her head like an aria, she danced through the house, flipping on the tube to the Oxygen channel, then boogie-wooing into the kitchen to pour herself a half glass from her dusty bottle of Gallo, then sipped it, still dancing. She started getting chilled from running around without clothes, but who cared?

Promotion. What a bubble-popping, orgasmic, rainbow-pretty word. Dollar signs paraded in her mind. Big, beautiful dollar signs. Now she'd have money to pay for the white carpeting. Money to upgrade the Civic. Money to pay off her Pottery Barn couch and the purple satin sheets and the museum print of the eagle.

She was gonna be…okay, not *rich*…but solvent, solvent, solvent.

And more to the point, oh, way, way, way more to the point…she was going to be a major player in the chocolate thing. It was actually going to be her baby. Seeing the advent of chocolate not dependent on rain forests. Developing the most fabulous chocolate products in the known universe. Creating products that no one else had—that no one else had even dreamed of.

Her.

Lucy.

Lucy Fitzhenry.

Was actually going to make history. Chocolate history. So it wasn't world peace or a cure for cancer, but sheesh. When push came to shove, what was one of the most absolutely critical things in life?

A rhetorical question, of course, as she sashayed over to her private stash by the computer drawer. One truffle before dinner. Oh, yes, all the rules were going by the wayside tonight. If those who called her an obsessive-compulsive fuddy-duddy could only see her now…having chocolate before dinner. With wine. Walking around the house near naked. No looking at the bills. No cleaning. No doing anything constructive.

And they said she'd never manage being wicked. Hah. She was just swallowing the last sip of wine when the doorbell rang.

She froze, then spun around, cracked her toe on a chair leg, winced, and then hobbled into the bedroom, yelling, "Hold on! I'll be there in a minute!" As fast as she could, she yanked on yoga pants and a sweatshirt, yelling out another promise at the top of her lungs, and then pedaled for the front door.

Because she was wicked—not crazy—she naturally looked through the peephole first. Her jaw dropped even as she hurled the door open. "Dad! What on earth are you…?"

She started to ask what her father was doing here, but since he was standing there with a suitcase, some kind of crisis was self-explanatory. The suitcase itself showed more proof of a crisis. It was one of those old-fashioned cases—hard-shelled like a turtle, gray, the kind that was too heavy to carry but you just couldn't kill it off; throw it off a cliff and it'd land without a dent. Only this one had three socks clamped in its teeth. One white, two black.

"Dad?" she asked more gently, by that time pulling him into the light by the front door.

"Your mother kicked me out. She told me to get out and stay out."

There. Her worst nightmare. The reason she'd stayed home so long and never moved away like every other self-respecting, independent adult woman. Only damn. She'd always feared her parents would argue each other to death if she wasn't there to play referee.

"Come on, give me your coat." He was just standing there with the suitcase, looking at her like a lost soul. Luther Fitzhenry was a surgeon. Cardiac. One of the most brilliant at Mayo—which was saying something. She'd inherited her slight height and skinniness from him. He couldn't be over five-six and was built leaner than wire. But his heart was huge, and showed clearly in his gentle facial lines and soft blue eyes.

At the moment, he looked a lot more like a confused, lost puppy than a brilliant surgeon. "She says I'm never home. That I'm always at the hospital. That we're already strangers so I might as well just leave."

"Okay, okay. We'll talk about this in a minute, but first let's calm down."

"I don't have anywhere to go, Lucy. If I could just stay here. For a night or two."

"For a night or two," she echoed, trying not to feel panicked at the terrorizing thought that he'd stay longer.

"I won't be a problem."

"I know you won't."

"I just didn't know where else to go."

"Uh-huh." She led him into the living room. He plunked down on her green microfiber sofa—the unpaid-for sofa from Pottery Barn—and looked around bewilderedly.

"I love your mother, Lucy."

"Would you like a drink?"

"You know I don't drink." He leaned forward with his long hands hanging over his knees. "On second thought, I would. Chivas on the rocks."

"Um, Dad. I can't afford Chivas. It has to be wine or beer."

"Oh." He looked at her hopefully. "If I gave you some money, could you go buy some Chivas? I don't want to put you to any trouble. It's probably too much to ask. Never mind." His thick, light hair was graying a little, and right now standing up in strange spikes. "I don't need a drink. Just completely forget I asked."

"Dad."

"What?"

"I'll go out, get you the Chivas. Just relax now."

"I love your mother, Lucy."

"Yes, you said that. I know."

"She says I never notice anything she does. That I was a spoiled young man and now I've turned into a spoiled old man. That I'm self-centered. That I never see her. I keep trying to figure out what brought this all on—"

"Her birthday?"

"No. It can't be that. I bought her that Mikado watch she wanted for her birthday—"

"That was last year, Dad."

"Well, it wasn't that. It was something else. I think…she may have reupholstered the couch. Or bought a new chair. Something like that. I walked in and she just seemed to get madder and madder—" He looked at her pitifully. "Whatever you do, don't go out just for me."

Okay. She went out, found a liquor store, bought his Scotch, came home. By then he'd fallen asleep— with his shoes up on her couch. She pulled off his shoes, covered him with a down throw, and then jogged back to the spare room.

She had a bed and various odd pieces of furniture in there because her parents had pawned off all the furniture they didn't want when she moved out. But since she rarely needed a spare bed, she'd tended to fill up the room with stuff. Unfortunately her dad could trip on things like the exercise bike and cross-country skis and snow gear, especially if he woke in the middle of the night, so it all had to be cleared out and cleaned up.

On the third trip to the garage, her stomach turned a triple somersault, making her stop dead. Not now. Not again. She hadn't had time—or she'd forgottén—to call a doctor that day, but then she realized, she also hadn't had any dinner. Except for the truffle.

The truffle was fabulous. When it came down to it, there was no such thing as a bad truffle. But it did seem as if she had a tiny propensity to get in trouble with chocolate lately.

That sudden insight was so unpleasant that she immediately hurled it in her mental-denial bin and aimed for the kitchen. Because her dad was still napping, she did the mac-and-cheese thing, finished making up a fresh bed for him, and then made the usual nightly calls…Ginger, her sister. Merry, her best friend. Her cousin Russell miraculously managed to connect between her calls—something was new with him, she could hear it in his voice, but he didn't mention anything except stopping over soon. And finally, her mom got a turn at the phone lines.

"Is he there, Lucy?"

"Yes. Do you want to—"

"No. I don't want to talk to him. I don't want him to know I called. And I don't care where he is. I just…" Eve sighed on the other end of the line. Lucy could picture her mother, so beautiful, her blond hair never looked fussed-over but always wonderfully styled, makeup just so, elegant as roses. But angry. "I just wanted to be sure he was all right. That's all. Kick him out, Luce."

"Mom, I can't—"

"Yes, you can. I'm sure he's talked you into staying tonight, so that's fine. But if you let it go on, he'll suck all the energy right out of you, taking and taking and taking. You're a grown woman. You don't have to take care of your parents. We're adults. Kick him out and don't look back."

It occurred to her around midnight that she hadn't had a chance to tell anyone about her promotion. God knew, she wanted to. There just never seemed to be a chance. She was just nodding off, so tired she hadn't even flossed, when a short, scrawny shadow showed up in the doorway.

"Lucy, are you awake?"

She jerked to a sitting position. "Yeah, Dad. What's wrong?"

"I just wondered if you had anything around to eat. I don't want you to bother. I don't need anything. Just tell me where to look. And then go back to sleep—"

If he'd opened the fridge or cupboard, he'd have found various kinds of food. But apparently he'd done that. And nothing he found looked like grilled chicken and green beans and a baked potato, which was apparently what he was in the mood for.

"I don't suppose you have any pistachio ice cream for dessert?"

"Nope. I've got chocolate. And Cherry Garcia. And some cookies. And bananas—"

"Your mother always has pistachio ice cream."

"Uh-huh. Dad. I'm not going out after midnight for pistachio ice cream."

"Good heavens, honey. I'd never ask you to do such a thing—"

"I have to work tomorrow. I've got a big day. I have to get some sleep."

"Me, too. Although I think I'd better cancel my surgical schedule for a few days. I've never done that, but I think I'd better. Only every time I start thinking, I seem to get more...unsettled. Which is probably why I couldn't get my mind off the pistachio ice cream. I know it's foolish. I know..."

Okay, she thought. He'd had a terrible, terrible day. He was afraid that Eve meant it this time. Lucy couldn't imagine her father surviving a divorce. He probably couldn't take a shower and find a towel on his own. He was brilliant in the operating room, but real life always seemed to bewilder him.

So she went out and found his ice cream.

It was past two when she tumbled back into bed, musing that this had been an extraordinarily wild day. Tumultuous. Filled with both exhilaratingly wonderful events...but worrisome ones, too. Still, through it all, she'd barely spared a moment thinking about Nick Bernard.

That was progress, she thought.

Major progress.

Only thinking about him last thing before sleep meant, inevitably, that every darn single dream had him in the star cast.

CHAPTER THREE

EVEN THOUGH Nick drove the satin-black Lotus from the house to the labs, the dogs managed to beat him. He could have walked, but the whole idea of driving was to avoid the slobber and dog hair. He had a business flight at noon, was hoping to stay clean until then.

"But that was silly thinking on my part, wasn't it, girls?" he murmured when he opened the car door and was immediately assaulted—lavishly, lovingly assaulted—by the two tail-wagging dimwits. Baby was the kisser. Boo Boo was the devil incarnate—trying to climb in the Lotus, nearly killing them both, threatening the soft leather seats, then after kissing him senseless with her long, wet tongue, taking off with his driving glove. Two pawprints the size of footballs showed up on his gray slacks.

"Women," he muttered, although he really didn't mean to disparage the gender. Not when the female gender was found in dogs, anyway. Women were another story entirely. Some days it just didn't pay a guy to get up, you know? Linnie had called that morning.

Their conversation was still sucking the energy out of him. When he first met her, Linnie had seemed every guy's daydream. She had no morals. No inhibitions. Money of her own. Nothing was too wild for her, in bed or in life. She was fun, crazy, unpredictable. Hell, when she dressed for a party, you never knew if even her critical parts were gonna be covered.

It had been an entertaining, worthless, fun affair—until he'd broken it off. It never occurred to him that she'd care. She'd never hinted at wanting more than an occasional good time. There were other guys in her life, he knew, and that was totally okay with him. He only called it off because he was so damned busy, really didn't have time to do the planning, the partying, couldn't just take off and vacation whenever she had the whim. He never thought it'd be a big deal to her. He just thought calling a friendly halt was being honest.

Apart from the ear blistering she'd given him—and that was several months ago—she'd kept calling ever since. She needed an escort for something. Then a favor about something else. This morning was another one of those "something elses." And when he couldn't—he honestly couldn't—she did the ear blistering thing again.

All his life—as of kindergarten anyway—girls had chased him. All his life, he'd liked it.

Only lately, he felt like he was batting a zero.

Nothing he did with women was right. "Including you girls." He crouched down to scrub both Baby and Boo Boo's heads before straightening again. "You can't go into the greenhouses. You know that."

They went up to the door anyway, wagging their tails, expectant. They knew Lucy was in there.

So did Nick.

Not a good idea to see Lucy when he was already having a bad-woman day, but there was no help for it. The new project loomed like a mountain in his mind. They needed to figure out how they could best work together, talk about both the details and the big picture, establish some timetables, put a plan on paper. Possibly Lucy didn't need every possible *t* crossed—but he did. Either that or he was going to drive himself bonkers worrying about it.

The truth was, that guilt had chewed on his nerves ever since the night—around seven weeks ago—when she'd called him with the news about her experiment's success. Until that night, he'd had no measure of how strong her crush on him was. Until that night, she'd never been this awkward around him.

He'd screwed up. Nick took all the blame because it didn't matter what Lucy had done. What mattered was that he'd been in a far better position, life-wise, to anticipate and cope with certain kinds of awkward problems. She was naive. He wasn't. It was as simple as that, and although he'd been ultracareful around her ever since, it hadn't helped. If they got a good working arrangement agreed on, though, he had high hopes they'd click a ton more naturally.

Right?

Right.

He pushed open the door, still mentally coaching himself into an upbeat frame of mind. She wasn't expecting him for another half hour, but he knew she always got in early. With any luck, they could get this conversation finished before she was really busy—or he had to leave for his flight.

The lobby was empty and silent except for the pitiful moans of the Great Danes left outside the door. The lobby, predictably, was empty, but right after that came the long hall to the offices. Lucy's was empty, but he heard the sound of her voice from the coffee room down the hall.

Reiko, the young mom of a four-year-old boy, seemed to be counseling her. "I just think you should go home. Get some rest, Lucy. You're obviously exhausted."

"Honestly, I would if I could get any rest at home. But he didn't go into work today, so I know he's still there…."

Nick hesitated just outside the door. He didn't want to eavesdrop, but he also didn't want to interrupt some personal, traumatic conversation. His pulse gave an unexpected buck at the idea of some man living in Lucy's house—someone keeping her up all night, somehow making her afraid to go home.

"You don't think he had an affair?" Reiko questioned.

"No, no. He'd never do that." Lucy's voice sounded wearier than a lead weight bell. "I just couldn't sleep all night. He was up every hour, needing something—"

"You can't work all day and take care of him all night, Luce."

"I know. But I couldn't turn him away in the middle of the night! And I don't know whether to try to help the two of them. Or stay out of their problems. Whether to let him stay, or insist he find another place. So far it's only been the one night, so I just can't see doing anything until he gets his head on straighter."

"You stayed with them forever." The cadence of Reiko's voice had a hint of her Japanese mother's. There was a musical softness, a rhythm and gentleness—with steel behind it. "Where my father grew up, a child was responsible for his or her parents their entire lives. But this is America. There should only be two people in a marriage."

"Yeah, well, as soon as I finally felt I could leave home, they almost immediately started fighting again."

"But that's not your fault. It's theirs."

"I know, I know. But that doesn't help me figure out what to do about the situation now. I mean, would you have turned your own dad away—"

Nick had been becoming more and more confused until he heard the word *dad*. Finally it clicked. She'd been talking about her father. Not a man. Not a lover who may or may not have been having an affair, who was wearing her out at night with his demands, with… Nick swallowed hard. Ridiculous, to realize how high and hard his blood pressure was pounding over something that was none of his business to begin with. Reiko spotted him.

"Hey, Mr. Nick, how's it going?"

"Fine, fine. How's the little one?" he asked, referring to her little boy, but at that moment Lucy spun around and spotted him, too. She promptly turned peach-pink and dropped her porcelain mug…which, of course, promptly shattered in a half-dozen pieces, coffee spilling everywhere.

Talk about immediate chaos. Both women immediately yelped, and then both talked ten for a dozen as they ran around for paper towels or rags. Nick just scooped up the porcelain shards and carried them to the closest wastebasket, both women fussing the whole time.

"You'll cut yourself, Nick—"

"Let me clean that. It was all my fault. Neither of you have to help—"

Okay. Once they recovered from that minor debacle, he managed to finally slip in a word. "I know I'm early, Lucy. But I just need a few minutes with you—" That wasn't strictly true, but he figured if they started out with a productive, short meeting, they'd have a better shot working out the hairier issues the next time.

"Sure, sure, of course. But unless we need to be sitting at a desk, let's walk toward the greenhouses, okay?"

He definitely liked the idea. It was always easier to walk and talk than to be stuck sitting still. Besides which, they had to go through the labs to get to the greenhouse area, and he always loved wandering through the lab. Bernard's major manufacturing kitchens had similar equipment—conchers, winnowing machines and all. But everything was in smaller size here, with more done by hand. And the best part, of course, was getting to sample some cacao nibs or the latest experimental chocolates, or just poke a finger in whatever liquid concoction the staff was stirring up next—at least if someone didn't slap his hand.

"Don't touch," Lucy scolded.

"The last I noticed, I own the place," he reminded her.

"I know, I know. But every process in here is a serious secret. And touching anything could monkey with an experiment's results."

"Nothing's supposed to be a secret from *me*," he said, his eyes narrowing on a fresh batch of roasted shelled cacao beans in a tray on the far counter.

She steered him firmly toward the door to the

greenhouse marked BLISS, saying patiently, "I know you're the boss. But you're just a teeny bit dumb, Nick, as much as we all love you. Your gramps has the touch. The understanding. The instinct. You don't."

"Hey," he said, in his most injured voice, but he wasn't offended—even remotely. It was always like this. Lucy was a wreck around him outside, or in the offices, or up at the house. But the closer she got to her own venue, the more comfortable and bossy she got—and the more fun. It was like watching the transformation from an obedient, boring Cinderella into a fine, confident, sassy wicked witch.

She key-coded herself—and him—into the greenhouse, then motioned him in first. "Now, Nick, I totally realize that you're the brilliant one from the business side of the fence. Orson has told me a zillion times how Bernard's was just a small-potatoes family chocolatier until you were a teenager and started nudging him with marketing ideas. And then taking the whole thing over. So I know you're brilliant. But you need people like me to do the dirty-hands stuff—"

"You're just saying that so I'll stay out of the chocolate samples."

"True."

"I'm kind of offended that you think I'd mind getting my hands dirty. It's not true. As a kid, I played in mud nonstop."

"That's nice," she said as she smacked his hand one more time—he'd almost reached another sampling plate right before they entered the greenhouse wing. After slapping him, twice now, she just went on doing the miniature wicked witch thing—albeit in sneakers. "You just don't understand how delicate the process is. You have no reason to. It's not your problem. But everything has to be right."

"You think I didn't realize that?"

"Oh cripes. I didn't mean to hurt your feelings. Of course you know all that, but in your job, you need all that knowledge at an intellectual level. Where in mine…well, I just don't know how anyone could do my job well if they weren't an obsessively fussy perfectionist." She said it tactfully, as if she felt sorry for him that he couldn't have that character trait. "You also have to be messy. And those two things usually don't go together. Which is why it's so darn hard to create really good chocolate."

He found it fascinating that she had the arrogance to think he needed a lecture on the chocolate business. But damn. She always saw things so differently from him that his curiosity was invariably aroused. "Say what? What does messiness have to do with creating good chocolate?"

"Well, maybe *messiness* isn't the right word. But you can't do everything by the book. You can't just tidily follow a recipe and hope it'll turn out. Because each cacao bean is different, every batch of chocolate has the potential to turn out differently. So to make the best stuff, you have to be flexible. Sensitive to the smells, the tastes, the textures. The nitty gritty of it all."

"I get it now. You have to be a hard-core sensualist. Like you."

Her jaw dropped. "No, I didn't mean that. I'm no sensualist."

"The hell you aren't," he murmured. And lightning suddenly crackled in the air. Not outside. Inside.

The Night of the Chocolate was suddenly between them, the memory in her eyes, in her arrested posture. The doors were closed behind them, locking them into the greenhouse environment. The climate wasn't hothouse here, but it was a world different from a freezing Minnesota March morning. A tangly jungle of cacao trees of all shapes and sizes looked exotic and wild. The air was warm and moist, every breath flavored with pungent, earthy smells.

But this morning, he couldn't enjoy it. He wanted to kick himself. Sometimes he got on so well with Lucy—he really liked being with her—when she was naturally herself. And he'd blown it up by bringing up that night, a memory that was obviously awkward and miserable for her.

Hell. He couldn't bat a run today to save his life. He tried pitching from a different stadium. "You know why I wanted to meet with you. We don't have to pin down everything this instant but we do need to talk about plans. How to work together. A time frame."

"I know. Orson filled me in that you were going to be stuck working with me."

"Not stuck." Damn, the woman started disappearing from sight the minute they got in her Bliss greenhouse. She wasn't being evasive. It's just that she checked the temperature on something and the water level on something else, and suddenly she was off.

He trailed after her. "The building of the greenhouses—I'll take care of that. Won't take that long if I get a crew on it. But I need your input on the details. You want this set up to be a model for all the new ones, or do you want variations? How many kitchen-labs do you want attached to the new project. All that kind of thing."

"No sweat. I'd love to work all that out for you— in fact, I could map out a drawing of the ideal layout—have it for you by tomorrow, if you want. One thing we need to immediately discuss, though, is trees."

"What about trees, specifically?"

"Well, for starters, cost. What exactly is my budget?"

"Hmm. As much as we love you, Luce," he said wryly, mimicking her own phrase from earlier, "I tend to think you've got the same money sense as my grandfather. Not that you're dumb. Just that you're a ton stronger at the creative, vision end than figuring out how we're going to pay for it. So how about if you just tell me what you need, put it on paper, and then let me worry about the budget side of things."

"Um, are you insulting me?"

"Definitely, yes. You and Orson are two peas in a pod about money."

"That was a really nice compliment. Comparing me to your grandfather. You know I love him."

"He thinks the world of you, too. But moving on…"

"Oh. Yeah. About the trees. The thing is—I need to start ordering rootstock now. It's such a major complicated process to get stock from South America and Africa. And if there's any chance you can get the greenhouses up and ready to rock and roll over the next few months—I really need to get those orders going pretty promptly."

"Okay."

She stopped carrying around hoses and a dirt-crusted fork and peered up at him. Those soft hazel eyes looked bruised-tired. Almost golden in color. Cat's eyes, he always thought. Sometimes sleepy cat's eyes, sometimes sensual as a kitten in the sunlight. Usually sensuality and innocence didn't naturally go together, but that was just it, in Lucy's case…

"Nick?"

"Sorry, didn't hear you."

"I said, do you understand how Bliss was created?"

She was getting formal and bossy and pedantic again. The way she got when she was nervous. What the hell'd he do wrong this time? "Sure I know how Bliss was made. Did you forget I've been part of Bernard Chocolates since I got out of diapers?"

"You've been part of the family business...but from everything you've ever said, I understand you were always part of the manufacturing and business side of the chocolate fence. All the parts involved in getting from the cacao beans to the candy. But I wasn't sure if you were familiar with the first part— how you get to the cacao beans to start with."

"I know the basics. The names of the beans. Where they come from. Where we get them. What they cost."

For some unknown reason, she handed him a hose—a dripping hose with a little mud on it—while she rambled down another aisle and ducked her head under some more plants. "But all those basics are really complex. In fact, I really believe the reason Bernard's chocolate is so fabulous is because we're meticulous about every single step in the process. Like in the roasting process, we're fussy right down to the seconds on timing. And we use way more cocoa butter than lecithin. And we don't just buy the best beans, we work really hard to discover unique blends." She surfaced for air, before ducking under another plant. "In fact, that's always been one of my favorite jobs. Experimenting with different blends..."

"Um, Luce, could we stay on target?"

"I am. This is the whole point. That we're meticulous about everything. The winnowing. The grinding, the dutching, the conching. The tempering...hold this for me for a second, would you?"

Out of nowhere she handed him a football-sized purple pod. Purple, as in ripe. Granted, he wasn't wearing a suit, just dress slacks and a decent shirt. His jacket was already hanging in the jet. But his intention was definitely to fly directly to a meeting in short order, which meant that holding onto a dripping hose and a prize-ripe cacao pod wasn't precisely an ideal situation.

"Lucy," he started to say—in his most patient, understanding voice. But she was still ranting on.

"Because that's the thing, Nick. All those parts of the process are like pieces of a puzzle. Every truly great chocolatier has its secrets that no one else has. Anybody could end up with an edible chocolate bar or a nice-tasting truffle. But Bernard's has always gone the long mile to find the better secrets, the better process, to do the work..."

He'd lost her. She'd disappeared somewhere where the pods looked the ripest. That was the whole problem with working with a perfectionist. She had to get every detail said and when she got on the subject of chocolate, she was like a windup toy with an ever-ready battery.

From the beginning, Nick had wished he'd had

Lucy on the sales force. Hell, he'd have hired her to *be* the sales force—if he could pin her down for two seconds when she was cleaned up. Almost the whole time he'd known her, though, she was invariably up to her knees in smells and water. Worse yet, she was even fussy about her mud.

He mentally snoozed as she kept talking. There was no point in trying to cut her off. Lucy was always going to dot every *i*. But time *was* dipping by. In principle he'd hoped to take off by ll:45—and he'd figured that the initial talk with Lucy wouldn't take more than twenty minutes. There were only a couple of things they absolutely had to get straight this minute. Only she was still talking. They hadn't settled anything. And he'd already been here a good hour.

Worse yet, as if she couldn't pause long enough to have a discussion about a project worth millions, she kept working. Moving. Bending. Lifting. Pinching. Turning on water. Turning off water. At the corner of one aisle, she was swiftly collecting a good-sized heap of purply-red pods.

"But the important issue, Nick, is that all chocolatiers concentrate on the same processes. What that really means is that the best are always competing with the best. All the great chocolate makers buy the best cacao, hire the best chemists, discover their own blend of the best beans. So there's been nothing to really…revolutionize the industry, you know? Until now, when…"

Momentarily he couldn't hear her, because her voice became muffled and indistinct when she disappeared deeper under the trees. But she emerged eventually with two more ripe pods.

"...What really mattered was when your gramps got into the rain-forest crisis. Experimenting with ways to raise and breed cacao trees in an environment that didn't require that rain forest climate. Which has been tried before, of course. But not successfully in a way that produced great beans. Much less unbelievably revolutionary great beans—"

"Yawn," he said aloud, trying to tactfully send her a signal that he knew all this. And whatever he knew or didn't knew, he couldn't listen to her ranting all day.

The signal didn't work. From beneath a branch she tried to hand him another hose—then peered out with an impatient glance when he didn't take it. How was he supposed to take it? He already his hands full. "Forget the hose. But hold onto that one pod, okay? I want it separated from the others. Anyway. We had two problems—first to find a way to grow fabulous cacao beans from a plant that would thrive in a non-rain-forest climate. A regular climate. And then..."

She hopped down from the forest level, looking like a kid who'd been playing touch football after a rain. Smiling. Knees and hands and shoes filthy. A swipe of dirt on her chin. "...and our second problem was to produce a superior bean. A bean better than anyone had ever seen before. And further, to

produce several new varieties of superior beans—
because you always need a blend to make different
kinds of chocolates…"

He gave up. Put down the hose. Carried the sacred
pod around as he ambled to the front work center,
where there was always a thermos of fresh coffee and
mugs. He poured himself half a cup, ambled back.
Undoubtedly she wouldn't notice his absence. She'd
forgotten him—which was a lot better than her being
weird and jumpy and flushing whenever he looked
at her sideways—but it was also a major comedown.
Women had chased him on three continents. He
knew his way around women.

Hell, he could usually find a way to cope with
Lucy, too, but not when she was near her chocolate.
No man could conceivably compete for her attention
compared to chocolate. Ever. And she was really
winding up now, her tone as breathy and excited as
a woman near orgasm.

"…So the thing is, the revolutionary thing is, the
experiments I've been doing for your grandfather
truly broke totally new ground. We weren't just
blending beans. We've been blending trees. Marrying a little Trinidad with a little Jamaica. Seeing if
the delicate 'Arriba' bean from Ecuador would dance
with the Rolls Royce criolla from Venezuela. And
from there, if we could find those offspring willing
to reproduce in a midwest climate…"

"*Lucy.*" He really doubted he'd manage to successfully interrupt her, but she'd climbed into another group of trees and tarnation, the day was wasting.

"….So that's what's so *exciting,* Nick. That's the thing. You want six more greenhouses, that's great—but I need to get the seedlings and root stock and stuff *started.* I mean I've got my own rootstock established now. I can fill a couple. But we need to repeat some of the experiments as well, because…"

Her voice dropped off. Which was impossible. Lucy never quit talking, not about chocolate, and when she was in that mid-orgasmic-beyond-excited stage, tornados could rumble and she'd never notice. He said immediately, "Where are you? What's wrong?"

When she didn't promptly answer, he plunked his coffee mug on the ground, set down the sacred cacao pod with it, and started jogging up and down the aisles.

"Where *are* you?" He was just about to get seriously testy when he finally located her. She was hunched over at the end of an aisle, leaning against the work counter by the coffee, holding her stomach and looking pea-green. "You're sick?" he asked.

"No. No. I'm just a little tired today—" She suddenly gulped, then whirled around and ran.

Completely confused, he chased after her. She stabbed in the code numbers by the door, and then tore out. He realized in two shakes that she was obviously headed for a restroom, but she was in such an all-fired hurry she never closed the door, just made it to the sink before hurling.

Nick had always been one to run a two-minute mile away from someone being sick that way, but Lucy…maybe she was slight, but normally she was stronger than an ox. He'd never heard of her taking a day off work. She had an exhausting amount of energy, never lost the whole bouncy bubble thing, always cheerleading even the lowest of the crew. So seeing her face look like pea soup shook him.

"What is it, you've got a flu, a bug, what? Could you have some kind of food poisoning?"

"Oh God, Nick. Go away."

But he didn't go away, couldn't. She was through being sick, but now she was cupping cold water to take away the taste, splashing cold water on her face, and just hanging over that sink like she barely had the strength to stand.

"How long have you been sick this way?"

"Actually for more than a week. It comes and goes. I was going to call a doctor, but that seemed so dumb. I feel *fine*. And I kept thinking it'd go away. And besides that—"

"What?"

"Besides that, my dad's a doctor. Practically every family friend is a doctor. They all work at Mayo. So trying to see a doctor without my family finding out and worrying and prying—" And then she repeated, "I'm fine now. Just go away. Give me a minute."

"You've been hurling for more than a week? And still trying to come to work besides?" He raised his eyes to the ceiling. Women. "I'll take care of this."

"You'll take care of what?"

"You," he said irritably, and reached for his cell phone.

CHAPTER FOUR

HAVING GROWN UP with doctors, Lucy not only failed to treat them like gods, but could easily tell the real silver from the tinsel. Dr. Jargowski was totally darling, with his gentle eyes and sneaky sense of humor and unshakeable patience. Unfortunately, he was a quack.

"Don't be silly," Lucy told him irritably. "I can't be pregnant."

"You are."

She redraped the cloth in a lot more modest fashion, mentally damning Nick from here to Poughkeepsie for bullying her into this waste-of-time doctor visit. "You don't understand. This has to be an ulcer. I have a great job. A job I absolutely love. But a few weeks ago, things changed—the job's even more wonderful, really, but it also become much more serious and stressful. And I'm a type A, you know? A worrier. A perfectionist. Anybody who knows me would tell you that I'm prime ulcer material—"

"You might find this hard to believe, but I'm usually the one to make a diagnosis, not the patient, since I happen to be the doctor," Dr. Jargowski said with wry humor, and gave a subtle nod to the nurse, indicating she could leave the room now that the pelvic, private part of the examination was over.

Lucy didn't care whether the nurse was there or not. "Well, the blood tests and exam have to be wrong. Maybe I have weird insides, did you think of that? Maybe I have a hernia or something making me nauseous. Maybe I have, I don't know, fibroid tumors in my stomach—"

"Try to trust me a little, would you? 'Weird insides' is not a medically descriptive term. And you'd be making medical history if you showed up with fibroid tumors in your stomach, since that's an impossibility. The symptoms, in fact, are not emanating from your stomach at all."

"Look, would you *listen* to me? I don't have a guy! I haven't seriously dated anyone in almost two years! And of course I go out. But I don't casually—" She waved her hand expressively.

"Ah. Well, even if you don't normally..." He waved his hand in the same expressive gesture "...it definitely appears that you must have. At least once. Around seven weeks ago."

Men. Men, men, men. Outside, Lucy found that the late afternoon had deteriorated into a drizzling, drooling rain—which was going to melt all the snow and make everything icy. That was probably a man's fault, too.

She dove into her car, locked the doors, started the heater and defroster on high and then sat there, freezing to death while she waited for it all to work. Eventually she thawed enough to move—or at least to lean over far enough to click open the glove compartment.

She used to keep pepper spray in there, but over the years she'd come to define "emergency supplies" a little differently. Thankfully she didn't waste time storing plain old candy bars for the serious crises, because now, she could go straight for the truffles. After downing three of Bernard's best, the steam had cleared from the windshield and her body was no longer stiff as an icicle.

Now she was just completely hysterical.

She drove home snuffling and blubbering and talking to herself. There was no one she could tell. No one she could face. Hell's bells, looking at the woman in the mirror shamed her. Twenty-eight-year-old responsible women just didn't make mistakes like this. And Lucy was more than responsible. She was *ultra*-responsible.

In the privacy of the car, she had to admit there was a slim, very slim, possibility that the doctor wasn't a quack.

It was even vaguely, remotely possible that the Night of The Chocolate could have involved some completely unplanned, unexpected, impossible-to-prepare-for—impossible-to-imagine—behavior on her part.

It was about the Bliss, she thought morosely. Bliss just wasn't regular chocolate. And the night she'd tested the new Bliss, she'd discovered right away that there was something chemically...extra...in the new beans. Something powerful. Something dangerous. That had to be it. What else could explain something that could change a sensible, practical, basically shy woman into a raving nymphomaniac?

Oh, God. She'd buried the memory so deep she was positive it'd never find its way to the surface again.

She moaned several times during the drive—every time that memory edged closer to her consciousness. On the inside, she felt like an eggshell with spider cracks, cracks that were slowly seeping over the whole surface of the shell. Her whole life was about to explode in a big, messy *phlat*. There was no way it'd ever go back together the same way.

Please God. Let this be a mistake. Let me have an ulcer. Let me have a tumor. Let me have anything but a pregnancy. Come on. You know this isn't fair. Nobody should have to pay for the one single thing they did wrong, should they? Cun't you find some really good sinners to vent on?

Her car swerved and she had to give up the sniveling. The temperature was dropping, turning the roads to black glass. By the time she reached home, she'd leveled the glove compartment's supply of emergency truffles and her chin had locked in a grim line. Her hands were stiff from controlling the wheel so hard. Whether her life was a disaster or not, she just wanted to get inside her house and put up her feet for a while. She was whipped.

She'd almost forgotten her dad was installed at her place until she pushed open the door and found all the lights on. "Dad?" The TV blared from the living room. It sounded like sports in a foreign language–although truth to tell, most sports sounded like a foreign language to her. Her fresh-painted white boxes in front of her green couch—the boxes that functioned as a coffee table, she thought—were littered with magazines, three dirty glasses, a bowl of aging cereal and a spill of loose pocket change.

"Da—?"

"Oh, there you are." Her dad strolled in from the kitchen, his hair unbrushed and sticking straight up, his feet bare. He'd been top of his class at Harvard Medical School, had students trail him down the hall whenever he spoke, had an international reputation as a heart surgeon. And he'd turned into a waif. "I was getting really worried. And really hungry."

"Hungry—"

"I don't care what you make, honey. You know I'm not fussy. I don't want to be any trouble. Don't you usually get home from work sooner than this, though? I've had a terrible day. Terrible…"

"Oh, Dad." She pushed off her jacket and reached out her arms. Luther made an attempt to fold into them. "Have you talked to Mom?" At the look in his eyes—holy kamoly, for an instant there, he looked as if he were going to cry, so she hastily changed the subject. "I don't always cook during the week, so I'm not sure what's around. But we'll look, okay?"

"Everything's such a mess...."

She noticed that. Oh God, oh God. The kitchen in her duplex was hardly state-of-the-art, but it was still *hers*. There was no one to tease her for keeping the counters spotless and the sink smelling like fresh Soft Scrub, and she'd slowly been collecting Staub. It cost more than she could afford, she admitted it— and suffered lots of guilt for indulging herself—but she'd only been buying a piece at a time. Which meant she had three. Her dad must have tried to heat something for lunch in the red Staub terrine. The remnants looked like baked cheese. All-day-baked cheese. Well-well-well-well baked cheese.

"My nurse cancelled my surgical schedule for another week, but eventually I have to go back to work. Obviously. It's just...I don't know where to go. How to function. I can't commute from here, but I can't go home...."

"Okay, okay..." She squirted soap in the sink, started the water running, patted her dad, ran back out in the cold to fetch the mail, started a pot of tea, opened the fridge. "I could do some fresh pasta with chives and mozzarella and mushrooms—"

"How about burgers?" Her dad sank in a kitchen chair. "What if I can never work again?"

Lucy pawed through the freezer again. "Or we could have some veggie lasagna. With a fresh salad—"

"How about pork chops? With your mother's mint sauce. Unless that's too much trouble." Her dad covered both his eyes. "I never cheated on her, you know. She's the only woman I ever loved. I adore her, Lucy. I don't know what I did that was so wrong."

"All right, all right. We'll have burgers."

"She said…she didn't love me anymore."

"Oh, Dad—"

"She said I couldn't find my own shoes. That I needed a keeper, but she wanted to be a wife, not a keeper. She said I couldn't find my own shoes, my own wallet. She said I couldn't find my own *life*. Lucy?"

"What?"

"She was right. I can't. What am I going to do?"

She gave him some lettuce to shred. Then some more tea. Then started working with some ground round—in the long run, she refused to stuff her dad with the cholesterol-packed diet he wanted, but tonight just wasn't the right time to argue with him.

She just didn't seem to have a choice about putting her own crisis on a far back burner. She cooked. Picked up. Cleaned. Listened to her dad. Tried to fit in a general plan for Project Bliss to give to Nick in between it all, but of course, the phone kept ringing.

Right before nine, someone rapped on the back door. She found Russell hunched on the porch. At nineteen, her cousin was cuter than an Abercrombie model, all boyish charm and shy smiles. He'd glommed on her when they were kids, followed her around like a puppy, and once she'd moved into her own place, he'd shown up regularly.

She gave him a big hug, but whispered, "Maybe it would have been better if you called first this time—"

"I couldn't, Luce. I had something really important to discuss with you." He only stepped in as far as the doormat, standing there in the dim light with too thin a jacket and no gloves.

"And you've driven all the way from Mankato—"

"It's not that far, but…aw hell. I just have to get this off my chest. And you're the only one I can discuss this with—"

"What?"

"I think I'm gay."

"Gay," she repeated, and thought, nope. This wasn't happening to her. Maybe she was the crisis counselor in the family. Maybe she'd been born with the assignment of being the Listener and Soother for the Fitzhenrys. Maybe with so many dramatic people in the clan, they naturally gravitated toward the nondramatic, boring one. Only for Pete's sake. Her whole world had fallen apart today.

And right now, if she'd even wanted to throw up, she couldn't have scheduled the time.

A voice called out from the living room. "Who's that, Lucy? Your mother?"

Russell mouthed, "Who in God's name is that? Your dad?" and she yelled back cheerfully, "It's Russ, Dad, just come for a visit."

"Well, tell him to come on in."

Russell whispered, "I can't."

She said, "You're going to have to now. Come on. I'll get you something to eat. Take off your jacket."

"I only wanted to talk to you. I don't want anyone else to know about this," he said desperately.

"And we won't be talking about this in front of my dad. But right now, there's no way to pretend you're not here." She would have thought she was stating the obvious, but Russ still had to be herded into the living room.

"So, I'll bet the girls are really chasing you, huh, Russ?" was the first thing her father said, making her wince—but it was typical family teasing. Girls had adored Russ from grade school on, and as far as Lucy knew, he'd adored them just as likewise. She had no idea when the gay question had started troubling him, but soon enough could see that discussion was going no further—not tonight.

Her dad immediately perked up for the company. At some point he miraculously found the beer at the back of her refrigerator, and a short time later Russell came back from the kitchen with her one and only partial bottle of wine. She raised a serious protest about his drinking and driving, but her father readily settled that by insisting that Russ could spend the night.

She made up the second twin in the spare bedroom, blinked a bleary-eyed good-night to them both around eleven, and crashed in her bedroom. Literally crashed. She pushed off her shoes and dove, headfirst, for the lilac-flowered duvet cover. Between the feather bed and down comforter, her bed was conceivably the softest thing in the universe. So soft that she determined that she was never moving. Ever again. Even for a minute. Even for a second.

She'd never gone to bed in her clothes—it was unthinkable—but honest to Pete, she couldn't move. For the first time all day, she felt…safe. Part of the feeling came from being cocooned in all the soft, luxurious down bedding. And part of it came from the purple. She'd really hard-core nested with color in here. The fake Tiffany lamp was lavender, the carpet a pale lilac. The old brass bedstead definitely wasn't purple but she'd found it thrown out in an alley, brought it home, and buffed it within an inch of its life. The dark purple satin sheets, the swoop of dark purple drapes…for a woman who dug in dirt most days, the room was an unabashed female hideaway. Exactly what she craved.

She'd had more than enough stress today. She'd

think about everything tomorrow, but for right now she just needed…

The telephone rang.

Of course her dad could have answered it. Or Russell.

But when the receiver next to her bed rang again, it was obvious no one else was going to pick it up. And it could have been her mother. Or Ginger. Or something wrong at the lab or greenhouse…worry built up so fast and thick in her throat that she grabbed the phone and then almost dropped it.

"I'll be back in town tomorrow, Lucy," Nick said, "but I had to know what the doctor said. Are you all right?"

That voice. It made her think of dark chocolate, but not just dark chocolate…a dark chocolate mint with brandy inside, or maybe with a little vanilla mascarpone filling in there, too. It was a voice that flowed into a woman's mind and seeped into her fantasies. It was a voice that tended to make bone tissue turn liquid. It was a voice with so much pure lusty male vibration to it that it could probably make a puppy puddle.

"Lucy?" Nick repeated. "Are you all right?"

"There's no ulcer, no tumor, nothing terrible. Thanks for calling, Nick. And thanks for arranging for me to get into a doctor so quickly. Don't worry about a thing. I'll see you tomorrow." She hung up.

Then unplugged the phone. Thank God there were still some land lines left in this world.

* * *

NICK BARELY STEPPED out of the car before the front door opened. Out bounded Baby and Boo Boo, accompanied by his niece.

"Hey, Uncle Nick! Bet you didn't expect to see me, huh?" Gretchen had turned twelve a few weeks ago. Nick had figured out that was some monumental thing to her because she'd changed her whole style of clothes, but what that all meant completely eluded him. This morning she had on a down jacket over a corduroy shirt that showed her skinny tummy—and here it was, freezing like a banshee outside. She was so gawky, all hair and big eyes and knees, so shy she could make herself sick in public situations. But not with him. She adored him almost—almost—as much as he adored her.

"Hey, shorty. What's this, you're already skipping school at your young age?" He pulled her into a hug, loving the smile she beamed up at him. She was smaller than the dogs. Although God knew, almost everyone was smaller than the dogs.

"Nah. There was a teacher in-service day. So I had it free. And I'm supposed to be at Dad's this week, but he's busy and he and Mom are fighting anyway, you know? So...I thought I'd come out and see Gramps and you."

Nick couldn't kick his big brother from here to the South Pole, but often enough, it was tempting. Clint and Gretchen's mother had never gotten married, thank God, but they still couldn't seem to resist fighting in front of the kid all the time. It killed him. The squirt likely wouldn't be half so painfully shy and misfit-y if somebody was around to actively parent her.

"Can I hang with you?" Gretchen asked.

"Hmmm…" He had to talk to Lucy this morning. Immediately. It wouldn't wait—not after hearing her voice last night—not if he was going to keep his sanity. The rest of his work, he could either shuffle or make-happen around a few hours with Gretchen. He'd done it in the past. "I need to have a half hour with Lucy at the lab. Alone. A real serious meeting."

"Oh. Okay." Her face fell five feet. "I understand."

He could tell she did. He could tell she'd had to understand too damn many things, too damn many times, for a twelve-year-old. "How about this for a plan? We can walk over together. You can hang with Reiko or Fritz or Fred. Or just wander around. In fact, you could help make sure I get that time alone with Lucy. We'll get our meeting over a whole lot faster if we aren't interrupted by anyone."

"I could do that! I'll make sure nobody interrupts you!"

"And then we'll do the day. I still have some work, but you can hang. Have to go over to the plant—but you'll love that anyway. And I'll finish what I have to and then we'll split, okay? You bring your fiddle?"

"Uncle Nick! I play the flute, you know that!"

"Yeah, I know. And you're so good I was thinking maybe you could play for me a little later, huh?"

"You don't really want me to."

Damn kid never thought anyone wanted to be with her. "Yeah, I do. Give me a second to pick something up from the house…and then we'll walk to the labs with the dogs, okay?"

"Yeah, that'd be great."

Okay. So walking with a twelve-year-old kid wasn't exactly a great way to get his psyche prepared for the talk with Lucy. But he usually had a gift for multitasking. Hell, he'd just traveled from Paris to Berne and back, did some moving and shaking to get the construction on the new greenhouses started, contacted security people, initiated a new contract with their Berne people—and that was just the last two days. Surely he could handle a reasonable discussion with a twenty-eight-year-old woman?

"So Uncle Nick…then Uncle Nick…and after that, we like…"

Gretchen, God love her, treated him like a hero. Sometimes, like this morning, it made him feel lower than pond scum. He adored her. He'd adopt her if there was ever a need. But he wasn't the kind of hero she wanted him to be. If the world were the right kind of place, she'd have a dad who'd earned that kind of respect, and a ton of other role models who could do a better job than him.

But right now she was chattering nonstop, at least

until they reached the doors to the lab. She quieted instantly, doing her shy thing. The dogs, by contrast, howled as if someone were killing them because of being left outside.

The place was as deserted as a carnival in the rain, no sign of life in any of the offices. All the noise and action emanated from the communal lab, where the whole staff clustered, bustling around some fresh chocolate tests. Reiko and Fred and Fritz called out welcoming hellos to both him and Gretchen. So did Lucy.

But he saw what she tried to pull off. She took one look, startled when she saw him, beamed out a cheerful hello and dove for the side door.

He caught up with her midflight, with what he hoped was an unobtrusive hand plucking her shirttail. "We'll be in Lucy's office for a few minutes, everyone. You okay, Gretchen?"

"Sure," she said, which was what Gretchen always said, but in this case, Reiko was already inviting her to try the new chocolate. The kid'd be okay.

Lucy would probably be okay, too.

Whether he was going to be okay was the real question. Because one look at her face and he knew this was going to go bad. Very bad. Maybe very, very bad.

As soon as they were out of sight, she said, "I know, I know, we didn't finish our Bliss project discussion the other day—"

"No, we didn't. And we need to get that done damn quick. But that's not all we have to discuss right now."

"What?" At the door to her office, she moved in first, quickly, as if allergic to being that close to him. He'd felt the startled tremor streak her spine when he'd touched the back of her shirt. And now she didn't hide behind the desk, but she moved as far as the windowsill, where she could lean, arms under her chest, chin up...as if she were braced for a blow.

He latched the door and leaned there, giving her some space, but for damn sure blocking the exit. "So," he said gently, "you're pregnant."

"Huh?" She shook her head as if disbelieving such an incomprehensible ridiculous statement.

Aw, hell. Politicians lied better than she did. Nick felt as if a lead ball—with spikes—had just dropped in his stomach. Yeah, he'd guessed the truth from her voice last night. From everything. Until that instant, though, he thought there was still a chance of some other answer. Fear of disaster didn't always mean a disaster was going to happen. Only he saw those hazel eyes shifting from his like a thief in a bank.

He wiped a hand over his face, wishing he could wash himself into a state of invisibility. "You're pregnant," he said again. "By me." For a second there, he wasn't dead positive if he was saying it aloud for her sake or his.

"For Pete's *sake*. I'm going to sue that doctor. I

realize it was your doc, but all the same, he can't just tell someone else a patient's confidential medical infor—"

"Luce—" He had to interrupt her. "No one told me. I just added it up. Your sudden throwing up, the timing, your swearing there was absolutely nothing wrong. Only you've never even taken a sick day, much less mentioned ever having an upset stomach to anyone. So…I looked at a calendar. The night you called me about the successful experiment—"

"That night doesn't have to mean anything. For all you know, I sleep with zillions of guys. Regularly."

He didn't say, when cows fly. But straight arrows like Lucy just didn't tumble for strangers. Or on a whim. Hell, her greenhouse floor was clean enough to eat from; she was that persnickety. "Look. You don't have to make up stories. We're in this fix together—"

"You're not in any fix, Nick. I am. This was totally my fault. You never came on to me. Never invited anything. Nothing would ever have happened if I hadn't…" She swirled her hands.

"Is that supposed to mean you didn't intend to tell me?" When she didn't give him the correct answer for that question, he said, very very quietly, "You just agreed to take on a mountain of extra work—to become an integral part of a chocolate project that could throw the cacao market on its ear and shake up the whole chocolate industry. Yet you didn't figure you needed to mention that you had a major health issue like a pregnancy on your plate?"

"Well. No."

Okay. He didn't have a temper, he'd told himself a hundred times. And if he did, there were very few people who could push it. But Lucy headed the list. Ramifications of this pregnancy—her pregnancy, *their* pregnancy—kept popping in his brain like mini-explosions. What to do. How. Where. When. But first, he obviously had to deal with that sick, panicked expression on Lucy's face.

"Luce…listen to me. We can work out whatever you want to work out. We can make happen whatever you want to happen." He heaved out a wary sigh. "Although you know my grandfather will only have one solution."

"No one has to know it's yours. And that includes Orson," she promised him.

"That's *no* solution."

"I'll get a mountain of pressure from family, too. Everyone will have an opinion about what I should do and try to railroad me into doing it."

"Caving into pressure from any side is no solution, either."

"So," she said, as if that single word were a finished thought.

"So," he echoed, and took a step forward, meaning to touch her. Why exactly, he didn't know, when he had never initiated a personal contact of any kind with Luce before. But the instinct to touch seemed to bubble up from a well of frustration and helplessness—feelings he had no tolerance for. This was all going crazy wrong. So far their whole conversation had been awkward and weird and unnatural. For darn sure, he'd *wanted* to face her, *wanted* to have this out. Wanted it down in black ink, what they were both going to do—if there really was a pregnancy.

Only in both his head and heart, he just couldn't seem to totally believe it. That single occasion, hell, it hadn't even been a whole night. One single crazy, crazy hour had led to this. In fact, when he'd wakened the next morning—in his own bed, alone—he thought he'd dreamed the whole thing. It just seemed incomprehensible that anything intimate could have happened between them.

And now Lucy was shrinking from him.

Nick couldn't remember feeling lost. The feeling was alien to everything he knew about himself. When his parents died, grief had overwhelmed him, but he'd had to take on responsibility and grow up so fast that he'd never had time to wallow. God knew, he'd made mistakes. And he'd played around plenty. But from the time he was a kid, he'd had the power to make all the major decisions about his own life with nominal outside interference. Now, though, there was Luce. Who didn't seem willing to even talk to him, much less include him in giant decision-making that affected both of them.

This wasn't just…upsetting and unsettling. He couldn't feel more lost if he'd been dropped in the South Pole without a compass.

"Look, Luce," he tried again. "Let's work from stuff we know we can agree on. I'll pay all your doctor bills. And for anything else you need or wanted related to this—"

"Actually, I don't think I'll need help. You know what great insurance I have from Bernard's. But don't worry. I'll ask if something gets beyond what I can manage."

Shit and double shit. Strangers could be having this conversation. Not people who were supposed to have been lovers. "Okay, skip any talk of money for now. What about…the pregnancy itself. I mean, I don't know whether you're scared or happy or angry or what. Have you thought about what you want to do?"

Her shoulders drooped just a little as she shook her head. "I just found out yesterday. To be honest, Nick, I'm still reeling."

It was the first honest, natural thing she said. "Me, too," he admitted. "I don't know what to say, what to do. But it seems like the place to start is with the sure things. If you're absolutely sure you want to keep the baby, that's one thing. But if you're considering—"

"An abortion? Or adoption?" She swallowed hard, as if trying to talk through a stone-size lump in her throat. "I'll consider everything. All the options. But the only thing I'm positive of right now, Nick, is that you and I don't even like each other. Not really. We had a moment. That's all. There's no basis for a marriage or anything crazy like that."

"I wasn't thinking marriage."

"I'm sure you weren't," she said swiftly. "I just wanted to clear the air, make sure you know that I'd never pull that chain in a hundred years."

She'd stiffened up all over again, as if braced for him to say something hurtful. He started to answer her, but then the doorknob rattled, followed by strange scratchy noises. "Not now," Nick called out, but the knob just rattled again.

"Uncle Nick, it's not me!" He heard Gretchen's voice pipe up, and glanced at Lucy, who was obviously as distracted by the child's voice as he was. Her lips twitched at Gretchen's obvious fib.

"If it isn't you, how come I can hear your voice?" Nick said wryly.

"Because it's Baby and Boo Boo. Somehow they got in the front door. And they ran all over the place. They're trying to find Lucy. And I can't hold them. But don't interrupt your meeting! I'm right here! I won't let them in! Don't you worry, Uncle Nick!"

Any other time, he'd have laughed—and Lucy undoubtedly would have, too. This time she just said quickly, "We can't discuss this now, Nick. Not at work. And besides that…"

Yeah, he knew. Besides that, outside the door was clearly bedlam.

Of course, pregnancy was a kind of bedlam, too, but for now, hell, both his personal life and Project Bliss seemed like trying to handle balloons in a high wind. He'd not only lost control. He couldn't imagine right then how the hell he was ever going to *get* control again.

CHAPTER FIVE

SATURDAY MORNING, just after ten, Lucy opened the bathroom door in a rush and ran smack into Russell—or, more specifically, her forehead rammed into his. Both winced.

Lucy recovered quicker, but her sense of humor was starting to slip on the subject of her cousin. God knew she loved him. Totally. The way you can only love good family—through their bad habits and the good stuff both. But damn. Ever since he'd shared his revelation with her, he seemed to think talking about it with her every spare second was going to make the subject easier to deal with. It wasn't that far a drive for him to commute from school in Mankato, but he was starting to become a dust catcher at her place. Last night he hadn't gone home at all.

When she'd first moved into her own place, she'd imagined—she'd actually totally believed—that she could go to the bathroom by herself. Indulge in her wickedness, by herself. Run around naked if she wanted to, by herself.

"I *know* you want to talk some more, Russ, but honestly, I just can't right now. I told you. I'm having lunch with my mom—and it's a solid hour and a half drive from here—"

She flew past him toward her bedroom, still zipping her favorite black jeans and toweling her hair dry at the same time. Russell, who seemed to think his announcement about being gay meant she wouldn't mind dressing around him, followed as far as her doorway. "I just don't know what I'd do if I didn't have you to talk to."

"That's crazy, Russ. You spent all last night talking to my dad, you get on with him like a house afire. You know you could tell him—"

"No. He's great, but I couldn't tell him this. Or anyone else."

"I'm just not sure why you picked me. I love you. You know that, but honestly, I know nothing about this kind of thing."

"That's not the point. The point is that you're the one person on the planet I completely trust. Not just trust that you wouldn't tell, if I asked you not to. But also trust that you wouldn't condemn me." He watched her pull on the white sweater with black stripes, a gift from her mother, and then attack her hair with a dryer.

"Are you sure you're gay?" Lucy asked over the dryer's whine.

"I admit I'm not dead sure. But I think I am."

"Did you actually sleep with another guy?"

"No."

"Kiss another guy, make out?" Cripes, she couldn't hear over the dryer so she switched it off, opened some pots, did the cheek and lip thing, then the earring thing, then grabbed her hairbrush. Somewhere she had some pull-on black boots. Dress boots. Soft kid leather. Heels.

"Well, no. But the feelings are there."

"Well, everybody gets feelings. When I see a beautiful woman in the movies, I notice her, and believe me, I'm not gay." The boots were in the very back of her closet. She rubbed off the dust, then backed out and hopped on one foot to pull the right one on. "For Pete's sake. I think everybody notices their same gender and can respond to their attractiveness and looks—without automatically thinking you're gay. Or that there's anything weird at all." She pushed hard—they were those kinds of boots that fit great once you had them on, but it took ages to get them on right.

"You think?" Russell asked. He still stood slouched in her doorway when she pushed past him toward the kitchen. He was wearing what he'd worn last night, when he'd claimed he wasn't sleeping over—the oversized shirt, the canvas pants, the no socks.

"Come on, Russell, you *know* that. It's just common sense. Only the homophobic types get hysterical if they have a *feeling* now and then. But I think you should ask someone with some life experience in this—"

"No," he said in a panicked groan.

"Okay, okay. But I knew one homosexual person pretty well. She's a woman. I met her in college. She was a good friend then, we just kind of lost touch after graduation. But I could try to track her down if you want me to ask her for some information or advice." She almost choked when they walked in the kitchen. Her pristine white counter and gleaming sink had disappeared. All she saw were beer cans. Coffee mugs. Leftover pizza. Crumbs. Mysterious and scary stains on the floor.

She had a fond memory from a few weeks ago— before the Night of the Chocolate—when the kitchen was still hers, all hers, and even the corners in the cupboards had been spotless. Even the corners of the *top* cupboards. Even under the refrigerator. Even behind the trash bin.

"Did you actually do anything with that friend? You know, experiment or anything?" Russell was now leaning in the doorway to the kitchen.

"No."

"But did you want to experiment? Did you think about it?"

"No. Cripes, Russell. It never occurred to me. I don't think it occurred to her, either. She was just a regular kind of friend." She grabbed her fringe bag, passed by the fresh round of messes in her living room, and shot a passing, desperate look at her picture over the fireplace. The only thing still normal in the whole place seemed to be her picture of the lone eagle flying over the lake. Her life was starting to feel like it had moved ten points off center and was never going to come back in focus again. Except for the eagle. The eagle was still all hers. She grabbed her coat. "I have to go. I'll be late for lunch with Mom as it is."

"But you're not getting…impatient…about talking with me about this, are you?"

"Of course not. We'll talk whenever you want."

"I know your dad's at the store. But I may stick around with him today. If he wants to go to a movie or something."

"Sure, sounds great. Only if I come home to find this place even more of a sty, I'm going to kill you both."

"Sure, Luce. Sure." He stood motionless and woebegone as she smooched his cheek.

She ran outside, only to feel a startling gush of wind. The ground was a muddy, soggy mess from all the melting snow, but even though the day was ugly, the sky polka-dotted with clouds, the breeze had a cocky scent to it. A springlike whisper of sweetness. She wanted to savor it, only damnation, guilt kept biting her conscience, so she ran back in the house. "Russell," she said irritably, "I love you. And you're going to be okay. All right?"

"Yo," he said.

Since she found him bending over the open door to her fridge, she assumed he really was okay and not as deprived of sympathy as she'd feared. Hightailing it back outside at full speed, she zoomed out of the driveway and flew toward the highway, mulling the upcoming lunch with her mom.

She'd already mentally debated whether to tell her mother about the pregnancy. She still wasn't sure. Her instinct was to stay quiet, to be sure of her own heart before bringing anyone else into the picture. But no matter how that worked out, Lucy couldn't wait to see her mom. She just wanted to be around a female.

For someone who ferociously guarded her quiet, boring, orderly life, hers seemed to be plucking apart, stitch by stitch. Russell had been hanging around enough to gather dust. Her dad seemed more and more installed. Her unpaid-for white carpet had an unknown brown stain by the couch. Her unpaid-for couch now had a building residue of Dorito, cookie and cereal crumbs. Her tidily rolled-up white bath towels had become heaps on the floor. Her clear glass shower door, that she'd thought was so decadent, so wicked, so fun...

She shuddered. It just wasn't a good thing for your dad to walk in on you when you had a clear glass shower door.

When it came down to it, the whole wicked thing

just didn't work when you had a parent in residence. Or when you discovered you were pregnant. The whole point of the wicked thing was to loosen up, change her fussbudget ways, live a little. But cripes. When a woman did that once—for less than an hour—over an entire life and got in this much of a mess, maybe she'd better go back to the boring saint scene.

The point, she told herself, was that she needed this lunch with her mom like she needed oxygen. It wasn't about the pregnancy. It wasn't about her sick confusion over Nick. She just wanted to be around another someone who communicated. Someone who talked the same language. Someone who said things in a way she understood them.

In other words, another woman.

Even speeding the whole way, she didn't reach the restaurant outside of Rochester until noon. She charged in five minutes late, but Eve didn't show up until ten minutes after that, so by that time Lucy was already installed in a booth with her jacket off and some milk ordered to settle her stomach.

The lunch crowd in Rochester was always the same, weekends and weekdays—all doctors and medical staff or patients. Eve drew every eye when she walked in, always had. Ginger had inherited their mom's looks; the elegant bones, the perfect nose, the layered blond hair that never looked "done" but somehow always looked right. It wasn't Eve's looks

Lucy had ever envied, though, but her presence and poise. She always figured she had the poise of a floppy pansy.

Her mom spotted her and zoomed across the restaurant. "Honey, you look as if you haven't slept in a week." She bent down to kiss her, and Lucy inhaled the warm cheek, the aroma of Samsura, the look of an elegant sweater over a simple navy dress. She'd know her mother, even blindfolded in a crowd, just from the textures and scents, and for the first time in weeks, she felt her defenses crumble. She didn't have to be strong. Not around her mother.

"To be honest, I haven't been sleeping, Mom—" Who knew how badly she wanted to let down, tell her mother about the whole crisis? But Eve interrupted before she could start.

"Let's order. I'm starving." The waitress was already jogging over. So lunch was ordered, and then Eve said, "I love you, Luce, but if you only wanted to have lunch to talk about your father—"

"I don't. I just haven't seen you in a while, and since Dad's been there, it's even harder. I just missed you."

It was as if her mom never heard her. "Because I'll tell you right now, I've had it. I know the lawyer I'm going to. George Grams. We all went to high school together. Anyway...when I was younger, I found your father's helplessness endearing. He needed me. He was so brilliant. Brilliant surgeon, brilliant in everything. I used to think it was cute that he couldn't tie his own shoes."

Okay. Her mom was a little frazzled. It was time to listen, not to talk. "So all of that means...?"

"That it's not cute anymore. I want you to realize I'm serious this time, Lucy. I'm going to get a divorce."

"So...have you been to see this George Grams?"

"No. But I will."

"Have you talked to Ginger yet?" Lucy already knew that answer, since the sisters e-mailed every few days. Ginger had the lucky advantage, though, of living far enough away to escape certain sticky family situations. At least she never got caught in the direct crossfire.

"No," Eve admitted, "but that's only because I haven't had time to hash it all out with Ginger. I don't have the energy for that kind of thing yet."

"Uh-huh. So. We've been down this road before. You don't really want a divorce."

There was a pause, when the waitress came back. Lucy had a small bowl of pea soup, while Eve had ordered two pieces of lemon meringue pie. Occasionally Lucy considered emergolating her mom. It just wasn't fair. Eve had the body of a model even though she shoveled in everything. Lucy shoveled in everything, too, and like the rest of the family, she never gained weight. But she also never got boobs, either; she just got zits. Particularly if she overindulged in meringue or chocolate.

Eve motioned with a finger. "I *am* serious about the divorce this time. I've had it with being in a marriage where I'm a nonstop nursemaid and mother. I want to be appreciated as a woman."

Oh, man. Did she need to hear this? She looked at her pea soup and then quickly covered it with a napkin. That green just wasn't going to work with a stomach that was suddenly roiling.

"Lucy, you listen to me. Do *not* get trapped by the surface traits of a man. Don't look at someone's brilliance and think—that'll be enough. He has to *like* being with you. You have to be able to laugh together. He has to *see* you. Instead of looking at you and seeing his work and his golf game and what you're going to make him for dinner and everything else but who you are."

"Okay," Lucy said gently, but her mom was just warming up. She decimated the lemon meringue almost as fast as she talked. Lucy let her spill. For a while.

"At least the sex was always good. Who'd think it, when a man's so selfish in other parts of his life that he could be great that way? But it was. Except that all men get to a certain age—not necessarily the Viagra age, but where—"

"Okay," Lucy said with a rare note of firmness. "I love you, but there's a line. Your sex life is the line. We're not crossing it. But since you're obviously willing to keep talking about Dad, let's just take that subject from a little different direction. He's at my house, for Pete's sake, Mom. This can't go on indefinitely. Tell me what you want me to do here!"

"No. That's exactly the question I won't answer. That's how it always is. Whenever he flounders, it's somehow my problem. Well, not this time. You do whatever you think you should. What I want you to do is make your father stand up. Wash his own socks. Not expect someone else to pick up his pieces."

"And you think I could force him to do this how?"

"I don't know. I certainly couldn't." Eve finished the last smidgin of meringue. "I think I'm going to have an affair."

"I'm going to pretend I never heard you say that," Lucy said cheerfully.

"I've even picked out the man. I'm not sure if this isn't really a very good answer. Sleeping with someone I don't care about. Just having a wild fling. Maybe then I could go back—" Eve suddenly seemed to realize that her daughter was having a heart attack. "All right, all right. We'll quit talking about this. Come on." She picked up the check. "Let's go shopping."

Shopping didn't help. Lucy pined after a Staub cocotte in just the pot size she wanted, but damned if it wasn't over a hundred dollars, far too much for a tightwad—much less for a pregnant tightwad who might or might not be supporting a baby in the near future.

"What's wrong with you?" her mom teased. "I thought you got a huge promotion."

"I did. Enough to pay off tons of things. Maybe even splurge a bit, too, but you know how it is. Some days the shopping gene doesn't seem to hit."

But it did for her mom, who bought lacy purple underwear and a loose silk robe. Sexy clothes. Ideal attire for a tryst with a lover, which was enough to give Lucy heartburn.

As she drove back home, night fell, bringing a gloomy, blotchy dribble of rain. At the turnoff for her exit, a genie seemed to control her hands on the wheel. Instead of taking her exit, she drove toward Bernard's instead.

She just couldn't face going home yet, face her cousin and her dad and the house that had stopped being hers. Somehow she had to figure out how her whole life had taken such a complete drastic tailspin. Somehow she had to get back in control of it again.

The grounds at Bernard's were deserted. The chocolate plant had a partial day shift working, but by Saturday night all the employees had cleared out. Gordon was reading a romance—which he quickly hid when he buzzed her through.

"Don't tell me you're working this late on a Saturday night, Ms. Fitzhenry?"

"I could say the same about you, Gord. How'd you get stuck pulling the weekend night shift?"

"Volunteered," he admitted. "My daughter, she's

getting pretty serious about her boyfriend. I have a bad feeling we're going to have a wedding in our future. A big wedding. I told her she should elope, but I think she has visions of a big expensive splash, so I figured I'd better add a shift now and then."

She chatted a moment more, because darn it, Gordon was a dear, but once she got past the last security gates and parked in front of her private lab, she felt a feeling of release inside. It'd be quiet here. Safe. She could think.

She key-coded her entry, pushed off her jacket and shed her purse right in the lobby. No one else was going to be here, no need to be tidy or formal. She surged down the quiet halls, past the offices, straight into the general lab—knowing exactly what she wanted to do. What she *needed* to do.

She aimed straight for the wall of stainless steel, temperature-controlled minivaults. Each of the researchers had separate ones, both so that experiments were protected and couldn't get mixed up with each other. She unlocked hers. Inside were chocolates left over from the first batches of Bliss she'd put together...there wasn't much left now, but still a box or two. She lifted one to the counter, opened it, closed her eyes and took a long, slow bite.

She waited, her eyes still closed in intense concentration. This wasn't about having a chocolate attack. This was a serious experiment.

She'd overindulged on this specific chocolate

that night. It had been a natural thing to do, because from the first taste, she just couldn't believe how uniquely fabulous it was. She'd tasted and tasted and tasted some more. Maybe she'd even gotten a little chocolate-drunk.

Was it possible that's what had destroyed her sanity? Was it possible that Bliss was dangerous?

Still fiercely concentrating, she let the nectar melt on her tongue, inhaling the smell, savoring the taste and texture.

Vague memories sifted and shifted through her mind—the memories she usually banished as fast as she could vacuum them out of sight. The memories had been right in this room. This crazy, cold kitchen-lab. Or at least they'd started here. It'd been a winter night, tons of snow outside, the fluorescent lights bright in here. And right here, she'd somehow met-amorphosed from the natural prissy old maid type she was into a complete nymphomaniac. With Nick. With Nick, who hadn't asked to kiss her, hadn't asked to have his clothes pushed and stripped off him, hadn't pushed to complete the wild seduction she'd started.

It was the chocolate.

Her parents' divorce. Russell. Her father. The pregnancy. Her behaving like a wanton goofball. Until that night, she'd had a totally quiet, normal life. She'd never messed with the boss's grandson. She'd never even considered such a crazy thing. Nick was completely out of her realm, completely different from her. Yet after several pieces of Bliss…

Lucy opened her eyes, plucked another piece, popped it in her mouth and closed her eyes again.

There had to be answers for the mess she was in. There *had* to be. It'd be a whole lot easier if she could blame it on chocolate, but one way or another, it had started with this delectable, unforgettable, unforgivable, uniquely intimately fabulous taste that was like absolutely no other…

"Lucy?"

She blinked—then squinted hard. Nick was in the doorway.

Nick.

Just as if she'd conjured him up from the taste of that wicked chocolate like she had the first time.

WHEN NICK REACHED the door to the lab, he was out of breath. Gordon had called him. The security guard had orders to contact him whenever anything happened out of the ordinary, especially now. Too much was going on in the lab, worth too damn much money, to risk any breaches of security.

Lucy was hardly a breach of security. She worked odd hours, always had. But Gordon contacted him because of the timing—it was a Saturday night, meaning there was no one else around, and Gordon was the old-fashioned type who fretted when a woman was alone at night.

Nick wouldn't have, normally, but Lucy was pregnant. When the call came on his cell phone, he'd just been having a beer and dinner with friends—an easy gathering to leave—and the whole drive here, he'd shaved his nerves raw. He just kept thinking she could have gotten sick, been alone, anything could have happened to her...

So he'd driven here hell-bent for leather.

Only now he could see she was fine. Beyond fine. She was sitting on the Formica slab, wearing skinny black jeans and an even skinnier black-and-white sweater, popping down chocolate. The good chocolate.

Damn woman had nearly given him a stroke, and here she was indulging in her favorite vice.

Besides which, she noticed him and turned stark white as if she'd suddenly seen a ghost. "Geezle beezle. You scared me half to death," she said.

"I scared *you?* You scared me. What the hell are you doing here at this hour on a Saturday night?"

"Hey. I have every right to be here."

Aw hell and double hell, now he'd offended her. He sucked in some oxygen and tried to calm down. "I know you do. I'm not questioning that. But there's no one even within shouting distance, and you could have gotten sick—"

"I'm not sick, Nick."

"But you could have been. And anyway, that's not the question. I'm just asking why you're here."

"Because I was testing something."

"What?"

The strangest expression crossed her face. By then he'd finally calmed down enough to take her in. Something seemed different about her. The snug black jeans and black-and-white sweater didn't seem particularly odd. And she was sitting cross-legged on the counter, the way she often did…nothing different about that, either. She had the same flyaway hair, the same freckles, the same kid-sister kind of looks.

But…maybe it was the harsh light? Her eyes looked deeper and darker than midnight. The long line of her neck looked whipped-cream soft. And he'd always noticed that she rarely wore makeup, had nice skin, but somehow it hadn't registered before that her skin was softer than silk. Sensual. Touchable.

"Lucy?" he asked again, more slowly. "I'm not trying to ask you a personal question. I'm just asking you about business. You're not going to suddenly spring more surprises related to Project Bliss, are you?"

"No, no. Nothing like that."

"But you said you were here…testing something."

She swallowed quickly. "I am, but…nothing like that. Nothing for the company. Darn it, this is embarrassing. Could you just forget it?"

He stood there, confounded. She was in his lab. At a strange hour. Alone. Claiming she was testing something, when her last experiments were likely to add millions to the Bernard coffer, and she wanted him to just forget it? "Luce…it can't be that embarrassing. Just tell me what you're doing and I'll forget it."

She pushed down from the counter, color flaming her cheeks, and then started repackaging the chocolate. Even when she was obviously nervous as hell, Luce was Luce and she was never going to be careless with chocolate. She resealed it just so, before carefully putting it in the stainless vault. Then locked the vault and checked it twice.

"Lucy." There were times he appreciated her fussy ways, especially as her employer. But hell, he'd hustled here and worried about her and was still worried about her. There was no way he was leaving without some answers.

"All right, all right. I just wanted to know if the chocolate was dangerous, okay?"

"Dangerous?"

She checked the lock for the third time.

"Lucy," he repeated, his tone of voice communicating clearly that he'd had enough of the nonsense. She must have realized it, because she suddenly answered even if she did have a hard time meeting his eyes.

"Not dangerous—as in something with Bliss or any of our testing on Bliss so far. Not dangerous—as in anything Bernard Chocolates needs to be worried about. Not dangerous—as in anything that could be a liability issue related to Bliss."

"Okay, but then…what other kind of dangerous could you possibly mean?" he asked, feeling more bewildered by the minute.

Exasperated and aggravated and huffy now, she blurted out, "For Pete's sake, Nick. I always sample the results of an experiment. At least my experiments. It's part of the job. But the night that first batch of Bliss came out…"

"Yeah?" Suddenly he had a worrisome, itchy feeling where this was going.

"You know it was good. Impossibly good. Which was why I tried another sample. And then some more. And that was when I called you, to tell you we'd hit serious success, and you came over with the champagne…" Her words came out fast and low. "And that's the point. Not the champagne. Not that you came over. But how much Bliss I'd taken in that night. You know perfectly well that there's a chemical rush from chocolate. People thought for decades that it was both an aphrodisiac and a sexual stimulant." She hiccupped. "And that isn't all nonsense. I mean, some of it is. But 600,000 tons of cacao beans were consumed every single year in the '90s…"

He swiped a hand over his face, disbelieving she was embroiling him in one of those pedantic lectures on stuff he already knew.

"It's not the jolt of caffeine or the sugar that gives

the kick, the way people used to think. It's the phenylethylamine, the same natural chemical that runs in the blood when somebody feels they're in love. Not that chocolate is about love. I'm not saying that. That's ridiculous. But I did have a lot of chocolate that night. And I started wondering—or worrying— if it was the nature of our Bliss. If it produced a stronger response than other kinds of chocolate. Because if so, this is something I never tested for. It never occurred to me that I needed—"

Okay. They were going to be here past midnight if he couldn't get her to stop talking. And apparently she was going to rant on unless they dealt with the embarrassment problem. "Lucy, are you trying to say that you think it was the chocolate that made you jump me that night?"

There. Her eyes met his. With a flash of emotion deeper than a well and just as unfathomable. "Well…the thing is, that otherwise I can't explain it."

"You don't think that possibly there isn't anything all that complex to explain? I mean…it seems pretty basic to me. A man. A woman. Alone. Late. Both ecstatic over a remarkable experiment's success. So there was a moment between us, that's all."

"A moment," she echoed.

"Yeah. A moment. When it all clicked between us."

She gestured. "But that's the point, Nick. I don't

understand how it could possibly have clicked, when you don't even like me—"

"Of course I like you."

"I mean *that* way. And from my side of the fence, I just don't…jump men. I never jump bosses. Positively I'd never remotely imagined jumping you. So I started to think—to worry—that possibly some mind-altering thing must have been involved or I'd never have come on to you."

He wasn't dead positive, but he was pretty sure she'd just insulted him. "So…you came here…to try some more of the Bliss, to see, um, if you felt like jumping someone else?"

"Well, of course not. I was just going to sample it. And then see if I lost my mind."

He stared at her for a minute, trying to analyze how he should answer her. It was like trying to communicate to someone speaking in Russian. She hadn't made a lick of sense since he walked in.

But then he realized the oddest thing. He wasn't talking to her from across the room.

He'd ambled closer. Distractingly closer. She'd gotten down from that counter, but she wasn't as short as usual. She wasn't wearing sneakers today, but black boots with heels. When or why he noticed those boots, who knew? But he heard himself saying—as if an ogre had sneaked into his mind and taken over his tongue— "Lucy, you didn't lose your mind. It wasn't the chocolate. You can stop worrying. I can prove it."

"You can prove it how?"

Right then and there, Nick mentally swore that if he ever had a daughter, he was locking her in a convent until she was thirty. Women like Lucy just weren't safe out there in real life. Not as long as there were guys out there, anyway. God knew, he wasn't the worst, but hell. When a woman aggravated and worried and tangled up a man's mind the way she had, come on…any guy was going to be tempted to seek a little payback.

She looked curious when he stepped toward her—curious, but not concerned. She took a backwards step, as if assuming he wanted to reach for something in the vicinity of where she'd been standing…making it damn clear that his wanting to kiss her never remotely occurred to her.

Even when he snagged her wrist, she didn't seem to guess.

Even when he tilted up her chin with his knuckle, her expression revealed complete confusion. She didn't have a clue.

But when his head ducked down, he saw those whiskey-brown eyes deeper, darken. He heard her breath catch. Felt the sudden trembly chill in her fingertips. And then his mouth dove down and settled on hers.

She tasted like warm, dark chocolate. Rich. Soft. Meltable.

Nothing in the universe tasted exactly like chocolate. Not good chocolate. Not the really exquisite chocolate.

But she did. And no, it wasn't the Bliss she'd been indulging in that put that exquisite taste idea in his mind. It was her. Her mouth. Her taste. Her lips molded under his, melted under his. Against his chest, for that instant, he could feel her heart stop beating. She went still, on the inside, on the outside.

And damn it. So did he.

He'd meant to kiss her. Meant to show her the obvious—that even people not normally tuned to each other could get a click of chemistry if the circumstances were right, a man, a woman, alone, night...

Only until that instant, he had no idea there was a deeper truth hiding behind his heart. Sure, he'd felt guilty about that night—very guilty. It wasn't his fault she'd come onto him. Not his fault he'd responded to a woman who came on like a Lorelei, willing, hungry, wild. He'd never have initiated anything with Lucy for a zillion reasons, the main one being she worked for Orson. But that whole night had been so...odd. It would be hard to guess whether she'd been more stunned, or he had. But that night, neither of them had any defenses because neither had a clue they needed any. By the time she was rubbing up against him and he was kissing her back, it was just too late to hope his boatload of ethics was going to row back to shore.

Now, somewhere inside him, that stunned feeling

was sneaking up on him again. He believed what he'd told his conscience—that all he was doing was showing her that a decent-looking single guy and a decent-looking single woman could kick up some chemistry—naturally. It wasn't Chocolate Bliss. It wasn't insanity. Rub two people together, you got friction. No mystery there.

Only…

Only…he suddenly spun her around so he was leaning against the cold counter, so he could pull her closer into the wedge between his thighs, so he could kiss her again. More deeply. More completely.

She lifted her arms, possibly as if she intended to push him away, but instead her palms slid up, slowly, to the slope of his shoulders. A sigh whispered from the back of her throat when he gulped in a breath, then, still frowning and furiously confused, dipped down to take her mouth again.

This just didn't make sense.

He and Lucy were chalk and cheese. He'd never been attracted to her. Yeah, of course there was that whole chemistry propinquity factor—rub a guy and a girl together, and guess what, he got a hard-on. But he'd never had a problem backing off from an inappropriate situation. He'd never leaped just because a woman offered him a "yes." And there were a hundred, thousand reasons for his natural inhibitions—and ethics—to go on high alert where Lucy was concerned.

But her mouth still had that delicious taste of dark chocolate. And that sigh of hers was throaty and wicked and sweet. Her fingertips stroked from his shoulders to around his neck, then tightened as if she was afraid of falling. Her arousal sparked his.

He got that part.

His head and his groin *both* got that part. It was the rubbing thing. The natural propinquity thing. But blaming Mother Nature just wasn't cutting the mustard. There was something far more complicated going on here.

He couldn't pin it down…but it was something in her taste. Something in her sweetness. Something in the way her small breasts nested against him, the way her head tilted to take in the pressure of his mouth, the way her hair sieved through his fingers like rich silk. Something about *her.* Uniquely *her.* That wasn't normal.

And whatever this terrifying Something was, it was making him behave and think and feel unnormal, too.

He found the force of will to stop kissing her, to lift his head. He gulped in some air, tried gulping in some more. It didn't clear his mind but it helped a bit. The scowl on his forehead seemed grooved deeper than rock. "For God's sake," he said.

Abruptly Lucy opened her eyes, and damn her, but those eyes looked more vulnerable than silk and satin and a baby's heart. When she tried to talk, her voice came out thicker than honey. "I don't understand…why did you do that?"

"Why did I kiss you? To show you that Bliss wasn't dangerous. To show you that this can just happen. Put a man and a woman alone, and nature kicks in. It's nothing to be afraid of."

"Right," she said. "Nothing to be afraid of."

When he drove home later, though, Nick's mood was itchy. They'd both said the right words. In fact, they both seemed to have the right words down pat. And maybe Lucy felt as unafraid as she let on…but the more he was around her lately, the more he felt like climbing K-2 in a howling wind had to be safer than this.

CHAPTER SIX

NICK POURED three mugs of coffee, leaving spills all over the blue stone kitchen counter because his hands were unsteady. Two o'clock on a sunny Sunday afternoon and his whole body was suffering hangover symptoms—only he hadn't had a lick of anything alcoholic.

If he wasn't hungover and he wasn't stressed out, logic would suggest that the hand tremor and the panicky pulse were caused by fear.

Nothing to be afraid of, Lucy had said the night before. Or was he the one who'd said that to her?

Either way, he hadn't slept worth a dime and he was antsier than a Mexican jumping bean. Scowling, he mopped up the counter, tossed the rag in his copper sink, and carted the tray of mugs into the living room.

His brother, Clint, was already sitting in a chair next to Orson—which meant there was another logical reason for a guy's hands to shake. Nick loved them both, but the rare times the two were allowed in the same room, there was always a chance the combination of gas and a lit match would explode.

Nick plopped down the tray, well aware the two of them were sitting like stones, obviously not having said anything to each other. He mentally sighed. "Rack 'em up," he said to Clint.

"We didn't come here to play pool," Orson said stiffly.

"No, We're here to talk some serious business. But there's no law we have to sit still while we talk. Come on, grab your coffee."

Getting the two moving was harder than herding goats, which was pretty silly, considering they only had to walk a few feet. Nick had called this impromptu meeting and set it up at his house, thinking that his place was more neutral so they might get along better. So far that was working as well as peace talks in the Middle East.

Afternoon sun poured in the long, tall windows, softening the male-starkness of his living room—navy curtains, navy walls, navy carpet. The white leather couches were as comfortable as pillows, but as soon as the men stood up, the two Great Danes—quiet as mice, just bigger—climbed on the couches and settled in for some serious snoozing. Nick was still herding family into the next room when his gaze chanced on the original oil over the white stone mantle.

The painting showed a long eagle winging its way over blue waters. Alone. Hunting. Lonely. Wild.

Years ago, Nick had seen a print of the painting, and loved it so much he'd spent months tracking down the original. He never knew why the painting moved him. It just did. He'd never been one to waste time analyzing. Just then, though, it streaked through his mind how totally unafraid the eagle seemed.

That was how Nick used to feel. When it came down to it, he really couldn't remember being afraid of much—until last night anyway.

Skydiving, he loved. Snakes, could do. Thunderstorms, climbing, deep-sea diving, flying, small spaces—all those things were a no-sweat. Occasionally shopping gave him the willies, just wasn't his thing, but that wasn't the same as a serious fear factor.

A memory seeped in his mind, of the afternoon he'd lost his virginity—and yeah, he'd definitely been scared about performance issues, but mostly he'd been so hot to get his rocks off that he didn't have enough functioning brain cells to be scared in any real way.

Actually he could only think of a couple times he'd been downright, beside-himself frightened. The first time was when he'd heard his parents had gone down in the plane. It was Gramps who'd told him, after the police had gone, and just hearing the words had hollowed out everything inside him, put him in an emotional state so achingly awful that he couldn't breathe, couldn't think, couldn't move.

It wasn't the kind of memory a boy of fourteen would ever forget.

There'd been one other occasion. A very different kind of fear. He'd been nineteen, driving with a bunch of kids—all roommates from college, happy, full of hell—skiing. God knew whose car it was, but it quit on a train track. Wouldn't start and wouldn't start. And then they saw the train coming.

He hadn't wet his pants. But he'd considered it. Definitely a major fear moment; he couldn't deny it.

And then there was yesterday.

It just didn't make sense, he thought in confusion. Nothing had happened that could compare to his other huge, life-altering events. He'd just kissed Lucy. Maybe more than once. Maybe each kiss had tended to quadruple in intensity. But still.

They'd just been kisses with a woman who was supposed to mean very little to him. Sure, she was important to Bernard's—and to his grandfather— and it's not as if he didn't like her. He did. Always had. But especially now, Lucy primarily represented a bucket load of worry and concern and aggravation and stress. So it made even less sense to have a hands-shaking, no-sleep, itchy-pulse fear reaction to a few kisses.

How many women had he slept with, for Pete's sake? What on earth was there to be scared of? And then a *really* scary thought popped in his head.

It couldn't *really* have been the chocolate, could it?

"Nick," his grandfather snapped his name. "You wanted to play this game, now where are you? We've been talking to you and you haven't paid a lick of attention!"

"Sorry. Woolgathering, I guess." Nick gave himself a mental kick in the rump and rounded the corner. The pool table was in the dining room. Actually, the pool table *was* the dining room. Business meals were catered at the mansion, and if he was serving food, it was invariably for a woman, which was much better done in front of a fireplace—or, for that matter, on a mattress. Which was to say, that he had absolutely no use for a traditional dining room.

So he'd covered the light walls with some tongue-in-groove red wood, shuttered the windows, bought a honey of a slate pool table. Orson and Clint both played, but just then they stood at the far end, holding sticks and chalk, still not speaking. God forbid the two of them try to share a pleasant thought without an interpreter.

"Clint, you rack 'em, and Gramps, maybe you could flip for the break," Nick suggested, which at least got them moving. Not talking yet, but at least moving.

For a short time he was distracted from thinking about Lucy.

Clint had walked in with a chip, which Nick had guessed the minute his older brother had driven in on the Harley. The motorcycle was guaranteed to annoy Orson.

When Nick looked at his older brother, he saw their dad. Carson Bernard had had the same brawny build, the big shoulders and bushy head of brown hair, the same brash smile. Driving his cycle on a cold March day like this, Clint was decked out in a leather jacket and pants that cost more than most people paid in monthly rent. Which was typical. Clint loved flying, cycling, climbing, deep-sea diving—anything that cost money and involved playing. The only thing in life he took seriously was Gretchen, whom he adored.

Clint had all the money to play he wanted. Orson had never cut him out of funds. He'd just cut Clinton out of any decision-making power of Bernard's as of thirteen years ago—when he'd gotten Gretchen's mom pregnant. Clint still had an office, but even showing up was an insult; the only thing in his in-box were charity and donor requests.

Nick had tried to get between the two a million times, always got bit in the butt for his trouble. Clint had stopped asking for anything meaningful to do, just made out like he wanted nothing more than to live the high, wild life. Orson made out like he didn't give a damn what Clint did, just kept pouring on the money—and withholding all respect.

It was a miserably touchy situation. At least from Nick's point of view. He didn't want his brother cut from the business, yet he had no way to push their grandfather. Orson had been father and mother to both boys, done everything, given up his own personal life to raise them—but hell, Orson could sure be unforgiving.

It was a trait Nick knew damn well he shared. Worse yet, the only time the trait kicked in for Orson was when the subject was honor. Clawing Nick's heart and conscience both was the constant awareness that he'd gotten a woman pregnant now, too—just as Clint had.

When his mind strayed back to Lucy again, he shut it down. God knew that was a crisis situation, but just then he had an immediate crisis that needed handling.

Orson won the break and landed the two ball in the side pocket. Conversation slowly edged into the business they'd come to discuss, but nothing happened easily.

"I'm well aware you have no interest in the business, Clint…" Orson lost his shot and had to give up the table. He also paused in case Clint wanted to argue with his comment, so that he'd have the chance to climb all over him, but Clint didn't bite. "But we both feel you should be aware of our current plans."

Clint lined up a shot. The three ball careened off the far edge, dipped in the side pocket. A brilliant shot. He never failed at anything—except for winning Orson's respect. He looked at Nick, not at his grandfather, for one unguarded moment revealing his hunger to be part of the Bernard business again.

"This Chocolate Bliss sounds phenomenal. Exciting, full of potential. But I'm not quite sure why we're talking about this so soon," he said. "No matter how outstanding the first experiments were, you're just initiating a major planting program right now, right? So it'll be another four years before the new trees are in production, then another four before they're really producing beans in any quantity. So sure, I understand, down the pike this could be huge. But right now would seem too soon to talk about major investment changes."

Typically, Clint revealed more knowledge of the business than Orson ever gave him credit for. Nick jumped in to answer, though, to avoid the two sniping at each other as long as possible. "Normally that would be true. But in this case, Bliss could have such long reaching effects that we have to develop a more complex strategy. Right now, only a handful of countries import cocoa. It's just too expensive."

"I know that," Clint said, already starting to sound defensive.

"But it won't be a luxury item if Chocolate Bliss succeeds. If we can manage to grow good cacao in a variety of climates, not just limited to rain forests, people everywhere could start enjoying it. Demand would more than double. Hell, demand could be limitless."

"Yeah...of course. I get it now."

Nick could see the wheels were turning in his brother's head, and in the meantime, it was his turn to take a pool shot. Although he could have made the shot in his sleep, he deliberately chose to miss it.

Sometimes losing was the only way to win. The truth of that grated against Nick's competitive nature, but letting Orson and Clint beat him was a sure way to keep them happy. "There's another huge thing that will drastically change if Bliss succeeds. And that's availability. The only time anyone could ever get cacao was limited to the span of October to February—when seventy-five percent was being harvested. But if we can grow it in more diverse climates and situations, we should be able to work with cacao all year round, not be limited by one country's drought or disease or anything else."

"You don't have to keep going on. I get it," Clint said testily. The brothers paused to watch their grandfather try and make an impossible shot—at least for an old man who was supposed to be fragile and majorly arthritic.

And it was Orson who intervened this time, directing a comment directly to Clint. "I wouldn't be cutting your brother short. You need to listen. We all need to understand how our Bliss experiment could affect the market long term. This isn't a small change. Availability, price, marketing, quality control, products—everything we know about the chocolate business today could drastically change if Bliss comes through for us."

Clint definitely picked up the bigger picture by then. "Man. People are going to try and steal from us right and left when news of Bliss gets out."

"I see that as a serious worry, too," Orson concurred. "Furthermore, other countries are hardly going to sit around indefinitely and watch us produce the only high quality cacao trees in this country."

Clint leaned against the wall, forgetting his turn. "They're going to want our trees."

"Exactly. So that raises another problem. We're used to working with patents on our chocolate products and processes. But how to patent and work with these multi-climate cacao trees is a whole different ball game."

Nick was afraid to smile, for fear of jinxing the moment, but damn. Clint and Orson were actually talking. He added, "And part of that problem is that we'll have forked over major investment dollars to experiment and produce the cacao. I don't believe we have any responsibility to give it away free. But I also really don't want to sell trees for a living."

"Hell, neither do I," Clint agreed. "Chocolate's our business. Not nursery stock."

Nick heard the *our* and was afraid their grandfather was going to clip Clint at the knees. But Orson was too busy zooming in on three balls in a row.

"Therein lies the problem. It's going to cost us a bundle to take this project all the way. For a long time, the risk is going to be all on our side. So one way to help finance it is to get a penny every time someone plants one of our rootstock."

Nick added, "Also, if we patent our cacao trees, we'll have some control over how the chocolate is released into the marketplace. Then we can prevent product flooding the market and really screwing up the price of chocolate."

It was Clint's turn, but he seemed to have forgotten all about the game. "You're talking about building an empire," he said slowly. "Hell. In the last ten years, we've gone from a highly successful ma and pa company into a multimillion-dollar player, but now, my God. This is a whole different world."

"I think 'empire' is a little too strong a term," Nick said wryly.

"I don't." Orson precisely hung up his pool cue. "This may be chocolate, not world peace. But it *is* a big deal, boys."

"It's a miracle that would never have gone even this far if you hadn't pushed for it." Nick gave him credit.

"It was an old man's idiotic dream that you catered to. You were the one who brought on research staff to run with it. And then Lucy, who heaven knows, took the ball in the last stages." Orson sighed. "But the point right now is simply to get the three of us on tap. I don't even want more lawyers in the picture until family is on the same page."

"You're giving me a vote?" Clint asked. "That's sure news."

Nick could feel it. Clint's comment turned the temperature down in the room thirty degrees. As if suddenly wakened by a sixth sense of something wrong, Baby and Boo Boo showed up in the doorway. They took one look at the guys, then flopped down where no one could possibly get by them.

Just like the men, Nick thought. When Orson and Clint drew their lines in the sand, neither could seem to find a way by each other.

Orson answered Clint as if he'd just been waiting for the first excuse to attack. "No, you're not getting a vote. But your brother insisted that you be informed. There's a good chance you'll have even more money to fritter away on toys and travel and boats and cycles and all."

"So…you think I've got a right to know what's happening. Just not a right to have a say." Clint took a slow, lazy step toward his grandfather.

Gramps took a slow, lazy step toward him. "You lost that right when you proved you couldn't be trusted."

"Oh, for God's sake. I'm sick of hearing that. I made a mistake thirteen years ago. You never once slept with a woman without protection, Gramps?"

"Never," Orson said.

"Well, it must be nice to be such a saint." Clint took another step, making them nose-to-nose.

Orson didn't back down. Nose-to-nose was just fine with him. "It isn't about being a saint. No man is that. But a man who doesn't have character is a man who can't be trusted."

"What in God's name does it take for you to forgive? You don't think it's a little ridiculous to hold one mistake against me for all this time?"

"One mistake? My great-granddaughter is not a mistake. And my great-granddaughter shouldn't be a bastard. She should have the Bernard name."

"You're saying it would have been better if I married a tramp?"

"It would have been better if you'd never slept with a tramp. It would have been better if you'd had the character not to get a tramp pregnant with a Bernard child."

Nick watched the color shoot up his brother's neck. "This is the oldest broken record in the book, Gramps. I can't take back what I did. Can't you just once look at how many years have passed?"

"I *do* look. And I see you playing on every continent. Wine, women and song is still your theme. Same old story. Never looking for responsibility, just a new way to have fun."

"Only because you won't give me a chance inside the company."

"You've got an office," Orson reminded him.

"Yeah. Only there's nothing there. No job, no role."

"But lots of money," Orson said quietly. "All the money you could want. You can't complain you were ever treated poorly, Clint. You're set for the rest of your life. And now, if Chocolate Bliss comes through, you'll have even more than you ever dreamed of."

Clint hung up his pool cue and stalked out of the room, his neck red and hot. The front door slammed. Outside, the engine on the Harley revved on high before aiming down the road.

Nick looked at his grandfather. Orson stood at the window, tracking Clint's leaving with old, thoughtful eyes, but his posture remained unyieldingly stiff.

"You two," Nick said quietly, "will never resolve this."

Orson turned to him. "I raised you boys exactly the same way—but somehow you turned out to be a man. And he's still a boy. When he's ninety, he'll still be a boy—unless he wakes up and stops blaming me for his problems."

"He wants you to give him a chance."

Orson shook his head. "I'm dying to give him a chance. But he has to take it. Not have it be given to him. Or it won't work."

Nick frowned. "I don't know what you mean."

Orson moved toward the door. "That's because it

would never occur to you to run away from a mistake or a problem, Nicholas." He found his coat. The dogs stood up, waiting for him. "Bernard's takes care of its own, son. But I'm not putting someone in a position of responsibility who'd have the power to financially hurt the rest of us and all we've built up, just because they may be family. You can change all that when I die. But as long as I'm alive, that's the way it's going to be."

When his grandfather left, Nick was too roiled up to settle down. Restless as a wet cat, he paced the house from room to room.

Normally, the place gave him a feeling of safe haven. As a young man, he'd lived at the mansion, in a separate wing from Orson, but it still wasn't enough. He needed his own space. When this house came on the market, he'd leaped. It was only a few minutes drive from Bernard's, and although the layout wasn't originally ideal, he'd hired an architect to make the place really his.

Now he wandered, up, down and around. He stood in front of a spare bedroom—the one he'd turned into a giant closet, half for clothes, half for sports gear. Everything was tidily put away, even his ragged jeans, even the boots with the holes and his favorite beat-up jacket.

Everything looked right, but there was no peace-pill there. He wandered into the master bathroom—which was, hands down, one of his favorite creations.

It had been no small construction job to put a live fireplace in a bathroom. He'd chosen it all, the step-up copper bathtub, the towels thicker than blankets, the recessed lighting. Ditto for his bedroom, which wasn't fancy, no mirrors or satin sheets or anything corny like that, just a bed bigger than a boat, sleek sheets, Swiss pillows.

None of it seemed to mean a damn. Not today.

Still pacing, he scraped a hand through his hair, trying to analyze why he was so miserable. As if there were a mystery.

Lucy's face popped into his mind faster than fire. Naturally the conversation with Orson had shaken him. Nick was unsure if his grandfather would survive discovering there was another bastard grandchild on the way. It would kill him even worse to discover the mom of the baby was Lucy.

But the most painful issue was that Orson would never likely forgive him for getting a woman pregnant. It didn't matter how different his circumstances were from Clint's. It didn't matter what else Nick had done with his life.

Hairier yet, Nick wasn't damn sure he could forgive himself, either.

Every time he tried to imagine himself as a father, his breath started coming in sharp, wheezy gulps. He'd survived losing both his parents. Survived inheriting the real work of running a business when everyone said he was too young. He handled his own life without help from anyone, just wasn't a fearful kind of guy.

Yet the idea of fatherhood tilted his entire personal windmill. And just as startling to his entire ego and esteem, one small, all-American shrimp of a girl kept scaring the holy wits out of him.

He didn't know what to do for her.

He didn't know what to do with her.

He didn't know what to do. Period.

CHAPTER SEVEN

THE WEEKEND HAD BEEN so stressful that Lucy couldn't wait to go to work on Monday. Her personal problems never chased her to work. She loved the job too much, and now with Bliss, had so much to do she could hardly think.

That was the theory. The reality, by Thursday night, was that she seriously considered clicking her heels three times and hiding out in Kansas. That not being an option, she hung the do-not-disturb tag on her bathroom door, whipped on the bathtub faucets, poured in evening primrose and cranberry melon and started stripping.

She'd had it, had it, had it.

Except for hurling a bunch of times, the work week had gone well, in fact, splendiferously. She'd sent Nick extensive written plans on Bliss, which saved her having to talk to him—and enabled her to concentrate on a frenzy of further experiments. She tested how the chocolate held up to heat and freezing, how it performed in various applications, all kinds of things. So far, their new baby couldn't seem to fail a test. Tarnation. Bliss wasn't just good chocolate or great chocolate. It was beyond anything even Lucy had ever dreamed of, and God knew, she was a choc addict from way back.

Unfortunately, work wasn't everything. Her life kept sinking into a deeper and stinkier mire.

When the tub was filled, she lit two vanilla candles, turned off the lights, and sank into the soothing, aromatic water. With a sigh, she leaned her head back against the smooth porcelain.

It should have helped. It didn't.

She glanced down. No tummy yet. The only sign of the pregnancy—beyond the hurl habit—were achy, swollen breasts. For the first time in her life, she just might fill out a B cup. But what she wanted, what she *needed,* was time to think about this pregnancy.

Instead, she seemed surrounded by people nonstop. Her dad, much as she loved him, was completely obsessed with himself and his marriage problems. Her mom was just as bad. And Russell, who'd always been her favorite cousin, seemed to be parked at her place until he got control of his life and feelings.

Lucy lifted a washcloth and purposefully dripped it over her head. The problem here, she knew, was her. Everyone brought her their problems. That's how it always was and how the family liked it. It was how *she* liked it. Only now, when she had a serious problem of her own, she couldn't seem to find a blink of time to dwell on it.

She was running her life wrong, she thought direly, and then ducked under the water altogether. She came up, hair soaked and dripping and sank back again.

Come hell or high water, she was determined to soak in the tub for a full twenty minutes. She was entitled to twenty minutes off from her life. It should be a rule, she thought. No one should have to live one's own life 24/7 without a break now and then. She'd just reached for the soap when the door suddenly zoomed open—bringing in a gust of chilled air and a man she didn't know from Adam.

"Oh, I'm sorry," he said.

"You didn't see the do-not-disturb sign?"

"Well, yeah, but I didn't know the house, and I had to pee."

"You must be one of Russell's friends," she guessed. It's not like it was a *Jeopardy* question.

"Yeah. Who are you?"

He was still standing there, tall, skinny, wire rims, still letting in gusts of cold air. Yeah, the angle of the tub pretty well covered her, but for Pete's sake...

"I'm the owner of the house," she said. "Go away."

"Is there another place for me to pee?"

"Yes," she said. "Outside. Or in your own home."

"Okay."

When he closed the door, she thought, no, that was too bizarre, it couldn't possibly have happened. But it had. Between Russell and her father, strange people were regularly invading her duplex. Eating her food. Making messes. Playing poker in her kitchen with her cards. Dropping pop and peanuts on her white rug. Peeing and missing the toilet.

Granted, they were all guys and there was only so much you could expect from the male of the species. But the women in her life, she had thought she could count on. Instead, her mom was likely to cause her a heart attack rather than be supportive right now. Ginger was too far away. Reiko was wonderful, but she could hardly spill anything to someone at work. And then last night, she'd tried having dinner with Merry.

Merry Olson had been her closest friend since grade school. They'd suffered braces, crushes, embarrassing moments and Mrs. Larson in geometry together. They'd always been able to share anything, no matter how hairy or touchy. This time, though, she'd really wanted to see her friend face-to-face, so she'd taken off early, driven to the suburb of St. Paul where Merry lived.

She'd desperately, desperately needed to talk about herself. About this pregnancy. About the terrifying and confusing feelings for Nick. And almost the first thing that popped out of Merry's mouth was,

"I'm so glad to see you. I've had something to tell you I couldn't share on the phone."

"What?"

"Do you see anything completely different about me?"

Lucy had looked. Long dark straight hair, sleek as satin. Dark eyes. Red lip gloss. A figure to die for, even covered up in jeans and a purple MSU sweatshirt. "You look great," Lucy said.

"Yeah. That's the thing. Lucy—" she leaned forward over the plateful of French fries, so no one would hear, "—I figured it out. I'm bipolar."

"Say what?"

"You know how I'm always so happy. That's why. Because I'm sick."

"Wait a minute. Why can't you just be happy because you're happy?"

"Because no one's as happy as I am. It's not normal. And this guy at work—"

"I want his name and address," Lucy said firmly.

"Well, his name is Jerry. I think I told you about him. He's the best ad man out there. Hard to get along with for some, but not for me. We've gotten to be good friends, you know? And he got around confessing to me that he was bipolar. They used to call it manic depressive—"

"I can't believe he conned you into believing this."

"He didn't con me, Lucy. He recognized the symptoms in me because that's what he had himself.

Running a hundred miles an hour. Always laughing, full of energy, but then sometimes falling into a big moody low—"

"Merry, you're a bitch one day out of the month. That's not a major low. It's just a pain in the butt!"

"But not like *my* low. Or like *his* low. And he had some extra meds, so he just said try them and—"

"And you immediately said no. Remember, how you used to get all As and Bs in high school? So I *know* you did the bright thing—"

"It was just an experiment, Lucy. And I could see almost immediately how they changed how I felt. That was the whole point, to see if they had any effect. And if they did, then I'd set up an appointment with a doctor—which is exactly where this stands right now. My appointment's next Wednesday. But in the meantime…"

Lucy sank deeper into the bathtub and tried to relax. The scent of vanilla candle drifted toward her. With her toe she added more hot water. She wasn't leaving this tub. Maybe ever.

Her best friend wasn't mentally ill. Merry was just a tad prone to believing others. She was a born cheerleader, naturally enthusiastic and upbeat. That someone had convinced her this was an illness made Lucy want to get up, drive to Merry's place, find the address for that Jerry and murder him.

She couldn't do that, of course.

But she couldn't shake the unnerving sensation

that her life had somehow shifted to another galaxy. Merry had her irrepressible moments, but she'd never made downright crazy choices before. Her parents had argued for thirty years, but her dad had never shown up with a suitcase of socks; her mom had never talked about running off and having wild affairs. Her cousin Russ had always tended to turn to her with problems, but they'd been like flunking-algebra problems, nothing so soul-altering as a sexual-identity crisis.

The people in her life had always been a little bonkers. Who wasn't? Everyone had difficult relatives and friends. But everyone had seemed reasonably sane until…well, until the Night of the Chocolate. When they'd all started falling apart on her.

Softly Lucy pressed a hand over her tummy. Maybe if she could feel something, she could start to believe the *p* word was real. As it was, her heart filled with panic every time she thought of the pregnancy. Dread mixed with joy, anxiety with wonder, confusion with fear. Mostly she just felt as if she'd taken a free-fall skydive from ten thousand feet and couldn't seem to get back her sense of gravity.

She *had* to think about this pregnancy. Had to figure out what to do. Had to figure out what she wanted from Nick, how she should and could handle him. Only her life had become this crazy roller-coaster ride. She couldn't get it to stop. She couldn't even get it to slow down.

Someone knocked on the bathroom door.

"I love you, whoever you are, but *go away*."

"It's me, sweetheart." Her dad's voice expressed patience. "We're out of potato chips."

"Dad. I don't care."

"And someone's here to see you. I let him in, told him you were in the tub and he'd have to wait. Actually, I asked him if he wanted to join the poker game. He didn't want to, but he had a beer and we've been keeping him entertained. But then we ran out of potato chips—"

"*Dad*. Who is it?"

"His name's Nick."

She stopped breathing. "I know you don't mean Nick Bernard."

"I didn't ask his last name. It was obvious that he knew you, honey, and I didn't want to pry…"

She opened the drain and stood up so fast, the room suddenly spun. So did her stomach. "I'll be right out."

She only knew one Nick. And she told herself that it was totally strange that he'd have looked up her address and come here, but of course it wasn't. She knew exactly how much unfinished business there was between them.

She grabbed a towel, roughly dried off, applied two layers of deodorant, brushed her teeth. There were no wardrobe choices. Since she'd planned on disappearing into her room after the bath, she'd only brought in navy sweats to put on, and she was hardly going to run down the hall in a towel to choose something else. Still, she had lip gloss in one drawer, and she found blusher in another. She didn't want to take the time to blow-dry her hair, not with Nick out there waiting, but that was no problem anyway. Her hair was already flyaway-dry by the time she wooshed open the bathroom door and let out several clouds of steam.

Immediately she heard voices coming from the kitchen, but none she recognized as Nick's. She heard her dad. Russell. Russell's friend who'd needed to pee. And another man's voice, maybe Dr. Anderson—her dad's buddy, who'd been regularly coming over to play cards with her dad in the evening. But no other voices.

Could Nick have left?

She hustled around the corner into the kitchen, only to stop dead. Her senses promptly overloaded. All the kitchen lights blazed hotly on the scene of carnage. The spillover of cards and poker chips. The two baskets of open, bulging trash. The crash of dirty dishes on the sink, the crusted-on pans and sticky counters. The smells of burned pizza, smoke, beer. It was enough to give a prissy fuddy-duddy, such as herself, a panic attack…but really, all that stuff she only noticed in a vague, peripheral way.

Nick *was* there. Her Nick. The one man in the universe that she didn't want to see…and yet, so fiercely, did.

He was leaning against a counter—primarily because so many poker players jammed around the table left only standing room. He was wearing an old leather jacket, unzipped, a black tee, jeans and boots. Those dark, sexy eyes found her in the doorway over all the noise and mess and confusion in two seconds flat.

She'd blocked the memory of the kiss in the lab the other night…just as she'd brilliantly, effectively blocked the night they'd made love, as well. But now, she suddenly experienced a short, hot flashback. With absolute clarity she remembered calling to tell him the experiment results of Bliss, her being so high, so totally high…his bringing over champagne…her dancing around, going on and on and on. About the chocolate. Only about the chocolate. She'd had no thought of sex, no personal agenda or thought or intention toward Nick in any way at that moment.

Only somehow, in the middle of all that dancing and prancing, she remembered being euphorically excited and happy and suddenly kissing him. Really, really kissing him.

It had been all her doing. All. He hadn't invited a single thing.

She blamed most of it on the chocolate. And a little on the two glasses of champagne on an empty stomach except for the chocolate. But some of it…some of it just wasn't a matter of blame.

She had been totally unprepared by the symphony of sensations. That night, she'd felt fiercely high on herself as a woman. She'd never thought of herself as powerful. Yet she was that night, with him. She remembered feeling…alluring…hot…hungry. Demanding—as if she suddenly realized she had a right to demand everything she wanted from life, from a man, from *him*. Her body acted as if it were an instrument playing an acute—exquisitely acute—musical crescendo in her breasts, her stomach, her groin, her blood.

Oh, how her blood had raced and rushed. Oh, how she'd kissed him and kissed him…and then stripped him.

God. The flashback came on so fast she didn't have time to block it, and suddenly Lucy felt the room spinning faster than a child's toy top…and then everything went black.

NICK FIGURED he must have fallen down a rabbit hole, only where the hell was the ladder back up? A loony bin had to be saner than this household.

At least he'd gotten her away from the madhouse in the kitchen. It was quiet in her bedroom, but when Lucy tried to lift her head, he gently, firmly pushed it between her knees again. "Let's just take it slow," he said lazily. "No reason to rush. Let's make sure you're not still dizzy."

From somewhere between her knees, she mumbled, "I know you must be thinking I can't take care of the Bliss project, but I *can*, Nick."

"Forget work. I didn't come here for that, Luce. Just practice slow, easy breathing for a few more minutes, okay?"

He didn't hear her agree, but at least she didn't do anything terrifying for the next few seconds, so he took the chance to catch his breath. Her bedroom seemed to be a vast ocean of lilac. Who could guess anyone could pack in this much purple? There were tufts of it. Smells of it. Candles and flowers and curtains and pillows of it. He'd never expected to ever see her bedroom, much less invade her private space. But when she keeled over, it just made sense to steal her away from the chaos.

It was definitely quiet in here, but as girly as it got. If she tried lying on the bed, he feared she could disappear in all those foamy, tufty covers. As it was, with her head between her knees, her nose might be buried somewhere in purple down at that level, too. Possibly he was smothering her.

She mumbled, "You can let me up. I'm better. Really."

"Yeah, well, let's not hurry it." God knew what he was going to do with her when she sat up.

When he drove here for a confrontation, he'd expected trouble. How could he not? Nothing he needed to say to her was conceivably easy. But her father answering the door had thrown him for a loop...and then there was a stunning jolt, when he'd stood inside the front door with a clear view of her living room, and saw *his* picture over her mantle. The one with the lone eagle winging over blue waters. The one he'd spent a fortune to buy the original of. The one that clutched him right in the soul…so it was eerie and unnerving to realize it had some kind of personal feeling for her, too.

Then came more shocks—one jolt after another. Nothing he saw in her house made a lick of sense. Lucy was as organized as a librarian, as fussy and meticulous as a mathematician. Hell, you could eat off the floor in her greenhouses. Yet here, in every room, on every surface, there seemed mess on mess on mess…none of which seemed to be hers. She didn't even seem to *know* two of the males in her kitchen. As far as he knew, she didn't even drink beer—much less smoke cigars.

He wasn't sure how many people were living here, but they all seemed to be living off Lucy. He remembered her saying one time that her dad was a cardiac surgeon, a big guy at Mayo. At first glance, the guy was a nice-looking, intelligent-eyed man—but his hair stood up in unbrushed cowlicks; he was eating out of a pan and throwing back the beer.

And damn it, she'd scared the *hell* out of him when she'd looked so sick and keeled over.

For that matter, she was still scaring him. "Luce?" Her hair was all soft, all flyaway, lighter than dust in sunlight when he reached over to touch her. He couldn't stay hunkered down on her bedroom carpet forever, trying to look at her face upside-down.

She lifted her head. God. Those eyes.

"I think," he said delicately, "that maybe you should tell me what's going on here. Somehow I just can't believe your house, your life, is like this all the time."

"It's not. It's the chocolate. That's all I can figure out. There has to be something in the chocolate that just totally turns your world upside down."

"I'm beginning to think that's possible. Which is pretty damn scary for a realist. But could we just backtrack a bit? Who are all those guys in your kitchen? Are they living here?"

When she lifted a hand to her temple, he figured she was still on the weak side, and since she was already sitting on that bed, he kind of eased her down to a pillow. And so she wasn't lying there in front of him, all cuddly and sweet-smelling and vulnerable, he draped a triangle of comforter over her.

Out poured this confused tale that started with her father, arriving with a suitcase of socks a few weeks ago, claiming he had nowhere else to go. And then her mother claiming they were serious about a divorce this time. And her dad, who'd never taken vacation time, now turning his life into a nonstop poker party. And then there was her best friend who'd decided to take medication for being bipolar even though she wasn't. And last, Russell was her cousin, who was worried about being gay.

"Eugene even called today."

"Eugene?" Nick was trying hard to keep all the players straight.

"An old guy friend. Every woman has a mistake in her past. He's mine. If you're going to make a mistake, I always say, do it all the way. I did. Anyway…"

"Anyway," he encouraged her.

"Russell isn't living here exactly. He just seems to be hanging out here a lot of weekends and evenings. Dad won't go home. He can't seem to make a decision about where he wants to go or what he wants to do. And I wouldn't mind—for Pete's sake, that's what family is for, to be there for you? Only there are stains on that couch, Nick. And I haven't paid for it yet."

"Okay."

"I love that couch."

"Okay."

"And the carpet—I've almost paid for that—but not yet. And I doubt you know much Staub cookery costs—"

"True," he completely agreed.

"And then you see that poster?" She motioned to the framed poster on the far wall, that read: Be Wicked For a Week, followed by a list of ideas—like sleeping late, giving up mineral water, not making your bed, eating dinner in bare feet, that kind of thing. "My life has turned into this terrifying joke, because I really meant it when I bought that poster.

I wanted to live a little wild. Break loose. Just like that. Only…"

She waved her hand. He got it. She wasn't the type to leave an unmade bed or to dine in bare feet. It just wasn't Lucy. And all these intruders had to be driving her crazy.

"You can't kick them all out?" he asked tactfully.

"It's my dad!" And since she'd turned on the faucet, she couldn't seem to stop a little more from gushing out. She'd always had the role in her family of being the caretaker. She'd never minded it before. She even liked it. It was just that right now, the whole world seemed to be caving in on her at once. She wasn't a sissy; she wasn't lazy; she wasn't irresponsible. But right now, for God's sake, she couldn't breathe.

He sat on her purple flowered chair, feeling his sense of gravity tilt. Lucy wasn't a complainer. She wasn't a spiller, for that matter. But it was as if she hadn't told anyone how much had been heaped on her head in the last few weeks—not even counting the major promotion and change in her job.

And he kept getting the needling feeling that she'd told no one about the pregnancy. Except him.

"Nick," she said suddenly, "if you came all the way to my place you must have really been determined to talk. About the pregnancy, I have to believe."

"That was the goal," he admitted. A massive understatement. Especially after the last to-do with Clint and Orson, he couldn't tolerate a waiting game any longer. He needed to hear what she wanted to do as far as the pregnancy. He could face anything if he just knew what it was, and he'd driven here to pin her down somehow, someway—even if he had to sit on her.

Only now he'd seen what she was living with, and it suddenly wasn't that simple.

Her eyes were closed. She was all snuggled up somewhere in those layers of purple down, and now he could see the pale smoky shadows under her eyes, the exhaustion. She said, "You want to talk…we'll talk. You want the whole truth, Nick?"

"Always." No question about that.

"I love kids. Totally. Unequivocally and irrevocably. Always wanted to eventually get married and have a dozen."

"A dozen?"

"Maybe more." She opened her eyes and pushed up on an elbow, although there was no sign of the usual high-energy, peppy Lucy now. Her tone was soft. Fragile-soft. "But I have serious fears that I couldn't be a good mother right now."

"Are you trying to say you want an abortion?"

"No. I'm trying to say that maybe an abortion would be the best thing." She looked away, as if searching for the right words in the ceiling, the far wall, and finally just met his eyes. "I don't know how you feel about this, Nick. But I really believe kids should come into the world with parents who are totally prepared and excited about devoting 24/7 to the parenting job. Or it's not fair. Not for the child."

"I couldn't agree with you more." He hunched over.

"And that's the reason I'm leaning toward an abortion," she admitted painfully. "The thing is that…frankly, I'm a late developer. Some might say a late developer beyond belief. It took me all these years to break away from my family. To finally get my own place. To set up my own life. And I *need* time. On my own."

"Of course you do."

"It's not just selfishness," she said, as if he'd criticized her instead of agreeing. "It's that I've never had a period of time when I wasn't connected at the hip to family, where people weren't depending on me. I've got to have a chance to test…life. To test myself. To know something about what I'm made of. Before just being thrown into the role of caretaker again."

"Okay."

"I'm afraid that if I don't, I won't be a good parent. That I won't have the experience at life, at doing things, to have anything to offer a child. How could I teach a child to be independent if I'm not myself? How can I teach a child to be strong if I've never had the time to develop strength in myself?"

"Lucy…did you think I'd fight with you about this? Because all I want to know is what you want to do.

Whatever that is, it's all right with me. We can work through whatever the best thing is for both of us."

She looked at him. And suddenly she didn't look like a young waif, but a woman in every way. Her soft cheeks and wise eyes and silky hair and the curve of her hip…he was supposed to be thinking about babies. About pregnancies. About how the hell in the twenty-first century a guy could have gotten himself in trouble like this? Instead, he seemed obsessed with the vulnerable line of her chin. With her eyes.

"You don't really want to hear what I'm thinking. You just want the problem to go away," she said gently. "And I don't blame you."

"I suspect you'd like the problem to disappear, too." He didn't know the next words were going to come out of his mouth, yet it seemed he had the same open-faucet problem she had. Who knew something was bottled up until there was suddenly a chance to let it out? "Lucy…there's an answer to this. The same answer that's been around since the beginning of time. If you want the child, we can get married. That gives the child the Bernard name and all the protection that comes with it. It gives you all the resources and protections that come with a marriage, too. We don't have to stay married. You don't have to stay tied. But if you want this child, there's no reason you should take the brunt of all the problems. It took two. I'm not looking to duck."

She cocked her head, and said gently, "I never thought you were." She hesitated. "Orson would have a heart attack if he knew you were the father, wouldn't he?"

"Yes." There was no denying that. "But that's not why I'm putting the option on the table. The fact is— it *is* an option. So is giving the child up for adoption. Or my adopting the child."

"Are those things you want to do?"

He wanted serious honesty between them, yet it wasn't easy to tell her the whole truth…simply because he wasn't dead sure what the truth was. Not for himself. "Right now, I think you have the biggest vote, because you're the pregnant one. But in principle, I have to admit I don't like the idea of adoption—at least adoption to strangers. This is a Bernard child, someone of my genes, my family. It'd really haunt me to have no say or knowledge in how a child of mine was cared for."

"That's how I feel about giving the child up for adoption, too. I know there are ways we could know ahead who we might be giving the child to, what kind of family, their whole setup. But I think I'd always worry that I wouldn't have the power to step in, to do something if there was a problem for a child. I don't believe I could give up a child that way."

"So we both agree that adoption isn't a likely choice for us."

She nodded.

"That answer wasn't so hard to come up with, was it? So that's how I think we should do this. Just start from what you need and want first. See if we can make that happen. Then worry about compromise if we have to."

She looked as if she wanted to quickly respond, but then changed her mind. She scooched up against the headboard, snuggling the comforter protectively close around her. Outside, a night breeze picked up, tugging at branches and brush, making a faint scraping noise against the windows...but he wasn't distracted. He focused intently on nothing but her.

"Nick...I'm serious about being against getting married—really, adamantly against getting married—for the same reason I'm worried about being a good mother at this time in my life. I don't want to be dependent on you. I need to stand on my own. To experience some life. I just don't see that I have anything to offer anyone as a wife, or a mother, until I've proven—to myself—that I can make it on my own."

"I'm not talking that kind of marriage," he said.

"No. You were talking about a business-arrangement kind of marriage. But I don't believe for a minute that you'd *want* to marry me, Nick, if it weren't for the pregnancy. I don't see you comfortably fitting in my life, or my fitting in yours. True?"

He couldn't duck it. "True." He wanted to add more, to gentle that blunt answer, because he meant no insult or criticism of her—or of either of them.

They were simply night and day in personality and background. It wasn't that some kind of living arrangement couldn't work. It was just that in any normal life scenario, neither of them would likely consider the other for a potential life mate.

As swiftly as he'd clipped out that word, though, she'd turned her head. Shadows hid her expression, but her words came out cool and careful. "So marriage is off the table. But we do have especially one terribly touchy situation with your grandfather. And I've thought about that. Orson never has to know you're the father of the child, because I'll never tell him, or anyone else for that matter...if you want that kept private."

"Luce—" He scraped a hand through his hair. She was thinking of him. His needs. His problems. But through the thread of it all, he kept hearing his heart thump with stress.

In the old days, the honorable thing for a guy to do—when he got a girl pregnant—was marry her.

These weren't the old days. But in some ways, he seemed to be his grandfather's grandson all the way, because damn it, he *did* believe in honor. It just seemed that the honorable thing to do for Lucy, with Lucy, was whatever the hell she needed him to do.

Not what he wanted.

She suddenly said, "Nick, I don't want you worried about Bliss. Between the two of us, we'll get the Bliss project on its feet and thriving."

"I'm not worried about the project," he said.

"And I don't want you worried that I'm going to be clinging to you, either. We may be in this together, but you don't have to pretend that you love me. Or like me. Or that we'd ever have had that one night together if it hadn't been for that one, crazy moment in time."

He stood, thinking that the light scents of lavender and lilac were getting to him. They were everywhere, in her hair, on her petal-soft skin, in the air. They were going to his head. He couldn't breathe.

Minutes later, when he was outside striding for his car, gulping in the chilled night air, the same thoughts kept drumming in his mind. She was underwater. With her family. With the job. With the pregnancy.

The pregnancy might be complicating his life— but it was making a chaotic hell out of hers.

The baby mattered.

But she mattered more.

And the way Nick saw it, he only had one honorable choice in this deal. Everyone else in her life was making her circumstances worse, not better, so it was up to him to ease her way. To make things workable for her. To make things right—on her terms.

God knew how. But there had to be ways.

It was up to him to find them.

CHAPTER EIGHT

"OKAY NOW…almost ready." Lucy pressed a palm to her stomach. For the last two weeks she'd wondered if that serious talk with Nick had miraculously worked to help with the morning sickness business. It's not as if the queasiness disappeared, but she'd found all kinds of great methods to cope with it. Soda crackers and pickles and graham crackers all seemed to help. Pickles combined with peanut butter seemed to work exceptionally well.

But this afternoon, nothing seemed to settle her stomach down. She'd been working nonstop on preparations for today's experiment, and if it wasn't for the tummy threat, she'd probably be dancing on the ceiling with excitement.

This was not meant to be a major scientific test, but still, it mattered enough to take major security precautions. The lab door was locked tight, security sealed tighter than the Pentagon, Gordon ordered to close down chance visitors for the next couple hours.

No one had been invited to this particularly elite

experiment except for key players. The group was congregated around the central work table. Fred and Fritz had the far stools; Reiko had perched next to Gretchen, Nick's twelve-year-old niece, and Orson had naturally chosen to park at the head of the table.

"You've all been so patient and this is it. I'm about to bring the last two dishes to the table...." She'd arrived before daybreak and had been running all day to get the tests ready. Midafternoon sun beamed through the windows, as spring-bright as her mood.

Inside, the kitchen work area of the lab resembled a movie set for mayhem and madness. Cups and bowls and cooking tools littered every work surface. Vast quantities of the experimental ingredients—notably eggs, sugar, chocolate, brandy, and mascarpone cheese—had long transferred themselves to Lucy. She was well aware there was chocolate in her hair, likely on her face...along with flour and sugar...also that the red T-shirt and jeans she'd worn to work no longer looked pristine. The dark chocolate was likely never going to come out of her white tennies.

Still, a girl did what a girl had to do for the sake of science.

The huge table in the center of the room was covered with a spotless white cloth. A red ribbon divided the table in two parts. The offerings looked like a feast for gluttons—with two dishes of chocolate ice cream, two of chocolate cones with apricot sauce, and two with chocolate berry tarts. Lucy hadn't brought over the chocolate roulade dishes yet, but only because she was still garnishing them with fresh red strawberries before those two dishes could join the others.

If she said so herself, this was not just a brilliant plan of hers, but also an unbeatably fun way to spend the day. Certainly the boys were drooling, and Reiko and Gretchen looked on the verge. Orson, being Orson, was simply letting her do her job her way.

Obviously the staff already knew that Bliss was her project—and they couldn't help being aware of the new greenhouses being constructed. Innovation was hardly headline news at Bernard's, and everyone understood the need for secrecy while new processes were being developed. Now, though, Bliss had developed to the point that the core group needed to be included in the big picture. Lucy had come up with an experiment as the most effective means to both show and tell them what was going on.

"We've all tested new products before, so y'all know the procedure…." She carried the two roulades to the counter, heard the oohs and aahs from Gretchen and Reiko, and then finally sank on a stool herself.

Her stomach was churning, her hands shaky, but her face was as radiant as the sun. Man, this was fun. And fascinating. For the first time in ages, she'd been able to concentrate on nothing but work—and God knew she loved the work.

"Okay, go. Remember to taste only one dish at a time. I don't care if you start with the roulades or the tarts or the ice cream or whatever—but sample both dishes of the same type before you go on to the next…." She had to remember to take a breath. "You all are too smart not to guess what's going on, so I'm telling you straight. We're comparing our best Bernard chocolate against a new chocolate. To get a fair test, I'm giving you samples of both in various forms—heated, chilled, plain, mixed with other flavors…."

Orson gently nudged her foot, as if to say, it was probably all right to move the test along. Lucy recognized that she had a tiny tendency to rant on, but damn. It was so important that everything be exactly right.

"All right, go for it. We want to hear every detail you can think of. Not just which chocolate tastes better, but how. Why. In what way. Everything you can say to describe what's going on with the different tastes—"

A sudden knock on the door made her jump. No one else was in the building but the group in here, and if security needed to contact them, the guards could have used the phone or pager. A spare second later, she heard the click of the door keypad being operated, and then Nick stuck his head in as if he owned the place.

Well, he *did* own the place, but that wasn't the reason Lucy's heart suddenly went kerplunk. Nick wasn't wearing business duds today, just old jeans and a black sweatshirt and scuff boots—in other words, Nick at his sexiest—which made her pulse feel even more aggrieved.

Darn it, she'd done her absolute best to avoid him for the past two weeks. The night he came over, she'd felt embarrassed to death about fainting all over him...but overall, talking had helped get her mind clear. It was obvious how responsible Nick felt. Also obvious how willing he was to do anything she asked him. Talk about a hero. How could she not be drawn to a man who was so damn great?

Only his whole attitude made Lucy even more determined to not be a problem for him. She'd given him the statistics and plans for Chocolate Bliss on paper, so he wouldn't have to talk to her. And she'd made crystal clear that the pregnancy wasn't his fault—which it really wasn't. The old "two to tango" adage didn't apply when she was the one who'd thrown herself at him. She was the one who'd goofed up both their work and their personal lives.

So she'd tried to make that right by absolving him of responsibility, and especially, by not acting as if he meant anything to her.

But he did. The damn man only had to show up for her heart to do that clanging, clunking, kerplunking thing, and he wasn't in the lab two minutes before he'd wreaked havoc on her experiment and her nerves.

The problem was that he immediately noticed the table of delicacies—and honed there like a bee at a picnic, stealing a spoon en route. At least until Lucy galloped over to cut him off at the pass. "*Not* for you," she said firmly, and took the spoon right out of his hand.

Gretchen immediately started giggling. "But he's the boss, Lucy!" she teased.

"I know that, Gretchen, you darling. But that doesn't mean he always knows how to behave himself." To Nick, who pulled up a stool next to his grandfather, she pointed a lethally dripping chocolate spoon. "If you try sampling any of the dishes again, I'm going to make you sit out in the hall."

"Until recess?" Reiko laughed.

Orson's lined face creased in a smile. "You tell him, Lucy."

"I was *helping*," Nick informed the group.

"You were stealing," Lucy corrected him, thinking that he was. Stealing. Her heart. Their lives were already mucked up because of the pregnancy. She'd screw them up even more irreparably if he thought she was in love with him. Then what would happen to her job? Her chocolate? Her life?

She had to stop thinking this way. Feeling this way. So she turned away from those devil-blue eyes and gave her samplers the rest of the testing instructions.

Complete silence reigned—for all of a minute—

as each scooped up a forkfull of the chocolate berry tart with blackberry sauce...until she saw Nick stealthily poking a finger at the bottom of the dish again.

"Nick!"

"I wasn't going to say anything. I just wanted a sample myself."

"But you're the boss! So your reactions will affect everyone else's!"

"You don't think Orson's response won't give everything away?"

"No. Because your grandfather keeps his feelings hidden. And because everyone will start looking at you, to see if you like something, and that'll affect their responses..."

Nick heard out this criticism with a bland face, but he still said, "It's just not human to be so mean."

Gretchen cracked up again, which made it hard for Lucy to stand tough. Everyone at Bernard's watched out for Gretch. How could they not? The Bernard family were all guys, so whenever the twelve-year-old wandered into the lab—or the main plant—everyone honed in on her shyness and tried to make her feel welcome and a part of whatever was going on. And dabnabbit, seeing Gretchen so happy—giggling happy—practically forced Lucy to keep playing the role.

"Are you going to send him out in the hall, Lucy?" she chortled.

"I might," Lucy said darkly.

"You said you would!"

"Yeah, but now I think that's not a serious enough punishment. Come on, you guys. If you wrote down your response to the chocolate berry tarts...talk to me now. Did you like it? Could you see the difference in the chocolate? I'm dying here."

"You're not serious," Orson said quietly.

The older man always seemed comfortable with Lucy being just who she was—Lucy often thought he hungered to be around normal, natural people, people who didn't always feel they had to kowtow around him. But just then, something in his soft old eyes made her heart catch.

"Which version do you like best?" she asked.

"You know what version," Orson said.

Reiko had turned spellbound-quiet, too. For a few moments, so did even Gretchen. "We all know chocolate," Reiko said. "But the chocolate in this dish—" she pointed to the offering on the left "—is beyond anything I've ever tasted, Luce. I don't know what to say...except oh-my-God."

Fritz and Fred nodded, neither smiling, either. "None of us have patience with less than excellent chocolate," Fred said. "But that one..." He pointed to Bliss. "I've never tasted anything like it. Here or anywhere else."

Orson nodded. "I would think this group would

be as picky about chocolate as anyone anywhere. But that one flavor…" He shook his head expressively.

Gretchen piped in, "There's nothing this good. Anywhere in the whole universe."

Lucy felt her heart ease. Heaven knew why she'd been so worried, when she *knew* how great Bliss was. But this was a first exposure for Fritz and Fred and Reiko and Gretchen. And although she'd personally tried Bliss in every possible application, she wasn't sure if she brought bias into the picture. Now, she could see from the faces that their response to Bliss was the same as hers. And this time when Nick started sampling, she said nothing, just studied his response, as well.

"Okay," she said finally. "Try the other dishes now. You may not have the same reaction if the chocolate is in cooked form—or chilled form." Suddenly her stomach turned over. She felt nausea rise, battled it back.

This was a long way from a serious marketing research study, but it was still a test. She needed to pay attention, not just to what the group said, but how they looked, how they responded to each dish. The lab staff had tested dozens of chocolates before this. They were all used to the nuances of different chocolate—excellent chocolates. Often enough, there wasn't a bad or good report card; it was simply a question of finding out what a particular chocolate was ideally for and using it in that way.

"You all know what we're really doing here," Lucy said. "This isn't that different from all the other times we've tested products. We'll do formal marketing research but not yet. You guys are the toughest judges. We need to be sure you all think we've got something special before we're even close to letting the cat out of the bag, so to speak—"

"Save your breath, Lucy," Orson said.

"Yeah, you're being dumb," Fritz announced in his usual tactful fashion.

Reiko murmured, "We all figured out there had to be something big in the works when the greenhouse construction started—something a lot more special than just expansion. But this... I never imagined anything like this. I've never tasted anything like it before. Any chocolate. From any manufacturer. From any chef. From anyone—including us. It's...beyond bliss."

"It'll wipe French chocolatiers off the map," Orson added, which was his often-voiced dream. The rest of the world valued French chocolate. Orson considered the Dutch to be true competitors and the French upstarts. No one ever suggested that he was a wee bit prejudiced, least of all Lucy, who'd always loved him, prejudices and all.

Now, though, watching the crew inhale her Bliss was better than any formal study. The response of every single one of them was identical. Orgasmic. And Lucy had used Bernard's best chocolate for the control comparison, so it wasn't as if all the dishes she'd created weren't beyond fabulous to start. But Bliss… She'd known when she roasted the first beans months ago…but not like now. Every which way she tried it, it came out the best—the absolute best—chocolate that she'd ever even dreamed of.

Eventually the group finished the tests, and typically, dispersed quickly. Gretchen popped up to take the dogs outside for a run, and then Reiko and the guys hustled back to their own projects. Lucy faced the cleanup alone, but that was status quo. The maintenance crew didn't touch anything to do with secret trials like this.

When she leaped to her feet to start carrying dishes, though, she just assumed Nick and Orson would take off. Yet both of them lingered. Nick said, "I came over today to track you down…to let you know we've got a new member joining your staff as of Monday."

"Pardon?" Lucy turned around with a confused frown. The lab had two high-powered dishwashers, but she'd just filled the sink with sudsy water to prewash the stickiest dishes. "Nick, I've been starting the interview process for employees in the new greenhouses, but honestly, there's no purpose in starting anyone for another couple weeks."

Orson was still sitting at the table, but Nick had stood up and started carting dishes when she did. Still, she didn't expect to find him so close. Touching close. So close she could see the whisker shadow on his chin, the spark of devil in his eyes.

"I know that. This isn't for the horticultural work. And normally, you know I wouldn't get involved with hiring people in your area," Nick said, although he didn't sound apologetic, only blunt. "But in this case, I knew you'd say no if I asked ahead. And I want you to try this out."

"Try out what?" she asked suspiciously.

From the far table, Orson seemed to be shrewdly studying both of them. Lucy suspected he was in on this, but he seemed to make a point out of staying silent.

Nick started threading dishes into the high-powered washer. "You've got too much to do. Or you will, once Bliss starts getting seriously on its feet. The whole kind of testing and experimenting you did today…I'm guessing you'd hate to delegate that, because you love it. And since you have a terrific sense of chocolate—we obviously want you to do the things you do best. Once we get into the nursery work, all the grafting and growing of the new cacao trees, that all involves more time than you can pull off. So as of Monday, you've got a personal assistant."

"What?!"

"His name is Greger Kristofer. His sister's name is Greta, and she's going to do some part-time stuff, as well. They're Swedish-American. Greger's got the general build of a rhinoceros, so you won't have to worry about doing any more heavy lifting. Besides the brawn, he's got some downright serious credentials. I'm putting him in charge of security for the project. He'll hire all the security staff you want, but he'll report directly to me, not to you."

Lucy turned around to squint at Orson. "I know you would never expect me to agree to this," she began, only Nick, damn him, seemed to accidentally move between her and her view of Orson.

"I know it's dictatorial, Luce," he said, "But it's the only way we can be sure you don't overdo. You're important to us. It's not a joke. It's not something we can take lightly. You *know* you have a tendency to overwork—so now if you try that, we'd have a spy to tell on you."

"For Pete's sake, I'd admit it if I got underwater!"

"No, you wouldn't," Nick said.

"I would, I would!"

"You never have before. We had to find out from other staff members when you were burning the candle at both ends. And they already know about Greger. Reiko agrees. So do Fritz and Fred. You'd work 24/7 if people didn't stop you. Everyone agrees we need a tattletale in-house."

He didn't mention her pregnancy, thank God. Not in front of Orson. But it was in his eyes, that he thought she was especially vulnerable right now. And that that gave him the right to boss her around.

"But what if I don't like this…Greger? What if he turns out to be a turkey and a half?"

"Then we'll hire someone else. All I'm asking is that you give him a try."

She ducked around Nick's arm. "Orson, do I have to do this?"

Orson looked sympathetic, but unrepentant. "Lucy, we already hired additional external security for the lab and construction site. And you know we're on the verge of hiring more security for Bliss specifically. You recommended extra staff yourself."

"Well…yes. That's totally true. But for the lab and greenhouses. Not for *me*. I can't even imagine trying to work with a shadow all the time."

Nick clattered in more bowls and spatulas and cooking tools—even those that hadn't been rinsed. She was going to object, but then she realized he was male. She should be appreciating his impulse to clean. God knows, she didn't know anyone with the Y chromosome who volunteered for KP duty—unless they were either bribed or threatened.

"He's not going to interfere with your work," Nick argued. "He's just going to be some extra muscle for you. He'll do the cleanups, the lifting, the running, the chores."

When Lucy glared at him, Nick rolled his eyes. "You know, there's a small possibility you could like it. 99.9 percent of the world wouldn't mind having some help. Instead of thinking of it like penance, couldn't you consider that it just might be a nice thing to have the grunt work off your back?"

"But then let *me* hire the person!"

Nick shook his head. "Then the employee would be loyal first to you. I want him knowing that I'm paying his salary. That he'd damn well better do what I tell him to do. Which," he added wryly, "is more than I could ever get you to do."

"Uncle Nick?" Gretchen poked her head in the door. "Can you take me and Boo Boo and Baby back to the house? I mean, I could walk. But if you're driving back—"

"I am. And it's easy to take you right now, G." But a long sexy finger poked at Lucy's nose. He was lucky she didn't bite it off. "I'm leaving. But don't try winding my grandfather around your finger."

"I *work* for your grandfather. Not for you!"

"Not on Bliss. On Bliss, you and I are glued at the hip, and that's how Orson wants it, as well."

She didn't slap him. She didn't punch him. She was a mature, professional woman who never lost her temper, and certainly not in front of Orson Bernard. Besides which, she'd never hit anyone in her entire life—but man, for a couple seconds, she was tempted to forget that.

Once Nick left the room, she found herself staring blankly after him...until she suddenly realized that Orson had moved, and was leaning against the

Formica counter now, studying her with a quiet, thoughtful expression.

"Sit down with me, Lucy."

"No, no, I've still got all this to clean up—"

"Sit down," he repeated.

All day she'd felt like throwing up, but now she *really* did. She'd always had Orson's respect, because she'd darn well tried to earn it from the very first day she'd met him. But something happened to her when Nick was around; her nerves and hormones and good sense got all tangled up—and then strangled up. She hated acting all emotional in front of a man she deeply, deeply cared about as well as respected.

But when she sank on a stool and started to make ardent, honest apologies, Orson gently cut her off.

"I'm afraid I've got a couple more surprises to spring on you."

"What?"

"First…I have to tell you that your Bliss is astounding, Lucy."

She flushed. "It isn't mine. It's really yours—"

"Yes, the original concept was. And our attorneys tell me that the patents and products belong to Bernard's, just like all the others developed in the lab. But I want to do something different in this situation, and so does Nick. You've been integral to Bliss. The raise we gave you related to the promotion is one thing, but we're going to give you a cut of the Bliss profits, as well." He named a percentage.

Her jaw dropped. Possibly five feet or more. "You don't have to do that."

His eyes crinkled at the corners. "I've fought with a number of employees about money through the years. But you're the only one I had to get tough with in order to give you more."

"But you already gave me more, in the form of a raise—"

"But that's for the work you'll be doing, the promotion. Also, Lucy, there's no guarantee what we'll make off Bliss. A new product is always a crap shoot, and will take extensive capital to get it off the ground. But all the same, this chocolate…" He shook his head. "It's more astounding than I ever dreamed. I felt it when I first sampled it. But today, to compare the product with our absolutely best chocolate and still have it test heads above…I'm near speechless."

"Me, too. I keep trying to find a flaw. A problem. But so far…"

Orson nodded, then went on. "There's a second problem I want to bring up, Lucy. A developing problem. From the beginning, I've watched you and my grandson spar with each other, go head-to-head now and then. I saw it as constructive. You both have Bernard's as your priority and you always seemed to come together when it counted."

All her worry buttons turned on. "Yes," she agreed immediately. "I think so, too—"

Orson's voice stayed smooth and quiet. "Nick didn't mention that someone tried to break into the lab last Sunday night, did he?"

"No!" Her face blanched of color.

Orson nodded. "Normally we'd have told you and the staff first thing. But in this case—because Bliss is potentially worth so much—we determined that an intensive, extensive private investigation was the best way to handle this. We've had thieves before. It's the nature of the industry, as you know. But if the secret was out on Bliss, we'd have to take huge and drastic immediate measures, which, I'm happy to tell you, wasn't the case."

"So the break-in wasn't about someone who knew about Bliss? For sure?"

"For sure," Orson reassured her. "It was just kids. Some very bright kids who managed to short-circuit the electric fence and hack through the first level of security. Apparently they thought it'd be some kind of lark to hit us for chocolate. But they didn't know about any of our research—this new project or any of our others."

"That's a huge relief."

"Yes. Actually, I guess you could say it's an 'extra' relief because the problem enabled us to discover we had an inefficiency in our security system that we hadn't realized before. So that was immediately corrected. But my point in sharing this, Lucy, is that both Nick and I have major security issues on our minds…yet I can still see that his attitude toward you goes beyond the mark. He was beside himself when we got the call from the security force, worried that you were at risk. And he hasn't backed down, even when he realized for certain that neither you nor Bliss were targeted in any way. I do believe he'd have hired an armed guard to trail you night and day if I hadn't called a halt to it. Something just doesn't make sense."

"It's the project. Because the research is potentially worth so much—"

"It's not the project. It's something about you." Orson faced her, eye to eye. Lucy had always been happy to lie for certain reasons. It was just that she'd never mastered the art of lying well, and Orson, darn him, was so ethical, so wonderful, that trying to color any truth would be like lying to a priest. He said deliberately, "I want the truth. You're ill, aren't you? That's the only thing that adds up, as far as I can see. It's the only thing that explains why Nick is acting so worried. It would also explain why he's so adamant about your no longer doing any physical work—"

"I'm not ill," she denied swiftly.

He leaned forward, clearly not buying it. "Lucy— I'm too old to play this by the usual employer-employee rules. You know how much I care about you. There's something wrong. I know it. I'm too old to be protected from a problem, and you know I'll help you if I possibly can. Just tell me what's wrong. Whatever illness you're dealing with—"

She never meant to blurt out the truth, but those kind eyes of his were relentless. It wasn't like lying to a mother or a lover. It was Orson, and she just couldn't stand to have him worried about her. "I'm not ill. I swear, Orson. I'm just pregnant."

The older man closed his mouth, the shock in his expression reflecting how unexpected the information was. Clearly he'd worried she had some kind of serious health problem, but nothing like this. Finally he said lowly, carefully, "Who is the boy, and is he going to marry you?"

Lucy could have bitten her tongue for saying anything at all. Orson was of the hopelessly old-fashioned generation who still believed that men protected women and unmarried pregnancies were tragedies. Naturally he was going to notice her growing stomach at some point, but ideally she'd have time to strategize the way she wanted to tell him. Now that she'd screwed this up by letting the cat out of the bag, she hustled to cover. "Right now, I don't know what I'm going to do. I'm still trying to work that out with…with the baby's father."

Abruptly she realized that only opened the door to more questions from Orson—questions she wasn't willing to answer. So she blustered through with a bit more. "Orson, you were right about Nick. He knows about the pregnancy, because he caught me being sick one time. So I'm sure that's why he's been so vocal about hiring extra help for me. He doesn't want the project jeopardized—"

"To hell with the project. He doesn't want *you* jeopardized by the additional responsibility and stress. And I agree with him. I raised him to be a Bernard. Neither of us have any tolerance for the kind of jerk who would take advantage of a young woman."

"It's not always the man who's responsible," she said desperately.

"The hell it isn't."

Orson never swore. Not in front of her. And though she wanted to argue with him further, his resolute tone shook her. It was one thing for her to let Orson down, to lose his high opinion of her. But it was another to have jeopardized Orson's respect and love for his grandson. Darn it, she never wanted to do that to Nick. He was Orson's pride and joy in every way.

She closed her eyes for one short, fierce second, fighting the sting of tears. "I didn't want you to know. I didn't want anyone to know. I don't want you worried I can't do the job, Orson. I *love* my job. I love the project—"

"No one's taking away your job, honey. You just should have told me."

She shook her head. "Please, please don't say anything to anyone. I mean, it won't be long before I start looking pregnant, and then obviously there'll be no hiding the situation from anyone." Until the words came out of her mouth, she hadn't realized how positively her heart had ruled out abortion. But that didn't mean she was certain of anything else, nor did she want to reveal any decisions or conclusions like that before telling Nick first. Right then, though, she seemed to have no choice but to handle Orson at whatever level she could. "I just really need some time. There's a lot to figure out. I just don't want the pregnancy to become public until I'm more sure of what I'm going to do."

He nodded. "I understand. Hopefully you can be married before the pregnancy is obvious to the world. But no matter what, Lucy, I don't want you afraid that you'd be stranded. I'm sure your family is telling you the same thing, but I still want you to know that you can count on me and Nick, as well. If you need anything, all you have to do is ask. And if you want to tell me the name of the son of a sea dog who—"

"No." She added desperately, "You know…everyone doesn't get married these days. Not just because of a pregnancy."

"The world seemed to work a lot better when they did. But I'm not trying to preach to you, Lucy. The opposite is true. I've known you a long time—long enough to know well what a tender and vulnerable heart you have. Anyone who'd ride rough over it deserves a good horsewhip—"

"Orson—"

"All right, all right. I'll keep my antiquated values to myself. Just know I'm there for you if you need help. Any kind of help."

"Thank you. So much."

Orson rose to his feet, clearly intending to leave now. "Don't be worried that I'll mention this to anyone. You know I won't. But please, let me know when your situation is more…decided. I also want you to discuss a more flexible work schedule with Nick."

Once he was gone, Lucy finished cleaning up…yet suddenly found herself staring into space in the silent lab. The experimental sampling had proven to be an overwhelming success, but all she could think about was the complete disaster she'd made of her life. And potentially of Nick's life, as well—if his grandfather discovered who the father of her baby was.

CHAPTER NINE

LUCY HAD GIVEN HIM some grief about his hiring extra security, but less than Nick expected. He made the last turn toward home, feeling grateful that testy meeting was over.

Leaves were budding out, red buds and azaleas splashing color on both sides of the road, new green forming a fragile umbrella above him. The signs and smells of spring lifted his spirits. Hard to beat a gorgeous evening when an impossible stress-load of a day was over and he could finally crash.

Lucy hadn't liked the idea of having Gregor watching over her, but that was no surprise. He hadn't seen any reason to fill her in on Greta's role until later. And Gramps had taken her on about the money. Nick figured Lucy had given Orson hell about that, too, but at least he wasn't in the target position on that subject. She'd never known he was behind the money plan.

The whole point, though, was that he'd finally found a way to *act*. Lucy now had some help, both at home and at work. She also now had a financial nest egg in the picture, so she could make choices about the baby's future more freely.

Lucy may have mentioned abortion, but Nick had been dead positive from the start that would never be a real choice. Not for her. Maybe he didn't know her well enough to know her religious or personal beliefs, but out front, she was a hard-core kid-lover and family person. She wanted the baby. She might not have realized it yet, but he'd bet the bank how her heart would decide the big questions—which meant that issues like security and financial matters needed to tackled by him on an a.s.a.p. basis.

It would probably be easier to do something for Luce if she were drugged and hog-tied first, he mused. But he suspected she was always going to be a pistol and a half. He couldn't change her. He could only change her circumstances.

Not like there wasn't a ton still to handle, but at least he'd made a start. Down the pike, he knew he had to address how he felt about becoming a father— but one crisis at a time. Right now, he was whipped. All he wanted from life was a frosted root beer, a red-raw steak on the grill and then maybe some hot tub time.

He took the last curve, spotted a car in his drive, and felt his mood promptly plummet. The car was sin-red and sleek low. Linnie's car. He hadn't seen it in months but, like his ex-girlfriend, no one was likely to mistake that car for anyone else's.

She was standing by his front door, looking typically expensive. So unlike Lucy, she was never without the right makeup or the right clothes. Her blond hair was artfully cut to frame her elegant bones. She was wearing a casually belted trench coat over sleek, slim pants and looked as if she'd been aimlessly walking around—which was a joke. Linnic never walked anywhere. She must own three hundred pair of shoes—none of which she could walk in.

"Hey," he said, as he climbed out of the car.

"About time you got home, stranger. You're working awfully late hours these days!"

"Just sometimes. But if you called, I missed it."

"I didn't call. I just missed you, so I figured I'd come by. If you were tired, I'd make you dinner. Or something." Her eyes elaborated on the "or something." She aimed toward him with a slow, sexy gait, intending, he suspected, to offer him an appetizer of that "something" before dinner.

She must have caught something in his eyes. Linnie was too smart, too sophisticated, to risk a rebuff. She suddenly smiled but stopped moving.

"You're not glad to see me?" She cocked her head, with an expression indicating confidence in the answer. Nick had always thought she had honest confidence rather than arrogance, because there likely wasn't a man born who wasn't glad to see her.

Him included. Nick'd have to be dead not to like

the unspoken invitation. The body. The look. The promise.

He unlocked the front door, letting her in. Inside, he started to worry. Was he dead? Was something life-threatening wrong with him and he didn't even realize it? Could he be dead and not know it? Because there wasn't even the first twitch below the belt. And yeah, Linnie could be challenging company, but in that one department, she was easy to be with…easy to let loose with…and damn, he'd been celibate for a while now. Yet…nothing. Nada.

"What's wrong?" she said as she came in, slipping off her trench coat and shoes. She might not have been here in a while, but she knew the layout well.

"Nothing, really," he said. "Just had an exhausting day." That was true—but not the problem. The problem was figuring out how he was going to tactfully throw her out, quickly, without please-God her raising a tantrum or being hurt if he could help it.

"I know what'll fix you up," she said teasingly.

He talked her out of a back rub, the hot tub, some fast, rash sex, a movie. He couldn't seem to talk her out of staying for dinner, though. She zoomed into the kitchen and just started pulling out pots and pans. He couldn't stop her without getting bluntly mean about it.

"I've got hours of work after dinner. That's just the way it is," he said flatly.

"You work too much. You need to relax. But at least we can have a dinner together, can't we?"

She wanted something, he knew it, and eventually it came out. Her mother was involved in some fund-raiser. Linnie was supposed to solicit the Bernard name on the list of donors not just for the money but for the support. Because chocolate was universally appealing, the name always perked up notice. It wasn't the same as getting money out of Herman's Die Cast, even if Herman gave a ton.

"That was a joke, Nick."

"Yeah, funny." He had a sudden image of her carrying a baby. It wasn't fair or kind, but man. He dropped the mail he'd been sifting through. She just...wasn't a woman he'd want carrying his baby, that's all. Not that he wanted a baby. Not that he wanted to be a father. Not that he wasn't completely terrified at the thought of fatherhood. But all the same, he'd want the mother of his child to be someone a kid felt...safe with. Someone who made a kid feel comfortably loved and valued and all that kind of thing. He'd want the mom of his kid to laugh easily and naturally, simply because she really liked the child. Really. Liked. Someone like...

Well, like...

"So what do you say?"

"About what?"

"Nick! You're turning into a dolt! About the fund-raiser! You're too young and sexy to get Alzheimer's—wake up!"

He tried. She not only fixed him a bloody rare steak and iced root beer, but concocted a salad with dried cherries and cranberries and some kind of vegetable that even a guy could eat. He was halfway through when the phone rang. He put down his fork and cocked his chair back to reach the wall phone.

"Bernard—" he started to say.

"Nick, I'm sorry to call you at home, but I needed to reach you, and I didn't dare call you at work because I didn't have any way of knowing if you were with other people...especially if your grandfather might have been with you. So it seemed like the only good way was to wait until you were hopefully home and alon—"

The chair legs dropped with a thump. "What's wrong?" Lucy didn't have to identify herself. He knew from first-babble that it was her. There was an uncharacteristic tremor in his voice that rattled his cage immediately.

"Nothing's wrong. At least not exactly. Well, actually, there is. I talked to your grandfather, and I—"

Then he remembered—he'd left right when Orson had been about to tackle her about giving her a share of Bliss. He should have known she'd call, that she'd be spoiling for a fight. "Don't even try turning down the financial deal. You're entitled to it."

"No, I'm not. Bliss wasn't my idea. It wasn't anything I did. It was all your grandfather's dream, and

I just helped put some parts of it together. And I don't feel I—"

"Luce. This is an argument you're going to lose, so you might as well not waste your breath." He was trying to reassure her, yet somehow the tremor in her voice sounded even more agitated.

"Nick, *listen*. The problem is that when I started to argue about the money with Orson, I got rattled. Not about the money. About the arguing. I know this'll be hard for you to understand because you don't get rattled. You're just not a ditz type, Nick. But with me, I can take work stress. I love pressure, for heaven's sake. It's not like I'm always a wuss. But when I have to fight with someone, I just can't *think*."

"You think you're the only one that happens to?"

"Well, I can't imagine you frothing at the mouth the way I do." She sounded so aggrieved and annoyed, that damn, he had to grin. Until she continued. "But that's not the point. The point is that I was shook up. Your grandfather guessed there was something wrong. He seemed to be thinking I had some fatal disease. I mean, he was really worried. *Really*. So I ended up blurting it out, because I just couldn't let him keep on worrying. I had to say something."

"Could you talk five miles an hour slower so I can follow all this?"

"I told him I was pregnant."

There went the smile. "All right," he said quietly, and then even more slowly, "All right. I can guess what happened after that. He responded by getting mighty upset—"

"You've got that right. But he wasn't upset at me. No matter what I said, he couldn't seem to see that I was at fault. To him, it was all about the guy." He could hear her gulp, then hiccup. "Nick, that's not what I led him to think!"

"I don't doubt that, Luce." He closed his eyes, trying to listen, to think. But suddenly he couldn't stop picturing his grandfather. Standing alone in the crowd when he'd graduated from high school, from college. There at every soccer game. There when he'd gotten his first driver's license. There when he'd broken his arm. Orson had always been there for him. Always. So much so that man, he really, *really* hadn't wanted to disappoint the one man who'd been everything to him.

"I didn't tell him it was you. I didn't name any father. But I *did* end up telling him that you knew about the pregnancy—because that's what started the whole conversation, why you were so protective, that he guessed you knew something. So that's why I'm telling you. So you knew when you talked to him next that he knows I'm pregnant, that he knows you know, but that he doesn't think it's you. Even so, I'm sorry…"

His mind was jumbled up in a verbal traffic jam, trying to figure out the he knows and she knows and you knows. But her last comment pulled him up short. "You have nothing to be sorry for."

"Of course there is. I don't want to cause a rift between you and Orson. I don't want to be a problem. For either of you."

"You're not, damn it. Stop worrying about everyone else. And I realize you didn't want the news out yet, but this is just a change in timing. There was only so long this secret could be kept under wraps. He was always going to know sooner or later."

"That's not true. Obviously I can't hide the pregnancy much longer, but he never had to know who the father was. Not if you didn't want it known. And now that I realize how upset—"

Linnie suddenly loudly piped up, "Who on earth are you talking to?"

On the other end of the line, Lucy changed tunes faster than popping a button. There was a millisecond of dead silence, and then suddenly her voice was as cheerful as silence. "Oh! I didn't realize you had someone there. Look, I'll let you go. I just wanted you to know what happened before talking to your grandfather again so you'd be prepared. And I'll catch you later—"

"*Lucy*—"

But she'd hung up that fast. Leaving Nick wiping a hand over his face as if he hoped he could somehow clean up his life, her life, their lives if he just rubbed hard enough.

Obviously not. But their situation seemed to be getting more catastrophic instead of less.

He only had one choice.

To step up.

To find a *lot* more ways to step up.

Quickly.

He opened his eyes to find Linnie staring brightly at him. "That was certainly a fascinating conversation to hear one side of. What on earth is going on?"

"What's going on," he said tactfully, "is that I'm afraid you have to go home. Right now."

That went over like a lead balloon—no surprise. His life was turning into nonstop lead balloons lately—but if anyone had the power to change that, it had to be him.

And nothing, right now, could be more important than insuring Lucy stopped feeling she was stuck facing this damned pregnancy alone.

LUCY OPENED THE DOOR to the company bathroom, and ran straight into the ungiving muscular wall of Greger's chest. Greger had a lot in common with a young Jesse Ventura. The part he had in common was being a Goliath-sized blonde with hands bigger than steaks, seam-splitting shoulders and a bow-legged stance because of the breadth of his thighs. Kind of a Mr. Clean come to life.

"Greger, this is not going to work," she said wearily.

"Yah?"

That was his answer for everything. A sympathetic *yah*. Having extra security around was actually very nice but if Greger had his way, he'd follow her into the bathroom. Hell's bells, he'd probably even wipe for her. He carried her mail. He carried her trees. He crawled into her cacao forest on his hands and knees right after her. He cleaned up mud; he cleaned up dishes. If she blew her nose, he had a Kleenex waiting for her.

And they'd only been together two days.

"I'm going home now," she said firmly. "Alone. Try to have a little faith that I can walk the distance of the hall without being supervised, okay?"

"Sure, sure," he said. "You make funny jokes, Lucy. I'll open the door for you."

"Greger. I know you're supposed to help me. And you are. But Mr. Bernard never expected us to be joined at the hip."

"Joined at hip?"

She gave up, even though she strongly suspected that Greger's English was just as good as hers. She knew he was a recent immigrant, but it was just too amazingly convenient for him to understand everything Nick wanted him to do and get confused about everything she did.

"Lucy, before you leave..." They were already at the door, with his holding it open and holding her purse, which she'd forgotten. "I have key for you."

"What key?"

"Mr. Bernard's house key. Mr. Nick, not Mr.

Orson. He said to give this to you before you left today."

"This time, Greger, I think you must have misunderstood," she said kindly. "There's no reason on earth for him to want me to have his house key—"

"Must be. Mr. Bernard said. Why, not my problem. He said something about you needing it."

"Honestly, I couldn't possibly need the key to his place," Lucy assured him, but Greger was still stubbornly blocking the door until they had this settled.

"Mr. Bernard, he would have given it to you himself, but he had to be out of town for two days. So he said to me, be sure to give it to you, yah?"

She gave up and took the key. It just wasn't worth continuing to argue once Greger started up with that *yah* business.

Nick was in Belgium. He usually made a trip there a couple times a year, but Lucy wasn't so sure it was business this time. If he had any sense, he'd have left the country to avoid her blistering his ears over Greger which she'd certainly do if he were within screaming distance.

With him gone, though, she'd managed to get in two relaxing, ordinary, wonderful work days. With nothing to distract her, she'd had some concentrated work time and concentrated think time as well. The first two new greenhouses almost had the lights on. New lab equipment had started to arrive. In the meantime, she'd been working on streamlining her grafting techniques for when the new trees got here. A fresh batch of Bliss was coming off the existing trees but right now, they weren't harvesting enough at any one time to make a "product," only for testing. Still, each new batch of Bliss kept her challenged to try new tests and new techniques.

As she climbed in her car, she yawned. A good night's sleep is all she needed to renew and recharge. That's what had been missing all this time. Rest. Enough rest so she could regain a feeling of peace. A feeling of control over her life.

A feeling that there were clear answers to her feelings about Nick.

She picked up milk and eggs, and was parked in her driveway less than forty minutes later. She opened the door to open, still feeling peaceful and serene, then immediately she stopped in shock. From somewhere inside her house came the whine of a powerful motor. Unfamiliar smells assaulted her nostrils.

She hustled in down the hall, only to find Dr. Armstrong—one of her dad's closest friends—bent over a carpet steam cleaner in her living room. The good doctor was sweating hard and peeled down to his white undershirt. "Dr. Armstrong?"

He didn't answer. Of course he couldn't possibly hear over the engine roar. She couldn't enter the room. All the furniture was pushed up against one wall, while the steam cleaner sucked at the carpet.

Rather than yell his name again, she jogged down the hall to the source of odd smells coming from her kitchen.

And there was her dad, wearing a surgeon's mask, kneeling on her kitchen floor with a pail and a brush. The liquid in the pail smelled distinctly like ammonia. Her dad had a foam rubber kneeling pad and long pink rubber gloves.

"Dad?"

Luther looked up, a panic-stricken expression in his eyes. Then he spotted her, and sank back on his heels. "Thank God you're home. We have to have all this done before she comes back."

"All what done? Before *who* comes back?"

"Greta."

Okay. She hadn't had a single truffle today, so there was no blaming chocolate for losing her mind. "And Greta is who?"

"Come on," her father said. "You know who. Greta is Greger's sister. Nick hired them both. She said you knew this. And Nick was right, Luce. You need help with all the work you're doing, honey, only my heavens. She seems to think that *I'm* responsible for some of the messes. I know that's ridiculous, but—"

Lucy put away the milk and eggs, shucked off her jacket. "But?" she prodded him.

"But she seemed to think that I should kick in a little help. And I said of course I would. Only her version of a little help…" He shook his head in horror. "And then Bill came over. Between the two of us, we almost got a double hernia, trying to carry the carpet cleaner in the house. But it's all got to be done before she comes back tomorrow."

Lucy sank onto a kitchen stool. "I'm getting some of this. I think. Only why is there a timetable on certain things being done before she comes back tomorrow?"

"Lucy," her father said with the patient tone he'd used when she was a child. "You know Greta. Six foot one, maybe two. Blond hair. And the build on that woman…look. I can't stop to chitchat right now. And neither can Bill. Don't be talking to him, either. You just go on."

"Go on?" Maybe she was crazy, even without chocolate, because less and less seemed to make sense in her life. Her dad motioned her toward the door as if it was obvious she was leaving.

"I know you're going to Nick's house tonight. Greta already told me. Mr. Nick, she calls him. She said you needed to get completely out of the way while we got this house back in shape. It won't take so much to upkeep once we give it a total rehaul. And you have work waiting for you at Nick's place. I don't know what work things, but Greta said you could be staying over there fairly regularly over the next few months. I don't know what the work issue is. I was just to relay the message that there were extensive notes at Nick's place."

"I'm supposed to go...to Nick's." When had all these plans gone on the table? Had the whole world tuned to a different satellite channel when she was at work?

"Take your cell phone, if you don't already have it. Merry called. And your mother. And Russell." Abruptly her father motioned her toward the door again, this time more forcefully. "Look, there's just no time to talk. I have a whole list to do before tomorrow morning."

"Or? What happens if this 'list' isn't done?"

"Come on, honey," he repeated. "You know Greta. She's the personification of an AK-47. And you have all those projects to do at Nick's, so just go!"

All right. Lucy didn't have a clue why she was really supposed to go to Nick's—she couldn't even ask him, since he was out of the country. But the bottom line was that she really didn't mind cutting out. This Greta had to be a saint if she'd managed to get her dad to lift a finger, much less do some serious housework. Lucy couldn't see interfering with a good thing. It wasn't that far a drive to Nick's besides. Going there was the only way she could find out for sure if there really was some work waiting for her.

She knew the way, not because she'd been there before, but because where Nick lived was common knowledge at Bernard's. A few years ago, he'd bought the house and property close to Bernard's—

distant enough to keep his independence, but close enough to watch over his grandfather.

The turnoff from the road led to a twisting, winding path through a canopy of maples. She passed over a wooden bridge, past a wild riot of azaleas, then under more venerable old trees.

Her breath caught when she spotted the house. It wasn't magical or fancy, nothing like the Bernard mansion, her first impression was of a protected, private haven. It was made of stone, a sprawling ranch style with three sturdy turrets and a long, slanted slate roof. Spreading evergreens reached to window height. The lawn was satin-green, soft and rich.

She saw no other cars as she parked in the curve of the circular drive. Still she hesitated, feeling like a trespasser. She reminded herself that Nick was out of town, that he'd obviously set up her coming here, made sure she had a key—and that even her dad was in on this deal. Still, she felt uneasy as she hiked to the front door, quietly unlocked it, and stepped inside

A note dangled from the hall chandelier, clearly written in Nick's black scrawl.

Lucy, don't hesitate to walk around. See the place, make yourself comfortable. Use anything in the house you want. I guarantee no one will bother you here. Take advantage and relax.

Relax? Yeah, right, she thought. But she was too curious not to poke around, at least a little. She started with the kitchen—because it seemed to have every techno-cool appliance known to man—but almost immediately she was diverted by a second note magneted to the refrigerator. The note promised her dinner on the top shelf. When she opened the fridge door, she found a fresh lobster salad, a chicken Florentine cooked and ready to reheat, and an extensive tray of fancy pastries—all chocolate.

She closed the door, shocked, thinking *good grief!*

Everywhere she turned, there were more goodgriefs. The navy and white living room looked stark and masculine…except for the box of magazines on the coffee table…everything from *Cosmo* to *Horticultural Digest*. For her? He'd done all this for her?

Beyond the living room, he'd set up a spare room as a home theater, with couches and shuttered windows and a giant screen TV. Again she found an arrow scrawled on a piece of paper, this time pointing to a heap of movies. *Charade. Truly Madly Deeply. Sleepless in Seattle.* All chick flicks. Nothing a guy would watch—at least not a guy she'd ever met.

She hugged her arms under her chest. She was starting to get seriously scared. This was beyond good-grief.

This was starting to all look planned.

Clearly she was justified in snooping further— how else could she know how far Nick had gone? Or try to figure out what he'd been thinking? It took her maybe a second and a half to find his bedroom. It was one of the rooms with a round stone turret, making for a cushioned window-seat area that overlooked the woods and grounds. Otherwise the room was all done up in the same rich navy—thick carpet, comforter and sheets. The mattress was as big as a small country, and ultra hard— she discovered by sitting on it.

She glanced inside his closet, a room-sized storage space with everything hung or tidily put away. Who'd have guessed Nick had a fussy side like hers? But she quickly closed that door; that was a little too much prying, even for her. Just past that door was the master bathroom, though, and one look took her breath away.

The bathroom wasn't just a good-grief. It was a straight oh-my-God. A gas fireplace divided the dressing area from the tub area. A short note had been taped on the white marble hearth. *Just turn this lever to the right if you want it on, Lucy.*

She did. A burst of warm yellow flames immediately danced in the grate. In front of the fireplace was a stand-alone tub, huge, with jets and copper fixtures. A copper cart had a tray of blueberry candles on one shelf, thirsty white towels on the next.

She stared at that hedonistic tub for a good long minute, thinking repressive thoughts, but they just didn't work. She flicked on the taps and started stripping—purse, shoes, cell, jeans, sweater, socks. She retrieved her purse to forage for matches. She'd never smoked, but she'd always carried enough in her purse to survive in Europe for at least six months. She lit the blueberry candles.

The fire licked and spit, warming her backside as she finished stripping down to the buff, then sank into the warm bubbly water with an earthy sigh. Later, she was going to think about why Nick had arranged for her to come here. She was going to worry. Mercilessly. Intensely. Obsessively. The way she worried best. Guilt would undoubtedly enter that equation, because Lucy always figured she was guilty for something.

But right then, she just mentally shoved her natural character aside. Even a saint couldn't have turned down this temptation. No one was here. No one would know. When was she ever going to be near a bathroom with a fireplace again in this life? A tub with bubbling jets?

She leaned her head back and lolled in lazy decadence for at least five dazzlingly long, wonderful minutes…until her cell phone rang.

She had to hop out of the tub, drip over to her pile of clothes and paw through until she found the receiver. She clicked it on as she climbed back into the tub…and heard Nick's voice.

"I was hoping you were at my place."

"I am. I just got here. Just took off my shoes and

was sitting on your living room couch. Still wearing my jacket."

"Yeah?"

It was so stupid. Even the way he said "yeah" sent a shiver up in her spine, and here she was, broiling between the fire and the warm water. "Nick, I don't understand what's going on here."

"I figured you wouldn't. That's why I called. So we could talk."

"I remember your mentioning Greta's name. But nothing about her being at my house. And why did you want me *here,* at your place? And as far as Greger—"

"Okay. One thing at a time. Did you find the food in the fridge?"

She leaned her head back against the cool edge and closed her eyes. "Yeah. I found all that fabulous gourmet food. You actually left that for *me?* You planned my coming here, down to even feeding me?"

"You asked me to, Luce."

"What? I never asked you to do anything like this—"

"No, of course I didn't. But indirectly you gave me quite a few clues about stress spots in your life. You figured out how to turn the fireplace on, right?"

"Sure, piece of cake," she said, and then suddenly realized he had to mean *this* fireplace, which meant he had to guess she was in the tub instead of sitting in the living room with her jacket like she'd said.

"Listen," she began, trying to swiftly formulate a good lie, only it was too late. He was already talking again.

"You said you needed time, Lucy. Time to think and get your life together. That between your dad and the job and family responsibilities and everything else, you were frazzled. So I tried to think of some way I could give you some peace and quiet. I'm gone a lot. You know that. My place is just sitting there. No reason you can't be enjoying it."

"But…"

"Yeah, I figured you'd have buts. The deal with Greta—you already know she's Greger's sister. She's a housekeeper. Used to working on big estates, but she hasn't found that kind of work here yet, and when I saw how crazy it was at your place, I figured you'd probably like a little top-to-bottom clean. Also that it might not kill your dad—much as he seems like a totally wonderful guy—to get a clue how much work he's causing you."

"But—"

"So while Greta's on a cleaning marathon at your place, you might as well stay at mine. I'll be home from Brussels on Friday—"

She was going to say something. She knew she was. Only suddenly she spotted a robe at the back of the bathroom door. A woman's robe. Long. Purple. With a price tag still hanging from the sleeve.

Purple, the same color as her bedroom. Which he'd seen. So the robe was for her?

"That robe, Nick," she began, having completely forgotten the rest of the conversation.

"Yeah, it's for you. But back to the original subject, your situation at home. You've got a cousin, right? Rock or Russell or something?"

"Yes. Russell."

"Well, you told me about your dad, your mom kicking him out and all. But I forgot what you told me about Russell."

"He's just...struggling. He's got this idea that he's gay. He may not be. I don't know. I don't know how to know. But I've loved him ever since we were kids, you know? He followed me around like a puppy. I used to put him in the basket on my bike and take him everywhere. Anyway. He's all confused and right now he just seems to feel safe at my place—like if he's with me, he doesn't have to think about it or do anything about it or worry or anything."

"Okay. Now on Greger..."

They talked about Greger and the staff and the whole Bliss project for a while. He seemed interested in every detail about their new chocolate that she could give him. Eventually, they both seemed to wind down.

"We're doing all right, working directly together so far, aren't we?" he asked finally.

"Yes. Totally," she agreed.

"I'd like to think we can keep talking about the pregnancy the same way. And I know you have to have reached some decisions by now on certain things—"

"You're right. I have." She used her toe to pour in more hot water. "I can't stop worrying about Orson. About how he would react if he found out—"

"No. Don't. You're not doing 'worry' alone, Luce. This isn't anyone else's baby. Or anyone else's business. It's ours. We're just going to forget about what other people think, or what other people think we should do. And concentrate on what we think is right."

Her heart went clunk...just to hear his voice say "our." She swallowed quickly, and then, "Nick, I did make a decision about something—"

"You want to keep the baby." He filled in the blank as if he'd known exactly what she was going to say.

She blinked. "How did you know?"

"Just a guess."

She closed her eyes. "I'm still really troubled about whether I'll make a good mom. Really troubled. And scared. That's nothing I can resolve with some fast, magic pill. But when I went in the grocery store the other day. I needed bread, yet instead of the bread aisle, I suddenly found myself in front of all those shelves of baby food. Mashed peas. They look so horrible. Only..."

"Only what?"

"Only I felt a wave of feeling so strong, it was unshakeable. That I wanted this baby. That in some way I already love it from my heart. Darn it, it's hard to explain—"

"You don't have to explain. If you want the baby, then that's the way it's going to be. All right. Then that's the way it's going to be. About everything. You figure out what you want, we find some way to make it happen."

She frowned. "All right. Why are you being so good to me?"

"What, you expect me to be mean?"

"Not *mean*. But you don't to be this nice, Nick. It's...unnatural. It's inhuman. It's downright unnerving."

"Okay. I'll try to remember to yell at you the next time we talk. But in the meantime, I want to ask you to do something."

"What?"

"Go in the living room."

"I've been in there."

"Maybe you have. But this time, I want you to turn on the light and go sit in the blue chair by the window and look around...I mean later, of course, after you get out of the bath."

"Why?"

But he never gave her a reason before he hung up. When she climbed out of the tub and dried off, she realized she was starving. So once she wrapped herself in the purple robe, she wandered into the kitchen and gathered up a plate of the lobster salad and other goodies. It was only then she remembered his request.

She flicked on a lamp in the living room, sat in the blue chair by the window, and then abruptly blinked. The picture of the lone eagle soaring over the water had a treasured spot in a reading alcove. It was in oil, not a print like hers, so that wasn't the point.

The point was that it was *her* picture.

Her sacred, private picture. The one that always touched her because it seemed to secretly reach the loneliest part of her heart. She wasn't like an eagle in any way, but the picture always made her think about how much she wanted to be brave and her own person, to have the guts to make her own path, not to live in anyone else's shadow…yet as hard as she tried to do that, she seemed lonelier all the time.

And this was Nick's sacred picture, too?

CHAPTER TEN

NICK KNOCKED on Lucy's front door at ten o'clock on Saturday morning. Waiting for an answer, he rolled his shoulders. The flight from Brussels yesterday had been brutally long and his brain was still foggy from jet lag. Even so, he'd driven to Lucy's house this morning as soon as he could get here.

"Hey." A kid answered the door. The cousin. Russell. The boy squinted up at him until recognition finally flared. "I know you. You're Mr. Bernard, right?"

"Call me Nick."

"Sure. I remember you from that night in the kitchen—when Lucy did a dive to the floor. You're her boss, right?"

"Actually, my grandfather is."

"Whatever. Come in, I guess. Lucy isn't here. She's with her dad. They're out buying tires. I can't remember whether his car needs the tires or hers does. Anyway…" Russell motioned him as if he owned the place.

Nick stepped inside. He already knew Lucy was tied up with her dad because he'd called earlier. He wanted to see Lucy—but not now. Right now, he'd hustled here specifically to get time alone with the sandy-haired cousin with the boyish grin. "Okay with you if I come in for a minute, wait around?"

"No sweat at all. There's coffee and stuff in the kitchen."

Nick trailed behind him, but slowly, poking a head in the living room, down the hallway. Although he'd never seen her place until the night she'd been sick, he was dead positive it looked more like her now. Every surface was polished. Tabletops gleamed. Pictures hung straighter than rulers. There were no crumbs, no cigar smoke smell, no cup rings.

It seemed crazy that he knew she was a clean-nik, crazier yet how he hungered to fix the things that bugged her. Of course, he felt responsibility for the pregnancy, particularly now that she'd decided to keep the baby. He'd done the obvious things about that—got her a cut of Bliss. Hired Greta and Greger. Made sure he had a better understanding of the stresses she was stuck with on the job.

Still, it struck Nick's sense of irony that he felt a fierce, building need to take care of her—when she was so adamantly against marrying him. She not only didn't seem to want him any closer; she never complained about anything. He had to push and prod to get even small hints about problems in her life—

but that was how he knew she was really worried about her cousin. She didn't know what to do about him.

God knew, neither did he. But since this was one of the very few areas where Luce had admitted worry, Nick figured he had to try. Even though he'd rather pay triple taxes—and wreck his Lotus—than tackle a problem as touchy as this.

"So," Russell said as they entered the kitchen. "You want coffee or something?"

"Coffee sounds great." Nothing, actually, was going to be great for the next hour. Nick cast a longing look at the back door—the closest exit. Other people were happy cowards. Why couldn't he be? What was wrong about being gutless? He could run out of here right now and no one would ever know— the kid'd never have a clue why he'd even come.

The idea was so tempting he could almost taste it.

"So…like…you run the whole chocolate company, right? What a cool job."

Russell was both friendly and gregarious, which at least gave Nick a few minutes to analyze the kid. The other night, there'd been so much noise and confusion that the boy hadn't registered in his mind that strongly. Now, he studied the boy's slight build, the devil's grin and bright eyes.

If Nick had the story right, Russell was hanging around Lucy nonstop because the boy was afraid of being gay. And he wasn't going to quit tagging tight to Luce until the issue came to some kind of resolution.

He steered Russell into talking about himself—the subjects he was taking in school, his goals, his hobbies, that kind of thing. The boy fiercely loved music and movies and books, but in school he was concentrating on math and sciences. "See, if you're in the Fitzhenry family, you have to go into some kind of health related field, or you get disowned. Like Lucy. She did the wild thing when she went into horticulture."

"Horticulture is considered...a wild choice?" Nick asked.

"I know, I know. It wouldn't be in a normal family." Russell slumped down in the kitchen chair across from him. "But man, you should have heard the arguments when Luce chose horticulture over medicine. See, she always had all A's. Our dads are both doctors. My mom's an anesthesiologist... I mean, everybody in the family has a second home at Mayo, you know? And Lucy was extra smart besides, so the family just assumed she'd go along the same ride—"

"Russ?" Eventually Nick had to interrupt. The kid could talk nonstop, without taking breaths, the same way Lucy could. And he liked the boy, but unless he got this show on the road, he was going to have a heart attack from building nerves. "Could I ask you a personal question?"

"Sure, sure." The kid looked at him expectantly, yet for a second Nick couldn't speak.

The truth was, he had no idea how to handle this. None, zip and zero. He reminded himself that this was for Lucy. That this was one of the few areas where she'd admitted feeling over her head. But damn. This was gonna be slogging uphill.

He started with, "Do you think I'm basically an okay looking guy?"

"Huh?" Russell responded blankly.

Nick slugged down another gulp of coffee, wishing the cup was loaded with whiskey—even if it was before noon. "I'm just asking your opinion. Whether you think I'm a decent looking guy or not."

Russell's face did the stoplight thing, flushing color, then going pale, then flushing color again. Like Lucy, he showed every emotion he'd ever owned and some he probably wished he didn't. "Well...yeah, of course. You're more than decent looking. You're cool. You know. You've got the looks, the moves, the sophistication. Everything."

Nick waited two beats of a second, because damned if he could make these words come out easily. "Let me ask you another question then," he said lazily. "If, say, you happened to be gay...would you think I was an appealing guy then?"

"Oh, God. Oh, God. Lucy told you? About me? I can't believe—"

Nick gulped fast. "Aw, hell. I knew I'd make a

mess of this. I was trying to…damn. Never mind what I was trying to do. Write me off as a bumbling idiot and let's start over, all right?"

Russell looked completely bewildered. "Okay. I guess."

Nick scraped a hand through his hair when a sudden terrifying thought occurred to him. All this time, he'd been doing all these things for Lucy because helping her was the honorable thing to do. But what if that wasn't the whole story? What if he kept trying to do things for her because he'd fallen in love with the most unlikely woman for him in the entire universe? Because hellanddamnation both, he couldn't imagine wading into a problem like this for anyone but Lucy.

Ever.

"This is the thing," he said, slower now. "You don't have to talk about this if you don't want to. But anything you say, I promise, will stay between us. And I thought maybe it might help to talk to someone who isn't family. Someone who isn't going to judge you no matter what."

"Yeah, well…I wouldn't know what to say. How to start."

"How about starting wherever you want? Like…when did you start thinking you were gay? Has stuff happened to you that made you pretty sure this was the way it was going to be?"

"Well…" Russell hesitated again, fumbled with

his coffee mug, then shifted in his seat several more times. "It all started with Sandra."

"Sandra," Nick repeated.

"Yeah. Sandra was my girlfriend. Not my first girlfriend," he added hastily, making sudden eye contact with Nick.

Nick got it. He'd had sex with someone else before this Sandra. They weren't talking about girlfriends. They were talking about sex. And Russell averted his face, fidgeting and juggling his coffee cup, as a long story awkwardly came out.

The first time, the kid had had sex with a prostitute. It was one of those rite-of-passage things in his high school, where the senior guys set up the junior guys with a hooker. Nothing new, but predictably more traumatic than the fun a teenage boy was expecting. "That went like the pits, I'm guessing," Nick said quietly.

"It was bad," Russell muttered. "I didn't think that was some clue at the time that I was gay. But then I started going with Sandra. We got closer and closer, you know?"

"Until you ended up in the sack."

"Yeah. And that wasn't like…the other. Only she'd been around a lot more than I had, so she knew things, you know? And I didn't. I thought it was okay. In fact, I thought it was great. But she started saying things."

"Like…?"

"Well. Like I kissed too soft. I was too nice. That kind of thing. I wasn't rough or tough or macho enough or something. And when she'd say that kind of thing—" Russell couldn't seem to finish that sentence to save his life.

"You wilted?" Nick asked straight out.

Once the real problem was on the table, Russell started talking at the speed of sound. "It never happened before. Shit. From the time I was like twelve, I could get hard just walking around, seeing a girl, looking at a picture, anything. But somehow with her...and then when she said like I was probably gay, it just clicked. I'd flunked the course twice with women now, you know? So it was me. It had to be me. And then..."

Nick closed his eyes, feeling so sorry for the kid he could hardly stand it. Broken hearts had a way of screwing with a guy's mind every time. Maybe the kid was gay, but it sure sounded like there was nothing wrong besides two rotten experiences that really messed with his masculine ego.

Normally Nick would rather suffer a tetanus shot than endure a touchy-feely conversation, but this wasn't really that. It was just two men talking together. And damn, but it felt pretty darn good to see Russell quit slumping and fidgeting and start to straighten up, lose the round-shouldered depression thing.

Nick finally got him laughing...and it was just

that moment when the back door burst open. Lucy charged in, with her dad right behind her. She took one look at the two men standing close together, at Russell's flushed cheeks and exuberant expression. "What on earth is going on?"

"We were just having a little talk," Nick said. "Good morning, Dr. Fitzhenry."

"Nicholas. How nice to see you again."

"Nick, when you called this morning—did I misunderstand? Did you need me for something? Because I thought I'd said I was going tire shopping with my dad—"

"You did."

Whether it was claustrophobia or some sleep-starved problem that kicked in, the kitchen seemed suddenly too close and too filled with people. All he had to do was look at her, and his brain function started rattling. He had to get out of there. He came through with the basic compulsory conversation and courtesy goodbyes, but then he pelted out toward his car.

As he might have expected, Lucy galloped after him. "What's going on?" she demanded.

"Nothing, really. Just had a little man to man with Russ. I don't think he's quite so worried about being gay now."

"Because…why? Because of your talk? What'd you *say* to him?"

"Just some guy stuff." He tossed his jacket in the backseat. The day was warming up—or his body seemed to be. Luce was wearing jeans and an oversized shirt, nothing on her cheeks but sunshine, yet he couldn't stop looking at her. A new, terrifying thought gnawed on his mind that he was feeling this way around her more and more. Rattled. Brain dead. Obsessed with looking at her. Something about the woman was turning him dumb. It was a scary thought.

"You're staring at me as if there's something wrong," she said pensively.

"No. Honestly. I'm just tired from the long trip."

She nodded sympathetically. "I'll bet you're headed home to get some sleep. And I'm driving into Bernard's in a minute—"

"On a Saturday? Why?"

"So I can get some things done without Greger breathing down my neck. Don't argue with me." She teasingly shook a warning finger in his face.

He had the oddest urge to bite that finger. To suck on it for a good long time. Then wanted to shake himself. Jet lag had never given him delusions like this before. "You like Greger. Admit it."

"And let you know you were right? Never. Not in this life."

"How much work are you trying to do this afternoon?"

"Not that much. A good hour. Not much more than that. I grafted some new trees last week. Technically it was just a duplication of the technique I'd done before, blending breeds and all. But I just want to check on them all, make sure they're doing okay."

"I'll do that with you. Then feed you lunch. How about that?"

She frowned. "You're taking me to lunch?"

"Yeah. You eat, don't you?"

"Of course. But I'm well aware you have a woman friend," she said firmly. "Work is one thing. But I don't want to steal any more of your spare time than we have to."

Hell, he'd forgotten about that—about how Lucy had telephoned and heard Linnie's voice in the background. "Luce...the woman you heard that evening...she wasn't a friend. She was an ex-lover who didn't want to let go," he said bluntly.

Lucy appeared to consider this. "You have a lot of those, or just one?"

He let out a breath. Until that instant, he wasn't aware how much it mattered to him—that she'd believe him. Or that her believing him would make him feel a zillion times more easy. Easy enough to tease. "At the moment, I only have one ex-lover trying to hang on. But if you're asking me how many lovers I've had—"

"Nope. Definitely, nope. Not asking that."

He could feel a hopelessly slow grin tugging the corners of his mouth. "You say that now. But feed you some Bliss, and God knows what you'll ask then."

"Neither of us," she said strongly, "are having any chocolate this morning. Not Bliss, anyway."

As it happened, she admitted being hungry, so he fed her first. It was an amazing experience, something Nick likened to auditioning for a slot in Ripley's Believe It Or Not.

She picked the restaurant. It wasn't Mickey's Diner in St. Paul, but it was a close clone to that infamous diner. The grill had to date pre-WWII, as did the jalousie glass and pitted hardwood floor and red ruby chairs. But they served Mulligan stew and blueberry pancakes, juicy burgers too big to put your hands around and old fashioned sodas.

She ate her burger. Then half of his stew. Her soda, then part of his. She stole at least half his mashed potatoes, then asked for an extra salad.

He stopped trying to eat at all. She'd never been bigger than a minute, yet she'd just eaten enough to fill a tiger or two and was still going. "No one's fed you since last Christmas?" he asked sympathetically.

"I had a great breakfast. It's just…"

She was looking over his plate again—like a Vegas winner in a jewelry store, certain there were treasures she hadn't evaluated yet. "We'll get dessert," he promised her, and then waved down the waitress. Quickly. God knew what would happen if her plate ended up empty while she was still hungry.

The waitress came through with a raspberry

cheesecake and a lemon chiffon pie. He pushed his choice in front of her, so she'd have two.

"So…you got new tires on your car?"

"No. New tires for my dad's car. I need a new car altogether. I just can't seem to get it on the schedule. Car shopping is a fate almost worth than death, you know? Or close." She forked in some raspberry cheesecake, then closed her eyes, clearly wanting to enjoy the orgasm without the distraction of conversation.

He leaned back, stuck a boot on a chair rung and just watched her, marveling. This was so, so like her— to find exuberant pleasure from something simple like a bite of cheesecake. Or sunshine. Or mucking in the dirt in the greenhouses. She always did everything heart and soul, whole-hog. Sometimes he did. But sometimes, too damn often, he got hung up on the stresses and the problems instead of taking the time to inhale the positive side of life the way she always did.

"Nick?"

"What?" This time he was the one caught woolgathering.

"You must have said *something* amazing to Russell. He looked happier than he's been in weeks."

"That's good to hear. Let's hope it lasts." Eventually he steered her back outside and in the car, thinking it was amazing she could walk after that meal. As he drove toward Bernard's, he asked, "You needed to help your dad get tires?"

It just seemed so unlikely. And she laughed. "No. I know zip about tires. But I wanted to talk to him. He's hard to corner in the house, but stuck in a car, he can't run away so easily. And I knew he was upset."

"About the divorce? I take it they haven't changed their minds about separating?"

She leaned her head back against the black leather car seat. "Nick, you don't have to hear about my family's problems."

"Is it illegal if I'm interested?"

"No. I just don't want to bore you."

"You're not boring me. I want to know."

She hesitated, but eventually spoke up. "Dad's been doing better. He quit drinking the minute he took on half his surgery schedule again. And when Greta got there, she really made him feel guilty. He got up off his behind, pitched in, helped clean up some of his messes—"

"Good. Didn't hurt him a whit to help, now, did it?"

"No. Not at all. But then I got home from work on Friday and found him sitting in a chair, crying. My *dad*. I hadn't seen him cry in years. And not like that. Ever."

"I assume he'd talked to your mom?"

"Yes. Exactly. She'd called and made an appointment for both of them to talk to a lawyer. A divorce lawyer. You know what she told him?"

"No, what?"

"My mom told him that in any normal divorce, the two people obviously hired two different attorneys. But in their case, my dad was too dumb and too absentminded to represent his own interests, so she'd have to do that for him. Which made her furious all over again."

"I want to laugh," Nick confessed.

"Yeah, so did I. If they weren't my parents, I would." Lucy sighed. "So anyway, Mom made an appointment with the lawyer for next Thursday morning. I asked him if he were going. He said, yes, what else could he do? She doesn't love me anymore."

Nick winced. "That's a hell of a thing to put on you, Luce."

"There was more. He said that he just couldn't seem to find his footing. He felt as if he were camping out in his own life. Without my mom, he couldn't seem to feel that anything mattered."

Nick waved past the guard and parked at the experimental station. There didn't seem to be anyone on the property but the two of them. "What did you say?"

"For a while, I just tried to listen. But he started scaring me. He said that a month ago, he was a person. Now he was just a shadow. He'd hear something in the hospital and think, I have to tell Eve as soon as I get home. Only now my mom doesn't want him home. She doesn't want to hear what happened. And he couldn't seem to find any point to getting up in the morning."

"Okay. Not good," Nick said firmly.

"Exactly. I tried to talk him into seeing a counselor. But he just said he didn't want or need a counselor. He wants my mother back."

"And what do you think the chances of that are?"

"Right now, zero," Lucy said wryly. "My mom won't stay in the marriage unless things change. My dad wants the marriage exactly the way it was. It's like a snake talking to a mongoose. No common ground."

"And you're worried he's depressed."

She shot him the warmest look, as if she were grateful he understood. "Terribly worried. My sister keeps saying, just kick him out, he's a grown-up, let him decide what he's going to do. But she's not here. And I found him *crying,* for Pete's sake. How am I supposed to just kick him out?"

"Lines in the sand," he murmured.

"Pardon?"

"I was just thinking that we all draw lines in the sand, Luce. My grandfather can bend for a lot of things, but when the issue is honor—that's his line. Your mom seems to have drawn her line in the sand. She wants some changes in her life, and whether or not she gets them, she's not going back to the way it was before. For my brother, Clint, he wants something from my grandfather. He's put his whole life on hold until he gets it. Craziest line in the sand I've ever seen. And for you—you can't possibly kick your father out. Love and loyalty. That's where you draw your line."

She glanced at him, startled. "I never thought of it that way."

"Don't you think it's true? It seems like everyone has some kind of a line totally unique to them. A line we set. A line we don't or can't cross, for whatever reason."

She was still looking intently at him. "So where's your line in the sand?"

"Mine?"

"Yeah, yours. Bend *my* ear for a while, would you? So I don't always have to feel like I'm the one talking your ear off."

By then they were in the lab. Lucy, turning on lights, led the way past the offices. Once inside the first community lab, she zoomed straight for one of the stainless steel units, spun the lock around and opened the chocolate safe.

He should have known—it had been nearly twenty minutes between feedings and she'd only eaten enough for an elephant for lunch, so poor thing, she was probably close to starvation. She didn't bring out the Bliss, he noticed. Was she still afraid the chocolate set off a maelstrom of hormones? Turned sweet girl-next-door types into brazen nymphomaniacs?

"Nick, you don't have to stick around. You can't help me. And I can nab one of the company wheels for a ride home."

"I've got a free Saturday afternoon. And I'd like to see what you're doing, if you don't mind."

"No, of course not. Although I confess I'm not doing anything very exciting today."

That word "exciting" seemed to promptly flash in neon lights in his brain. It kept happening, he thought edgily. Exciting wasn't a word that was supposed to apply to Lucy. From the very beginning, he'd mentally labeled her in the kid-sister class. Maybe he'd done that because she had a crush on him, and he automatically locked her in that "need to be treated extra kindly" category. But he'd just never imagined her in the sexual fantasy context.

Now, he seemed to be doing it all the time. It was unnerving. Especially because she was pregnant, and he could easily imagine her with a bulging abdomen or holding a little squirt in diapers—hardly X-rated images. Yet somehow he was increasingly getting X-rated ideas about her. And somehow he found himself shifting his schedule every which way to spend more time with her. How weird was that?

"Have you been back to the doctor?" he asked, thinking that maybe that reaction to her would disappear if he concentrated on down-to-earth issues.

"Yup. Got a clean bill of health. I also decided to stick with your doc. He gave me a list of ob/gyn doctors, but he's got a family practice with back up. And I don't have any special issues."

"You don't think you should have a specialist?"

"I would, if I had any interesting health problems, but I don't. And even more important, at least to me..." She hesitated.

"What?"

"I just liked him, Nick. I know a lot of doctors because of my family, but that doesn't mean I'm comfortable with them. He was reassuring. Easy to talk to. A straight shooter."

"Did he give you something for the nausea?"

"Yeah. But that's already getting better." By then they'd reached the lab and were headed straight for the Bliss greenhouse. She glanced at him. "If you're actually staying while I work, I'm warning you now, you'll have to tell me what your line in the sand is."

"I was hoping you'd forgotten that conversation."

"Fat chance," she teased. "Come on, you. I'm sick of the conversation always being about me."

"Well, I'll tell you, I swear. Just as soon as I think one up."

"A cop-out if ever there was one," she muttered, and punched in the code to the greenhouse.

And that was it. She forgot him. Once she started working, Nick had no illusions that he was any more important to her than, say, a gnat. Even that status was iffy, because likely a gnat was more important if it were a bug who could eat her plants.

He couldn't really be falling for a woman who rated him below beans on an interest scale, could he?

"So what are we doing here?" he called out.

She called back, "You don't have to do anything, Nick. Just relax. I just really wanted to check on some of my new babies. It won't take me that long, I promise."

"Babies?"

He figured he could track her down from the sound of her voice—which worked fine—but he should have known better than to ask a question. He found her already on her knees in mud besides a long trough of seedlings.

"This are my newest babies," she said, her voice throaty with passionate fervor. "Aren't they gorgeous?"

"Um…yeah, they sure are."

"This is my favorite part of the job," she confessed, and that was the last time he got a word in. It's not as if he didn't know better than to get her started about work. But damn. She got so revved up and bouncy. It was hard not to encourage her. She radiated more positive energy than sunshine.

"Chocolatiers have always done cross-breeding, Nick. You know that. But all these centuries, they cross-bred to get a superior quality of bean. It never occurred to them to try to change the nature of the cacao tree itself. That's where Orson had such vision."

"Uh huh." His gaze pinned the slope of her rump. If she'd gained a pound, he couldn't see it. But her rump was distinctive. Little and tight and sassy. The kind of enticing rump that made a guy just want to cup it and squeeze.

"I'm not boring you, am I?"

"Oh, no."

"Okay, then…you know the whole Darwinian thing about how the weakest tend to naturally die out, the strongest survive. Just like the strongest female wolf always seeks out the alpha male wolf. It works in plants the same way. So all those years chocolatiers had tried to cross-breed cacao for the flavor of the beans, they didn't look close enough at enticing more strength from the plant."

"Gramps was doing that years before you came on board."

"I know. And they hadn't had luck for years—as you know. He'd get the grafts going, but the result would be bitter or unusable chocolate. Or maybe the tree broke down in a short period of time. Whatever—something always went wrong. It was just three years ago that it all started to come together. With these babies…"

She motioned to her seedlings—the ones she was watering and patting and pampering as if they were newborns in an incubator. "What happened was our taking two specific cacao trees from two different continents. Both were dependent on their rain forest climates before, no different than all the others. But it was as if…they fell in love."

"The trees...fell in love," Nick echoed dryly.

"All right, all right, you laugh. But put it any way you want it, it was as if these two trees saw each other, were grafted together, and just exploded in growth and beauty. As if someone had given them joy juice. As if they finally found their natural soul mate. So it wasn't just that we got stronger trees, better able to adapt to a variety of climates. But we got Bliss out of their mating, as well."

"So, you think it's love."

"Look, I know that sounds corny. But otherwise, it's not that easy to explain. The relationship between the trees makes no scientific sense. They're just *right* together in a way they never were before. They thrive ten ways to Sunday when they're grafted together. Better than they ever did alone. Better than they ever did in their so-called natural environments originally."

He fell silent for a minute. Certainly there was no point in arguing with her. Arguing with Lucy when she got going on chocolate and cacao was like hoping to get run over by a steamroller.

But when she finally stood—with a groan—and then bent over to dust the dirt from her knees, her face was as radiant as a moonbeam. He vaguely remembered once thinking she was ordinary-looking. He clearly remembered thinking he'd never be attracted to a girl like her. That night they'd had together was still too hazy for him to totally recall it, as if he'd been delirious with fever—or insanity—and it just wouldn't come clear.

But right then, seeing the dash and splash of brightness in her eyes, her quick grin, that petal-soft skin and dirty-jeaned knees, something slapped him hard. Right in the heart.

"Luce?"

"Hmm? You ready to go? I need to clean up, but that'll only take me a sec. And then I have to lock up, of course, but   "

"Before, you asked me what my line in the sand was. The line I just can't or won't cross if I have absolutely any choice."

She stopped, cocked her head. "Yeah, I did ask you. And I really do want to know."

He said slowly, "There are certain things I can't walk away from. Even if I'm going to be hurt, even if it's the kind of thing that other people would be able to ignore...I can't. If it's a problem I have to face, I can't wait. I have to *do* it. Figure it out."

"Hmm. I think I get it. Like—?"

Her mouth was open. Of course Luce's mouth was often open. But this time he slipped in a slow, easy, "Like this. Exactly like this."

And reached for her.

CHAPTER ELEVEN

LUCY SAW NICK step toward her, saw him raise his arms. Self consciously she looked down, thinking she must have dirt or chocolate or something on her that he was going to brush away—Nick was one of those people that always looked put together, where she was one of those people who forgot her clothes as soon as she put them on.

Only in that millisecond when she looked down and then back up, he'd stepped closer yet. His hands hooked her wrists and then lifted them around his neck. She realized that fast that he was going to kiss her, and her lips parted to object, but suddenly her air was gone. His lips had swooshed down on hers.

All this time, she'd been good. She'd tried to never let on how fiercely she was still attracted to him, how much he dominated her thoughts and feelings. He'd made that even harder by doing so many ruthlessly provocative things...like setting up his house as a retreat for her. Like bullying her into taking extra money for Bliss. Like keeping her preg-

nancy and his impending fatherhood a secret solely
because she'd asked him to. Like…leaving her alone
to decide what she wanted to do about the pregnancy—exactly as she'd asked him, no matter how
hard it had to be to keep his mitts off decision-
making and controlling the problem.

In the beginning, she just thought the chemistry
was, well, chemistry. Physical attraction. A girl
smelled an alpha male and whoosh, there went her
hormones. But now, damn. Now she knew it was
more than chemistry.

He wasn't just adorable.

He was lovable.

So kissing her now was an ultra-mean, ultra-
unfair, ultra-cruel thing to do.

Her arms, already looped around his neck, tightened. Her toes, already pushed up on tiptoe, locked
in place. Her eyes shut faster than blinds and she
kissed him back. Fiercely. Furiously. Oh, God. He
tasted so good. Like chocolate. Like him.

She was a pregnant woman. She couldn't be held
responsible. Right?

Right.

She may not have chosen the father of her child
wisely—in terms of her life. But her heart had chosen him brilliantly. He was sexy and smart and a
man of integrity. He had a great butt. He honored his
family. Her baby was going to have downright fabulous genes, at least coming from his side.

That was another reason for going hog-wild in his arms, right?

Right.

Sensations bombarded her. The smells of earth and sweet loam. The filtering light from the green-house canopy. The distant whisper of spring wind. The silence between them, except for her thundering heartbeat—and his.

His mouth moved against hers, tasted, took, tasted some more, and then, on a low grumble of a breath, dipped down for some serious tongue.

She remembered that tongue of his...from the Night of the Chocolate. Only this time she hadn't had even a remote taste of Bliss. And it was broad daylight. So there was no scientific reason—at least that she could pin down—to explain why she felt so emotionally naked in his arms, but there it was. Every daydream she'd ever had was hanging out there. Every fantasy of her perfect man, out there. Every schoolgirl crush, every decadent dream, every unholy, unwholesome, shameless thought she'd ever had, out there.

And being vented on him. She rubbed against him, feeling her breasts tighten and swell—bigger breasts than they used to be, not huge, but definitely fuller than a month ago. And her tummy wasn't the flat board it had been, either, but had a little pudge to it, enough pudge to nudge against his abdomen. His erection ground against her with hard, hot urgency. In fact, his skin, his mouth, his hands all seemed to be suffering from a sudden, fierce increase in temperature.

He lifted his head and gasped for a breath. His eyes slitted open for that moment, stared at her. A frown of complete bewilderment appeared on his forehead...but then frown or no frown, he dipped down for another kiss. And another. His hands found their way to her shirt. He loosened one button. Then another. Kisses and buttons kept loosening, unleashing new sensations, new trouble. And from Lucy's boots, they were already in all the trouble they could handle.

She loosened her arms from around his neck. It was just no time to be holding on. She wanted her hands free. Her heartbeat soared when she pushed up his long-sleeved T-shirt, loving the feel of him, splaying her palms on the smooth, strong expanse of his chest.

She pushed the shirt up and over his neck. There was a hint of a grin on his mouth when it disappeared over his head. She tipped up, kissing him this time, and wiped that grin right off. He made a sound that rumbled between his throat and hers, caught inside that kiss, a groaned whisper of longing, and oh, yeah, she heard it. Her pulse started rushing like white-water rapids, wild, noisy...fierce.

He wanted her. That's what that hopeless, helpless groan implied. Imagine. A man making a desperate sound—for her. Nick. *Nick* making a sound of naked wanting—for *her.*

Her khakis were already unbuttoned—she hadn't been able to button pants for weeks now—which he discovered in a second flat. Then his hands slipped up and unhooked her bra. It was her favorite—chocolate-brown with lemon-yellow lace. And it was new, because none of her old bras fit her any more. Unfortunately, the sexiness and allure of the bra was completely wasted, because he never even noticed. Slingshot fashion, the bra flew off into the cacao forest somewhere…like somewhere in the general location of wherever her shirt and his were.

He spun her around, slammed back against the wall, and then pulled her to him, into him. Slowly he sank down, down, until he was sitting on the ground with his legs splayed, and she was tangled around him. Her pants were still on, more or less. So were his, more or less. But with her knees shucked up around his torso, she could feel him against her intimately, evocatively.

"This is crazy," he murmured.

"I know."

"For damn sure it isn't the chocolate, Lucy. Not this time."

"I know."

"I don't know if pregnant women are supposed to do this."

"I don't think you're supposed to deny pregnant women anything they want."

"Don't *tease,* Luce. Damn it. This is going to be my fault."

"I sure hope so," she whispered, and zoomed in for another kiss, this one on the side of his throat. He'd only done a Saturday shave, a swipe and a promise. But she could still smell the clean foam of shaving cream, already feel the tickle of stubborn little black hairs, taste the warm skin just under his ear. Then lower.

Her back arched so she could get a look at that luscious guy chest, forgetting momentarily that he was getting a look at hers. Which wasn't luscious or guy-like, but a source of sensitivity. He discovered precisely how sensitive.

They might have slunk to the floor in a slam-bam tumble, but suddenly Nick turned down the speed to slow motion. That hungry tongue suddenly traced a languid, lazy path down her neck. He lifted her, just from the weight of his hands, so that his mouth could trace the shape of her breasts.

She'd felt fire between them before, but how could she know how much hotter tenderness could be? Damn him, she couldn't think. Couldn't remember how to breathe. Felt a gulp of vulnerability so raw, so huge, she could barely swallow it back.

"Nick," she whispered suddenly, not having a question, more voicing a fear in his name alone. And he answered her as if she'd asked a question, as if he'd heard her. And maybe he really had heard her heart.

"Nothing'll happen that you don't want. Not with

me. Ever." He lifted his head, just for that second. "Trust me, Luce."

"I do."

"Damn it. Don't trust me *that* much."

"I do. In fact, I only trust you. This way. This much."

"I just don't want you regretting—"

"Nick, could you shut up?" she asked him. And when he did, she said, "thank you," and kissed him again.

It was a good thing he was an experienced lover, because she was completely confounded by the problem of getting her pants off. And his. Very quickly—she used to be an A student, after all—she figured out there was no comfortable mattress anywhere. Nick seemed to have realized that, too, which was undoubtedly how he'd come up with this sitting up position. Only to make that work, it meant getting their pants off and untangled, which was exceptionally tricky because she was completely unwilling to get off him. And he seemed just as zealously unwilling to separate from her long enough to perform such an acrobatic feat.

But he did, eventually, manage to get her pants loosened and unzipped and finally down and off. His were easier, although he yelped when his bare butt connected with cold cement. She had to laugh. She just didn't have time to laugh for long.

When he slid inside her, every nerve ending in her

body burned with exquisite awareness—of him, of her, of the snug, sleek fit of the two of them. She thought she'd remembered the first time they made love, but this was daylight, with his eyes open on hers, with her tuned to every expression on his face, in his gaze. Before, she'd had champagne to loosen her inhibitions...and Bliss.

Now...she just had him. The touch of him. The sound, sight, taste of him.

How could she not fly?

"Jesus, Lucy...how long have you had all this locked inside you?"

"Just for you," she whispered. "Just for you."

Out it came. All that need. All that hunger. All of those years of repression—well, some of it had definitely slipped free before on him, particularly the night of the Bliss caper. But she knew him better now, knew he had a tender, gentle side he kept well hidden, knew he was as heart-sore lonely as she was, even if he'd never said it. Her heart trusted him, so much that she simply felt freed. Free to fly with him, to soar with him.

She knew, instinctively from her soul, that there'd never be another man like Nick. Not for her. No matter what happened, she wanted this moment with him. She wanted these feelings with him.

And she wanted this baby. By him.

That bombardment of emotions and instincts conspired into making her feel more powerful than a superhero, happier than joy. And en route, she seemed to pick up all the wicked, bad ideas of a red-hot woman who'd forgotten to take her inhibition pill—either that, or Nick did something magic to make any normal shyness disappear.

He pumped inside her, building the pace, creating a rhythm wilder than a drumbeat, taking her to emotional places she'd never been…inciting need she'd never felt, feelings she'd never yearned for before now, before this moment. Her skin flushed from impossible heat. Sweat beaded both their brows. She saw his eyes, on a level with hers, wild like hers, mirroring her face as her eyes mirrored his.

"Please, Nick," she hissed. "Take me, take me…"

He whispered something back…she thought he said, "Love me, Lucy"…but that seemed as impossible as this whole crazy dream. Nothing real could be this perfect. No other man or woman could possibly have experienced this level of wonder before. Maybe she didn't hear his words, but she still heard him. The cry from his heart, for her to come to him, come with him, come, come, come…

Release washed over her in silver spasms, clenching her from the inside, spilling a gush of sweet, intense pleasure. And then he erupted on a yelp of shock—and again—until he was half laughing from the sheer force of his orgasm. Finally they both sank against each other, his head on her shoulder, her head on his. Both of them were breathing like gasping freight trains—diesel freight trains. Noisy. Gusty.

Eventually she caught her breath, yet she wasn't inclined to move. Maybe ever. She couldn't think of a single reason she couldn't nap right then, still wrapped around him, still semifilled by him, in one of the places she loved most in the universe. But possibly he wasn't quite as comfortable as she was.

"Ah…Luce?" he murmured.

"Hmm?"

"We're both completely out of our minds."

She lifted her head, turning serious for a moment, and framed his head with her hands. "Please. Don't regret this."

He seemed to sense how painfully he could hurt her with the wrong comeback. "I'll never regret this," he promised her.

There. Her heartbeat eased.

Maybe it was too late, far too late, to deny how deeply she'd fallen in love with him. But some things she was absolutely sure of.

Her heart had picked a pricelessly wonderful man to fall in love with. Maybe she had no faith that he'd ever feel the same. Maybe dealing with the pregnancy and being a single mom was going to be extremely hard. Maybe the rest of her life wasn't sorted out or even close.

But she hadn't picked the wrong man to love.

With him, she felt like the wild, free woman she'd

wanted to be for so long. She didn't mind being a prissy, set-in-her-ways fussbudget for the rest of world. But deep inside, she'd wanted to know there was more. That she could be more. And with Nick, she could be…and was.

She had no illusions that he wanted to be married to her—or would ever have chosen to be with her if the pregnancy hadn't surprised them both. But she kept trying to accept that. Being with him, loving him, still opened her life the way nothing else remotely had. If she never had more, she still had this.

ALMOST TWO WEEKS LATER, Nick still couldn't forget that afternoon. Right now—considering he had his hands completely full with Orson—it should have been impossible to dwell on Lucy. Yet her face seemed imprinted in his mind, their situation shadowing every thought.

His responsibility for her was crystal-clear. It didn't really matter who was most to blame for that one wild night. The rest of Lucy's life was affected by the advent of a baby. His baby. She needed to be protected and taken care of. That was a cut-and-dried.

Still, his resolve didn't begin to explain his increasing strong feelings for her. Of course he liked her. He'd always liked her. But she wasn't like any of the fast-lane women he'd known. Actually, he knew what to do with high-maintenance women.

He had no idea what to do about a woman who didn't want a thing from him—and didn't seem to particularly value what he did have to offer. For a guy who'd been chased nonstop for years, the experience of a woman who hardly hustled to give him the time of day was humbling.

She was attracted—obviously. That one night could never have happened if she didn't have feelings for him then…and now, every time he kissed her, she melted. Whew, did she melt.

But the minute they were out of touch range, she seemed to forget him. Revert back to talking business. To treating him friendly-like. To going out of her way to keep her distance.

She'd made clear she didn't want to marry him, but hell, she didn't have to rub it in so hard. Besides which…

"Let's get this damned show on the road!" Orson barked impatiently.

Madris, Orson's driver, shared a commiserating glance with Nick. Neither had wanted Orson to stay inside this morning. Thunder growled in the west, bringing on an imminent spring storm. The new leaves were all rustling, restless. Clouds punched and bunched overhead, looking like dirty gray fists.

Orson had been unable to see the greenhouse construction project for the last ten days because his one bad hip had been acting up. This morning the hip was worse, yet he'd called up first Madris and then

Nick. He'd had enough catering to his ridiculous health. He wanted to see how the new projects were going and that was that.

When they arrived at the experimental station, Orson turned and caught the two men exchanging glances. "Don't either of you say a single word."

"I won't have to," Nick said easily. "When Lucy sees you limping, she'll blister your ears better than I could any day."

"Lucy shows me respect. Unlike the two of you."

Madris, who'd looked like a wizened octogenarian when Nick was a kid, rarely wasted time arguing aloud with the boss. He just said to Nick, "I'll be waiting right here."

"You will not," Orson snapped. "You'll go home until I call for you."

"Yes, sir." Behind his back, Madris mouthed, "I'll be here."

Nick nodded. Technically he was supposed to be in a marketing meeting for the Christmas packaging and products, but when his grandfather called, he'd quickly hiked over to the house. The only time his grandfather ever got testy or mean was when he was in pain. Unfortunately, that invariably meant Nick was called, because no one else could deal with Orson—and live to tell.

By the time Orson climbed out of the car, Nick had a cane ready. He tried to be subtle about moving ahead fast enough to open doors.

"I spoke with your brother last night," Orson said testily. "Clint tells me he wants to take Gretchen to Brussels this June."

"That seems like a great idea."

Orson arched an imperious eyebrow. "He asked me if I wanted to go with them."

Nick smelled a skunk in the woods, even if he couldn't see it coming yet. "Well…that'd be an awfully long trip for you."

"I've traveled with tougher health problems than this hip. I'd go if I felt like it."

"But…you don't want to go?"

"Of course I'd like to go. It'd be a chance to show my great-granddaughter the culture of Brussels. And to see so much of where the chocolate business—the important chocolate business—really started."

There was a problem coming in the conversation. Nick just didn't know where or when it was going to kick in. "So you told Clint…?"

"No. Of course I said no. I told Clint if he wanted to invite me to something, I'd enjoy a dinner celebrating his doing some worthwhile job. Or, for that matter, any job. Any kind of useful work at all."

Nick mentally winced, guessing the rest of the conversation between his brother and grandfather had been a ton of fun. Like getting poison ivy on a vacation. Or throwing up in a restaurant.

His grandfather hucked ahead, using his cane more like a battering ram to stab the floor than as a stabilizer. "Reiko!" he barked a hello. Reiko looked startled, shared a glance with Nick, and then gently popped in the doorway to greet the old man.

Orson suffered an affectionate greeting, then scowled on past Fritz and Fred.

No one was in the general lab. Nor was Lucy in the Bliss greenhouses. Outside, past another gated round of new secure fences, were the new greenhouses. The first one appeared completely done. The others had completed skeleton frames. They resembled long white caterpillars, stretching almost five acres.

Nick noticed a plumbing and heating truck, and just past that, Greger and Lucy. Lucy was wildly gesturing to the tall, blond-bearded plumbing contractor—naturally Orson had hired the best in the business, but apparently Pete Olson couldn't please Lucy. Not today. She looked a bit like a female David challenging Goliath, but the way she was shaking her forefinger, Nick was darn happy he wasn't wearing Pete's shoes.

"Orson!" She spotted Nick and Orson at the same time, and left Pete wiping his brow to pelt straight over to them. "What's going on? How come you two didn't let me know ahead you were coming over?"

"I just wanted to surprise you, Lucy." Orson managed to lean down to get a kiss from her. Nick didn't get a kiss, but her gaze slid to his with petal softness and clung for just a moment before turning away.

"Well, there's going to be a big rain, you silly, not a good day to visit."

Nick watched her take in his grandfather in a swoop of a female glance. She hooked Orson's arm, bolstering him without saying a word, and started up a chatter about how the Bliss expansion project was coming. The first shipment of seedlings was due in the next couple days—which meant that a ton of things simply had to be ready and working ahead of time.

"Which it will be," she assured his grandfather. "Would you like me to show you?"

"That's exactly why I came," Orson agreed.

"Okay, but I'm so tired today…." Anyone could see she was lying through her teeth. Her cheeks flushed like a kid's. "So…if you don't mind, let's use the golf cart to run around, all right? That is, if you don't mind not walking. You'd really save me some energy—"

"No problem at all," Orson said.

Nick knew damn well the old man would have fought tooth and nail if *he'd* suggested using the cart, but Lucy did it, and she could do no wrong.

Greger brought the cart around, but Lucy drove, chattering nonstop about grafting and cross-breeding and soil types and moisture levels. When the two waxed on ardently about fertilizers, Nick zoned out.

She was dressed unusually well for an outside-work day. The jeans had no holes; the Teva sandals looked clean; a perky madras scarf haphazardly tied her hair back. Naturally she wore no makeup. She'd managed to accumulate dirt on her knees and hands and elbows and one cheek. Just her right cheek. And dirt on that rose-soft porcelain cheek struck him as an unbelievable abomination....

He realized he was obsessing over a woman's cheek. In the middle of a workday. A bolt of lightning suddenly crackled overhead, even though that didn't stop Lucy from lathering on about botany and cacao—Orson foaming at the mouth the same way.

"Really, I was glad about the stormy forecast," she told Orson. "The trees aren't here yet, so they're not at risk. And if we have a bad storm today, it'll really test all our systems—security, power, durability, everything. So it's perfect timing."

For the first time Nick spoke up. It was the first he could possibly have gotten a word in. "But, of course, if the lightning comes any closer, you'll be going straight back inside."

She smiled at Orson. "It's like having two bullies in my life. Him and Greger. I'm not sure which one's worse, but it's a close contest..."

Suddenly something pinged. It was just a small sound, but Orson heard it and so did Nick. He had no idea what it was, but Lucy must have, because her face suddenly flushed beet-bright and her hands flew to her stomach.

"Darn it, I've lost another button," she said with embarrassment. "I swear I'm getting fat as a slug."

It didn't seem like a big deal at the time. Lucy's cell rang several times, and the plumbing people were waiting for her to finish their instructions. She was so obviously in the middle of major work that a visit—even from the bosses—was an intrusion. Orson readily agreed to cutting their progress tour short.

Nick saw his grandfather to the house, and then peeled over to the plant and offices for the rest of the day. He stopped back at the mansion after six, though, partly because Orson had asked him to pop by—which wasn't happening often these days—but even more, because Nick had been naggingly worried about his grandfather's health. Although the house had an excellent security system, no one personally watched over Orson once the housekeeper and cook left for the day and Madris took off.

By six, the clouds had rolled in closer and settled overhead like a smothering mattress. Rain was coming down in slick gray sheets—a healthy spring soaker, if it weren't for the whining wind and lightning. Nick let himself in the back door, shaking water from his hair and jacket, and was greeted immediately by Boo Boo and Baby. The dogs were beside themselves with boredom and bounded around, bringing him a collection of toys, ropes, bones, squeeze balls, socks, a shoe. Boo Boo had stolen a towel from somewhere and wouldn't give it up. Baby wanted to moan and get petted.

Eventually he worked his way past the canine gauntlet and tracked down his grandfather to a tall chair in the front living room, a tray barely touched next to him, no TV on, no warming fire, his cane still within thumping distance—and the scowl on his brow even darker than it had been that morning.

"I'm going to hire a private investigator," he started out, his voice more belligerent than a bullhorn.

"For Clint?" Nick asked, confused where this was coming from.

"Of course not for Clint. Your brother tells me every sin he's ever committed. Most of the time before he's even done anything. I mean for Lucy."

"What? Why on earth—?"

Orson pushed out of the tall brocade chair—Nick's grandmother's favorite chair, once upon a time—wobbled a moment and then started to pace the living room with a heavy lean on the cane. "I'm going to find out who the father of her child is. And then I'm going to raise holy hell."

Nick froze. Then crossed the room to the small sterling table with the decanter of brandy. He hadn't had dinner yet. God knew when he was going to get any, but he figured he could likely down five shots or more and his heart would still be thundering worse than the storm outside.

"Gramps," he said quietly, "you don't have the right to interfere in her private life."

"I don't care. You saw how it was this morning. She's starting to get a tummy. It isn't much because she's so little to begin with. But not long from now people are going to start noticing, and then they're going to start asking. I cannot fathom why her parents haven't intervened—"

"Possibly because it isn't up to her parents, or anyone else. She's well over twenty-one. Well capable of figuring out what she wants to do without interference from anyone."

"That may be what you think. It's not what I think. I think the father of that child should be horsewhipped. I don't understand it. How a man can get a woman pregnant and then just disappear from her life—not if he expects to call himself a man."

"Gramps, you're not being reasonable. You don't know what Lucy's opinion is—"

"I don't *care* what Lucy's opinion is. I can hire a private investigator without her knowing. I can do all kinds of things without her knowing. No young woman knows what it's like to go through a pregnancy alone, or bear a child alone, or rear a child alone. It seems fine to her right now because she's young and strong—and because she doesn't realize everything that's involved."

"Gramps—"

"The older generation gets a reputation for being old-fashioned for a reason. The reason is that we've been through more life. I don't care what the current mores of society are. They're wrong. She's a wonderful young woman. Whoever did this to her—"

"Orson—"

"I'm going to find out. And one way or another, I'm going to—"

"You're not going to sic a private investigator on Lucy. Period. Not just because Lucy wouldn't want it, but because there's no reason to. I *know* who the father is," Nick blurted out.

Odd, how complete silence fell for that one brief moment. Orson turned to look at him. Nick had poured the bowl of brandy but had yet to take a sip. He didn't want it. Didn't want to sit, either. Outside, rain was battering the windows like a nightmare desperate to come in, hurling and spattering and pelting noisily. Yet somehow there was nothing he noticed but the shadowed glint in his grandfather's eyes.

Orson clipped out a single word. "Who?"

"Me, Gramps. I'm the father."

"You can't be."

"I·am."

"That's *my* great-grandchild?"

"Yes."

"You took advantage of a young girl?"

"She isn't that young in age."

"No. But she's an exceptionally vulnerable young woman—which you've said yourself. I just can't believe this." Orson didn't yell, didn't swear. Just looked at him as if no one had ever disappointed him this painfully. "Not you, Nick."

A knife stabbed in his gut couldn't hurt this bad. "I wanted to tell you before. Even knowing how upset you'd be, I still wanted you to know—because I knew you were worried about Lucy. But I couldn't. Because she didn't want anyone to know. At least not for a while longer yet."

"Marry the girl."

"I can't."

"It's the one thing you can do. Have to do."

But it was the one thing he absolutely couldn't do. It was the one option Lucy had made almost violently clear that she wanted nothing to do with.

His grandfather's respect had always mattered enormously to him. Risking that loss was no small thing yet until that precise moment, Nick hadn't realized how hugely silence had grated on his conscience. Hiding his responsibility had made him feel like a coward. Still, coming clean brought no relief. The emotional blade in his gut just kept hurting. He tried to answer Orson with the truth.

"Sometimes taking care of a woman means doing what she needs rather than what you think is right for her."

"Horse shit," Orson said, then more slowly, "I still can't seem to believe this. You got that sweet girl pregnant? You slept with a young woman who's never been remotely near the fast lanes you have?

You slept with an employee? And further, someone you didn't even have a personal relationship with?"

Orson shot out the words like pellets, but even if Nick was given the chance to respond, he couldn't have. If hell froze over, he'd never have revealed that Lucy had come on to him, that he would never have invited that initial contact in a thousand years. To hurt Orson's love for Lucy? Never. Equally true was that Nick already felt the weight of guilt, of wrongs, not just from Orson's viewpoint, but from his own.

Orson said, soft as a whisper. "Get out. Get out of this house."

Okay. Now it came. Not just the sharpness of a blade sliced into his heart—but shame, fiercer than grief. He'd never let down Orson before. He'd scale mountains before disappointing the one person who'd been there for him from the day his parents died.

Through a thick clot in his throat, he said quietly, "Gramps, we need to talk about this. Not for my sake. I understand you're beyond unhappy with me, but you're going to see Lucy in the days ahead, and—"

"Get out. I'll talk to you later. I'll talk to you plenty. But right now, I don't even want to look at your face, Nicholas. Just…leave."

He'd been so braced for an explosion that he just had no idea what agony Orson's soft tone would cause. The silence in his eyes was more hurtful than a thousand bruises. Nick didn't want to make up stories to defend himself. There were no stories he could make up. No stories he could tell.

He'd feared letting his grandfather down from the time he was a boy…but somehow it never occurred to him that it could happen when he was a man. A rock shifted from under his feet, a foundation he'd never believe could crumble.

But right then, at that moment, there was nothing he could say or do beyond what his grandfather asked him to do, and leave.

CHAPTER TWELVE

LUCY WAS DETERMINED NOT to come unglued. The last three weeks had been nonstop chaos, but she kept telling herself that she *liked* chaos. So her parents were still on the noisy divorce track. So her dad was still having friends over at her place at all hours of the day and night. So every encounter with Nick seemed to raise the confusing tension between them, with that only getting more hyper instead of less. So work had gone plumb crazy, thinks to the Bliss Project being put on the fast track. In fact, the first two greenhouses were already up, checked out and prepared for the arrival of the first cacao seedlings.

Okay, so she hadn't stayed perfectly glued through all that, but she'd held onto her sanity. More or less. Some more, some less. It was just today that her emotional glue was suffering a complete meltdown.

It was the seedling thing. She'd choreographed every step in the procedure to handle the incoming cacao plants as only an anal-compulsive fussbudget could do. But the shipment of plants was supposed to be carefully staggered. Positively only one shipment of plants was scheduled to arrive this week. Not two. *Never* two.

All the plants needed on arrival was the obvious care—being located in a protected, controlled environment, treating them for travel shock, their food and watering needs tended to. That kind of thing Lucy could do in her sleep. But she only had two hands. And what she couldn't possibly do was graft that many plants at the same time.

She'd anticipated every single piece of the work but that one. She'd just never expected to need a clone of herself. And once the plants were past the shock stage and all settled in—once she really had a take on the quality and nature of the seedlings—she had to get that grafting work done. It's not as if she could wait until the trees were four feet tall. It had to be done at a certain time.

Like today.

"Look, I don't want strangers anywhere near here," Lucy told Greger frantically. "I don't want anyone touching the plants. The soil. The temperature, the controls. *Nothing.*"

"Gotcha," Greger said placidly. "Sure and you're a little upset—"

"I'm not *remotely upset.*"

"Yah. I can see that. But don't forget you've got me. I won't let anyone in here. And I can do all the carrying and staging and picking up so you won't have to."

"Which is good. Because I need to do all the grafting."

"Gotcha," Greger said again. "Except you can't possibly do it all yourself. Thankfully I've been watching you for weeks now. So I'll be right beside you, and you can watch every single thing I do, so you won't have to worry a bit."

That sounded right, but Lucy didn't trust him. That was, she *trusted* him—Greger was an overprotective, sneaky pain in the butt, but she had no doubt whatsoever he was a good guy. It was just that trusting him with something minor—like her life—was entirely different than trusting him to touch her precious plants, to do every graft and cut and planting the right way.

Which, of course, meant *her* way.

Life would have been so easy if the plants had just arrived in staggered fashion, the way they were supposed to. If *she'd* been in charge of the shipments, they'd have come in on schedule. Only now...well, she'd just have double hours until it was done. That was all there was to it.

At noon, Greger said, "You're leaving for lunch now."

"I am, I am," she agreed.

At one, he brought her lunch. Possibly she may have absently mentioned that she was starving for seafood, because he brought her a crab salad, an apple, a tuna fish sandwich, a lobster dip with crackers, and a bowl of clam chowder. Because Greger was being such a bully, she polished it off, and then lickety-split, headed back to the greenhouse.

At three, Greger said, "You're going to take a break now."

"I really could use a couple minutes," she agreed.

At three-thirty, he said—in that aggravating slow, placid voice of his—that she was either taking a twenty-minute break with her feet up or he was calling Mr. Bernard.

She agreed to take an immediate break.

At four Greger brought in Reiko, who'd been working at the same feverish pace on another project in her own private lab. She knew what was going on. "What? Are you trying to completely wear yourself out so you'll be too beat to work tomorrow?"

When Reiko was gone, Lucy rounded on Greger for being a traitor and a tattletale and not her keeper. Possibly because she was dirty and sore and so tired she couldn't see straight, she ended up firing him.

She'd never fired anyone before. It made her feel guilty and ugly and all pinched up on the inside, but when he left the greenhouse, she closed her eyes and gulped it all down, because darn it, this was Bliss. *Her* Bliss. Because of her, the company had invested all this money, and if it didn't work out right, it was going to be her fault. Or it was going to *feel* like her fault, which was totally the same thing.

Minutes ticked by. Long, silent minutes. Working with the cacao cuttings took intense concentration and she'd been at it all day. Still, it wasn't work. Not really. She loved it too much to call it work; if so much wasn't at stake she'd be loving it even more. Every single tree was different. The cuts were never the same. She loved the challenge of it, the smell of the dirt and the trees and the light and everything else…it was just that her back ached. So did her knees. Her toes were squished-dirty inside her tennies; her fingers were gritty; it seemed as if she had to pee two dozen times a day lately and her eyes were burning from focusing so intently for so many hours.

When the greenhouse door opened, her head shot up, not sure whether she felt more aggravated by yet another interruption or relieved. She ended up neither. Nick strode in, wearing old chinos and a holey sweatshirt, but as if it were first thing in the morning—instead of thirteen work hours into the day—his stride was quick and vital and full of zoom.

"Damn it. If you're here to yell at me, too, you can just turn right around and head back out."

"Rough day, Luce?"

"You know it is. I'll bet everyone and his mother have already told you it is. And don't tell me you didn't already hear about my firing Greger." She gulped. "It's killing me. I feel so terrible. I know I hurt his feelings."

"Yeah, that tends to happen when you fire a guy. But don't get all eaten up by guilt. You can make it up to him when he shows up for work tomorrow." He stopped in front of her, shook his head with a grin. "My God. You look like something the cat refused to drag home."

"Didn't you like playing in dirt when you were a kid?" Possibly she'd already considered that issue— that Nick wouldn't let Greger stay fired. But at least he wasn't rubbing it in.

"You bet. Still do. Just don't get much chance these days." He pushed up his sleeves. "I've got a plan."

"What plan?"

"The plan is…you're going to tell me exactly what you still have to get done today. Not what you *want* to get done. But what you absolutely *need* to get done. And then, whatever's on that list, we're gonna boogie until it's accomplished."

"Just like that? No arguing? No treating me like I have to have a rest every two and a half seconds? No making out like pregnancy has turned me into a half-wit?"

"You're the boss in here, shorty. You give the orders, so heap 'em on. Go for it."

She really, really didn't want anyone doing her cuts. But Nick didn't argue with her about being obsessive to the nth degree. He just set her up like a surgeon's assistant, carting the tools, making it possible for her to move from just one cut and graft to the next, arranging it so she didn't have to bend and twist so much.

She never glanced at her watch, had no idea how long they plugged at it, but they seemed to zoom down one row and up the next and then another. It was amazing how much faster the work flowed, when she had someone helping who both watched and anticipated what she needed next.

Because she was getting way overtired—and because she was having a majorly self-centered day—it only gradually occurred to her that something was wrong. Not with her. With Nick.

He'd barely spoken, which was fine; God knew she could talk a magpie out of the tree, but not when she was concentrating. But over that long work stretch, Nick's silence slowly seeped into her consciousness. The only time he smiled was when she directed one at him. He offered no extra conversation. There was something tense in his shoulders, a shadowed strain around his eyes.

Midway through the last row, she said out of the blue, "Okay. What's wrong?" And then looked at him straight on so she could read his expression.

"What? Nothing." When she kept squinting at him, he admitted, "All right, I admit I'm tired." And when she persisted in still staring him down, he said,

"When you have a minute where you don't have to concentrate so intensely…there is something I need to tell you."

"What?"

"Orson knows I'm the father."

She dropped her sacred grafting knife. "What? Why? Why did you tell him? Nick, you *promised* me—"

"I had no choice, Luce. He was determined to hire a private investigator to find out who the father was all so he could beat up the guy."

"He what? Oh. God." A chuckle chortled out of her throat. "Darn it, I'm not sure whether to tear out my hair or laugh." But then she said swiftly, all humor gone, "Damn, Nick. I'm so sorry. I feel terrible. That had to be a miserable and uncomfortable conversation for you to handle." Because she noticed how quickly he stiffened up, she ducked her head and returned to work.

"It wasn't easy but at least the news is out now. We both know it was going to get out sooner or later."

Again he fell silent, as if that was totally the end of the story. Sometimes he was so male that she just wanted to smack him. "Look," she began, "I'll talk to your grandfather—"

"No, you won't."

"I know how old-fashioned he is, so don't try telling me he isn't blaming you. And that isn't right. You and I both know whose fault it really is."

"Luce." He stood up. "There were two of us. Remember?"

Oh, she remembered. She remembered the Night of the Chocolate…and she remembered making love two weeks ago. She remembered every scent, every touch, every groan of need, every burst of an unexpected smile tucked between them. She remembered the feel of his skin. His mouth. His hands.

She especially remembered that afternoon in the lab…when they'd been on the concrete floor, their clothes and bodies still in an abandoned heap…and realizing that it had happened to her again. There was no blaming Bliss on that occasion because she hadn't had a single bite. But *something* that happened. Something had transformed her into a Wanton Wanda again.

And damn, but she liked it. Liked being Wanda instead of Lucy.

Except for the end of the story—when she went home to sleep solo that night, suffering uncertain dreams all night long, fretting why he'd felt driven to make love to her this time.

But right now was no time to allow herself to dwell on any of that.

"You know what?" she said suddenly. "I'm really beat. Could we quit?" She fully realized that he didn't want to talk about his grandfather. But now she understood where the strained shadows around his eyes came from. She could have worked for another couple hours at least, but he obviously needed some serious rest.

"All right," he said, "If you're sure."

She gave herself credit for doing a fine job of manipulating him, only her satisfaction didn't last long. Nick got it in his head that she should stay at his place, and nothing would talk him out of it.

"Look, it's just silly for you to drive all the way to your place. You're in the middle of a major project. You're whipped, and you're going right back to it early tomorrow. My place is just a hop and skip from here."

"But I have to go home," she said reasonably.

"If you're afraid I'm going to bug you, don't be. I've got at least two hours of desk work to do, so I'll be disappearing from sight. You already know about my bathtub—the one with the fireplace and the sound system and the TV on the far wall—"

"All right, all right." Of course she hadn't forgotten his tub. No woman in her right mind would ever forget that tub, and since every muscle she owned was sore from overwork that day, she just couldn't find the will to turn him down. Still, she came through with a couple more token protests. "But I don't have any clothes at your place. And I have to call my mom and sister tonight—"

He had answers for everything. A cell phone with unlimited usage. A big, fat, white terry-cloth bathrobe. A chick flick put on the wall TV screen. And food. She didn't remember mentioning that she had a sudden hankering for nuts, but almost from the moment they arrived at his place, he started coming through with goodies—a peanut butter sandwich for an appetizer, and then later, a big catered to-do of a Waldorf salad, crisply roasted chicken with mandarin oranges and almonds, carrot & nut muffins.

If any other guy had pulled this nonsense on her, she'd have assumed that a demand for payback was imminent. But Lucy knew this was about nothing but the pregnancy. She knew how responsible Nick felt.

She knew how much she'd goofed up both their lives with that single impulsive action months ago. But sheesh. Somehow *her* pregnancy had gotten tangled up in a multimillion dollar chocolate deal, and the fragile relationship between a man and his grandfather, and everybody's pride and sense of honor, and relatives spilling terrible troubles all over her life until her normal world seemed in complete shambles.

At least in cavemen days, a pregnancy was just, well, a pregnancy.

Nick didn't seem to suffer her same feelings of confusion. They shared conversation all the time, but he always seemed calm and calming. And tonight, he did just what he said—disappeared into his office a few minutes after he fed her. He told her to just yell out if she needed anything, but she didn't need a thing, and he didn't intrude on her in the slightest. She finished eating, then soaked in the tub, then did all her payback phone calls to her mom, and then Merry and her dad. After that, she curled up next to the fire in the voluminous robe and watched *Turner and Hooch*—which she hadn't seen in ages.

She'd hoped the movie might distract and relax her, but it didn't seem to. Her palm kept straying to the soft swell of her abdomen. From nowhere she'd suddenly picture a baby with a shock of dark hair and startling blue eyes...or sometimes a skinny blond baby who wanted everything her way. The mental pictures came with a burst of fierce maternal feeling, so big it just seemed to explode inside her.

But the more the baby became real to her, the more problems between her and Nick festered on her heart. She couldn't stop fretting that Orson had found out about Nick being the baby's dad. She wanted to do something to make the situation better between the two men, yet what? It troubled her even more that they'd made love a second time—especially because she couldn't seem to regret a single moment of it. And more than anything, it festered that her feelings about the pregnancy, about him, had changed so much since they first talked.

Since she was stuck at his place that night, it seemed an ideal time to have a fresh, long talk with him. Far too many issues had been left gaping loose. So that was her intent, to talk with him. But after the movie, she sat down on the big navy-blue comforter on his bed for a few moments—just to gather her thoughts before seeking him out.

The next she knew, she was snuggled up in navy satin sheets and bright morning sun was bathing her face.

IT WAS THE FIRST MORNING in a blue moon that Nick hadn't been to work before seven. He stood at his kitchen window, hands stuffed in his pockets, staring intently at a mama deer and her newborn fawn outside.

The baby was a little package of white and butterscotch with scrawny, splindly legs. The fawn wasn't old enough to run without stumbling, but when it came to suckling, it latched on with the power of an industrial magnet. The doe looked around with nervous, wary eyes, yet she let her little one nurse.

Nick didn't want to breathe, afraid she'd run, knowing she'd run. He wondered how long it'd been since he'd taken a moment like this to just…be. To just look around, smell the roses, notice life around him like that mama deer. And then he thought, Lucy was gonna be just like that mom—fiercely protective, but still a sucker for letting the baby do whatever it wanted.

His phone rang. The doe couldn't have heard it, yet Nick must have responded with a sudden movement, because the deer darted into the woods with the fawn cavorting at her side.

Nick clicked on the phone and reached for the coffeepot at the same time. As far as he knew his brother never rose before ten unless there was a dire emergency, yet Clint's bark was distinctly wide-awake.

"What in God's name happened between you and Orson?"

Nick finished pouring his third mug of the morning. So much for smelling the roses, he mused wryly. "Feel good not to be in the hot seat yourself for a change?"

"No." Clint sounded annoyed now. "It feels bad to have my brother beat up on and not having a clue what it's about—or what to do about it."

"I didn't leave you a message to embroil you in my mess. I just really want you to watch out for him. You know damn well he's not half as healthy as he makes out. And I wouldn't care if he was mad at me—except that suddenly I can't be around enough to keep a close eye."

"Well, it's not like he ever gave me a chance to watch over him," Clint said.

Clint went on. Initially his tone was hesitant, as old angers and old hopes surfaced. He'd had no opportunity to do anything for Orson that wasn't so spiked with emotional darts that his defensiveness wasn't automatically on high alert. Nick heard him. And cared. But it was at that moment that Lucy walked into his kitchen.

After eleven last night he'd found her, lying on top

of his bed, no cover over her, out for the count. She stayed asleep when he pulled out the comforter. Her thick white bathrobe slipped, just a little—but enough. From the hall light, he saw the soft white swell of her tummy. The baby.

He'd covered her, got her tucked in, then sank into the navy leather chair in the bedroom and sat there for God knew how long.

His conflicting feelings for Lucy were tearing him up. Orson's virulent rejection was tearing him up worse. Nothing was going right—between the stress of getting Bliss going, the usual business pressures, and his personal life deteriorating into complete confusion. But the baby. How come it never hit him before?

He'd thought about the pregnancy nonstop for weeks.

Not the baby.

Somehow it finally occurred to him that it was *his* baby growing in that soft swell of a tummy. That he was going to have a child. Not just Lucy. *Him.*

Thoughts bombarded his mind from every direction. He considered how his dad had fathered him and Clint. Then how Orson had fathered Nick's dad. He analyzed family. What it meant. And what he wanted family to mean to the pint-sized child coming into the world.

So he hadn't slept last night. And the day before, he'd had to cut short a critical meeting with their European bankers because he'd heard all about Lucy firing Greger and taking on the entire greenhouse work alone. His grandfather wasn't speaking to him. And besides everything else, there seemed no way he could resteady his life until Lucy decided what role and place, long-term, she wanted for him in the baby's life.

All this chaos was caused by her. The barefoot waif in the oversized robe who stumbled into the kitchen with a huge yawn and panicked eyes. She opened her mouth, then noticed he was on the phone. He ended the call in two shakes.

"I've *got* to get to work," she said.

"I'm pretty sure it'll be okay with the boss if you're a few minutes late." He turned around, opened a cupboard.

"It won't be okay with my trees. After a few more solid work hours today, things can settle down a bit, but I have to—"

He waved two cereal boxes in front of her face.

There went her German resolve. The look of weakness in her eyes was kin to orgasmic. "Oh God. I haven't had Golden Crisp in ages."

"We'll head to work right after breakfast. But you have to eat something first, right? And I do, too."

Truthfully, he was fine on a few cups of coffee and an apple most mornings—and he'd never even seen Lucy eat for the first four years she worked for Bernard's. Now it was all he could do to keep it coming. It wasn't as if he regularly stored mountains of food in his pantry.

She went through two bowls of cereal. An omelet with mushrooms and cheese, and then more cheese, and some chives and pepper. O.J. No coffee. A slice of toast. A bagel. An apple. A banana.

He sat across the table from her, just to watch in awe. "I guess you're not still having trouble with stomach upsets, huh?"

"Nope. I can't believe it. One day that whole sick feeling was completely gone. And all I wanted to do was eat."

"Where in God's name are you putting it?" He glanced under the table, noticed her bare toes were painted shocking pink. "No hollow leg anywhere in sight."

She chuckled. He told her about the doe and her fawn. She asked him about Clint, then about Gretchen. He asked her how things were going with Russell and her dad. Considering that his nerves were in complete shreds because of her, he couldn't fathom how conversation kept flowing easier than a spring stream.

She stopped eating suddenly, said, "I never expected it. To be able to talk with you so easily."

"To be honest…neither did I."

For the first time in ages, she looked at him the way she used to…something unguarded and warm and pure female in her gaze. But that was over in a blink.

While he waited for her to run and get dressed, he

found himself staring out the kitchen window again. The doe and fawn were nowhere in sight, but the yard was dripping, the grass a brilliant Irish green with spring dew trapped in the sunlight. He told himself that he was increasingly frustrated and stressed by the whole situation, yet this crazy thing kept happening. When he was with her, he forgot the stress. When he was talking to her, he forgot how different they were, how impossible their relationship was. When he worked with her on something—God knew she could get fussy and anal and tedious—but damn, they really got the work done. No matter what the work was.

"I'm ready, I'm ready…"

She charged out of his bedroom, wearing the clothes she had on from yesterday—not that fresh clothes mattered. She was going to do nothing but play in the dirt again today. "Listen, you," she said, as if she were a general about to instruct an underling.

He wanted to shake his head, see if it cleared the water from his ears. Women talked to him with lust. They talked to him with affection. Sometimes they even talked to him with awe—awe of his money if nothing else. But no one had ever talked to him as if he were kind of a nuisance appendage in her life, the way Lucy did. What happened to the hero-worship? The crush?

"Are you listening?" she repeated.

"Yes."

"Well, yesterday was goofy. An aberration. I was beside myself with work, and I know I overdid. I appreciate your helping, your being patient. But the way I put you out—and took your bed—that's just way out of line, Nick. For Pete's sake, you even threw my clothes in the washer and dryer. So I just want to get it straight. I don't want you afraid I'd ever do this to you again. It was just a totally off day, all right?"

She never expected anything from him. It was starting to grate. As if his doing anything decent was a shock. As if his doing anything nice for her boggled her mind.

She tore outside, opened the passenger door, tossed her bag inside. "Nick? You heard me, right?"

Since she hadn't climbed in yet, he took the opportunity to grab her arm. She glanced up, nothing more than an idly curious expression on her face. And that was enough to tip him over.

He leveled her against the car, getting her backside all wet from the morning dew, not caring. He took her mouth and kept it, kept it until he'd tasted and molded and brewed their flavors together. He kept it until he was harder than wood. He kept it until the taste of her, the smell of her, was so under his skin he couldn't think straight. And then he lifted his head.

She looked—finally—as shaken as a baby leaf.

Her lips were red and damp, her eyes huge and dark. Hot. Oh, yeah, she had the need on her face now, none of that crappy you're-such-a-nuisance expression.

He told himself he had a reason for doing that. A damn good reason. He couldn't remember what it was at that specific second, but he had one.

"In," he motioned her, and she folded into the black leather seat as if her legs wouldn't hold her up another second anyway. "You're working until three today. No later. Because we have absolutely critical stuff to do after that."

"We do? What?"

"Shop."

"Huh?"

"I saw the tummy. You need pants. Pregnancy clothes. And if we're stuck doing that, we might as well get a bunch of stuff for the baby, as well. Get it all done in one fell swoop."

He didn't slam the door on her side, just closed it. But when he got in on his side and started the engine, she said in bewilderment, "You want to shop? With me?"

Of course he didn't want to shop. He'd rather sleep in a bed of hornets. He'd rather rip off a toenail. He'd rather watch the Oxygen channel. He couldn't think of a single activity he liked to do less than shop.

But damnation, he *had* to get this woman and this

situation figured out—a lot faster and a lot better than he was doing it now.

If that took some serious suffering, then that was just how it had to be.

CHAPTER THIRTEEN

ONE OF THE MAJOR SUBJECTS in the boardroom that morning was Witch's Broom.

"What's that?" Clint whispered next to him.

Clint rarely attended board meetings, but he'd showed up for this one and glued himself in the seat next to Nick. Clint's sudden bold interest in the company seemed in direct proportion to how furious Orson was with his youngest grandson.

Nick figured that somewhere there had to be a god with a mighty ironic sense of humor. His brother and grandfather were finally taking a few slow steps toward each other—but only because of his screw-up.

Clint usually knew more than he let on, but Witch's Broom was a mighty obscure reference for any but hard-core chocolate people, and this particular board meeting was both wild and fast. The group, fourteen members, were antsier than rabbits at a fox farm. The crisis was cocoa futures. Cocoa had been part of the coffee and sugar exchange since 1979.

"I *know* that," Clint muttered.

"Then you also know," Nick muttered back, "that three-quarters of the world's cacao is harvested by the end of February. Which means the numbers for this year are in. Decimation of more rain forests cut the crop, but the most serious crisis this year was the disease factor of Witch's Broom in two countries. That sucker really did some damage. And it's primarily because of those two problems that the price of chocolate is sky-high."

"I know, I know." Clint's whisper took on a testiness. He always said, "I know, I know" when he felt sensitive about not knowing something he thought he should. Nick never meant to overexplain anything, but he couldn't guess what Clint really did know. Sometimes his brother paid sharp attention; sometimes he didn't give a damn.

"So then you know that the price could climb higher than $6,000 per metric ton if it keeps on this way."

"But what about all those buffer stock programs that were supposed to stabilize the cost of chocolate?"

"Hell, they've been trying that for forty years. As soon as they get a quota system going, some country backs out. Then they tried liquidating it. Then they pushed the program again. One way or another, it just hasn't worked historically. And then there's the European Union thing."

"What European Union thing?"

"The EU allows the replacement of cocoa butter with cocoa butter substitutes—for up to five percent of the weight of the product. Only the U.S. has never agreed to allow that. In fact, we've forbidden it. Some say we're protecting the quality of chocolate. Some say we're artificially forcing the price to stay high because of restrictions. So in a tricky year—like this one—with high prices, the EU is extra mad at us."

"Okay. So all this adds up to a tough profit year for us. I get that. But in the long run, it actually means a fantastic financial future for Bliss, right?"

Orson, at the head of the board table, thumped his gavel. He didn't look at Nick. He hadn't looked directly at Nick in days now. But the side discussion Nick had been doing with his brother only echoed the education Orson was giving the rest of the board. Stockholders were shareholders, but only minor shareholders. Family had seventy percent of the stock.

Back when Nick took charge—and doubled the company size—they'd opened the company to shareholders in order to get capital. And it worked. Those few who showed up at board meetings, though, tended to be chocolate-lovers more than business-decision-makers. They knew little. They just wanted to feel part of the process.

So far, the board had never voted against anything Nick put on the table, primarily because he'd given them a sizable profit since they'd first invested. But they *did* take all morning asking questions.

The lack of sleep was catching up on Nick. His eyes felt grainy, his mood itchy and irritable. His mind kept leaping to that kiss with Lucy this morning. He never remembered feeling that hot, that needy, that wired from a single kiss. For any woman.

It ticked him off.

A few minutes before noon, Orson finished the board's agenda, and the group shuffled out, still discussing issues as they filed down the hall. Orson continued to gather papers from behind the podium. Nick had almost reached the door—the last one out—when his grandfather said, "Wait."

Nick turned around.

His grandfather said, "Close the door." And then, still, stacking the papers together as if it took an infinite period of time to even up the edges, he said, "You need to marry that girl."

"Is that how it's going to be? Every single time you see me, that's all we're going to talk about?"

"Probably. Until you do the right thing and marry her." Orson seemed to finally grow tired of stacking the papers and smacked them back down on the podium.

Nick straightened his shoulders, not moving from the door. "I can't."

"Of course you can. It's the only honorable way to handle a problem like this."

Nick was bristling for a fight. Had been ever since his grandfather turned on him the first time about this. But damn it. He'd never fought with Orson. Disagreed, sure. Discussed, a million things, a million times over. But it was hard to get into a serious fight when the stakes were this precarious and important. "Marriage," he said, "is *your* generation's definition of honor."

"It's everybody's definition." Orson shot up his chin. Three generations ago, his family may have been humble immigrants from Brussels. But Nick still pictured him as an antiquated Robert E. Lee, sure of who was right—even when he was dead wrong.

"No. It's *not*. My definition of doing the honorable thing is doing what's best for the woman involved."

"She's not The Woman! She's Lucy! She's the mother of my great-grandchild!"

Nick lifted a hand, then dropped it again. He started pacing the south length of the room...just as Orson started pacing the north length of the room on the window side. "Something you don't see, Gramps, is that in your generation, you had it damn easy."

"I beg your pardon!"

"It's the truth. Everything in your generation was more black and white. If a woman got pregnant, the man married her. She'd want that, and the man knew he was expected to do it. That's how the problem got solved. Only these days, that's a luxury we don't have."

"Luxury?" Orson's tone turned thunderous. "You call it a luxury to do the right thing?"

"Yeah, I do. Because if you were a guy then, you knew exactly what was expected of you. There was no question about it. Your choices were either to marry the girl or be a total jerk. No in-between. No confusion. These days trying to do the right thing is hairier than trying to learn a foreign language."

"A child needs two parents."

Nick lifted a hand again, this time in a stop motion. "We need to get this straight, because I'll be damned if we're going to argue and snipe every time we see each other. I can't *make* Lucy marry me. I can't fix this situation the way your generation would have fixed it. All I can do, all I keep trying to do, is be there for her. I'll help her any way she lets me. And I'll be there for her, every time I discover something she needs help with. That includes marriage. It includes her work. It includes anything she wants. But damn it, Gramps—I can't force her to do something she doesn't feel right about. And that's just the way it is."

Orson had stopped pacing. He'd clearly become hung up on something at the start of that monologue. "You asked her to marry you?"

"I put it on the table in the very beginning. But

she made it clear—crystal-clear—that she doesn't want a marriage." Nick glowered at him. "I don't care if you pressure me until kingdom come. I don't want you yelling at her. I'm *not* pushing her. And I'm not about to let anyone else push her, either. I don't care if you think she's wrong. I don't care if I think she's dead wrong. We're still doing this *her* way."

He'd probably have ranted on a while longer, except that he suddenly realized Orson had stopped looking so rigid and self-righteous. His grandfather was staring at him with downright puppy-soft eyes.

"Damnation," Orson said slowly. "You're in love with her."

Yeah. Like that solved anything.

Nick stalked out and let the door slam behind him.

"IT'S TWO-THIRTY, Lucy." Greger stood in the doorway. "You told me to let you know—"

"I know I did." And she was more than ready to hang up her spade and grafting knife for now. If she said so herself, she'd done a fabulous job. Her gaze caressed row after row of her new baby trees. The grafts were all clothespinned in place. Her eagle eyes searched the soil for any hint of a weed, any threat of anything that wasn't perfect. But even pacing the width of the greenhouse one more time, every darn thing seemed as close to perfect as she could make it.

"Okay, you get to go home early, Greger." When he just looked at her, she said, "Come on. I'm trying to make it up to you for being such an insensitive creep yesterday. So let me, okay? And there's no reason for you to stay, because I'm leaving early myself."

"I'll leave when you leave."

"I'm going to take a shower. Here. Alone," she added, just in case Greger was under the misapprehension that she needed assistance. "A fast one, because I've got to clean up lickety-split—Mr. Bernard's picking me up at three—so try to believe me, all right? You really can take off."

Greger was harder to herd than a goat, but eventually she shooed him off, and then hightailed it for the staff shower. With her work, she always kept spare clothes around, but nothing she'd normally chose to go out in. Still, at the dot of three, she was as ready as she could be. Her hair was dried, fresh lipstick on, and thankfully her navy sweater was long enough to conceal her waistband, because there was no way in the universe her old jeans were going to snap or zip any more.

From the window, she saw Nick pull up in her car and grabbed her shoulder bag. He'd just opened the lobby door when she charged toward him, lifted up on tiptoe and kissed him hello.

It was a soft kiss, unlike the scorcher he'd sprung on her this morning. Still, she didn't hustle it. There was time to season that little kiss with a few promises and a few reckless suggestions and a clear, honest offering from her heart.

Maybe she didn't exactly intend to bare her heart—that part just happened. But she'd definitely intended to make him suffer some pure, simple payback. No one was around. No one could have seen it. And tarnation, if Nick was going to pull these dangfool crazy things on her, she was going to pull them right back.

She was out the door before he'd even moved, much less breathed. She opened her own car door and slid into the passenger seat.

When Nick got in and started the engine, he said, "You, Ms. Fitzhenry, are an amazing amount of trouble."

So he'd felt some response to that kiss. It did her wicked heart good. "Had a rough day, did we?"

"You can't imagine."

"So spill it out. I know there was a board meeting this morning. I know your brother went. I know the price of chocolate is sky-high. And—if someone didn't already tattle to you—Orson came over to the lab after lunch this afternoon."

Nick slid her a glance. "How'd that go?"

"Just like always, he was a darling. We walked up and down the aisles together. Talked graftings and cuts and feeding schedules and fertilizers until we were both hoarse. Even Greger got so bored he wandered off. But we had a great time. "

"That's all?"

She affirmed, "He was totally kind, no mention of the pregnancy or you or anything else. Just Bliss. He loves checking on Bliss. And there was nothing really new about his visiting—he's always popped over to the lab several times a week—but this afternoon, I had the feeling he was making a point of being with me."

"So he didn't bug you?"

"Not about anything."

"And he was in a good mood?"

"Totally." Unlike Nick, she noted. She thought it might lift his spirits to hear that Orson had been so good-humored. But Nick seemed...wary, somehow. He was smiling the right way, saying the right things, but something in his posture was defensive and preoccupied.

Bossing her around, though, seemed to loosen him up considerably. "I Googled where to shop." He named an anchor department store in a high-end mall.

"That's quite a drive."

"There was nothing closer that had it all. I mean, we don't want to have to go ten places, do we? That store seemed to have maternity clothes and baby furniture and everything else."

Offhand, she'd bet he'd never put *maternity* and *clothes* together in a sentence before, and she still wasn't sure why he'd felt compelled to push for this outing. The same-old sense of responsibility, she assumed. Which unfortunately seemed to inspire his bossy streak, as well.

"You've been so busy at work," he said, "that I'm guessing you haven't had much catch-up time at home. The last I knew, you really wanted to pay off some of your furniture...."

"I did that. Paid off my carpet, as well. Big raises are mighty enabling." She grinned. "One more paycheck and my credit card might even start to look solvent again."

"What about the new car idea?"

"I'll get around to that. When I have a little more free time."

"I know you like your car. When you talk about it, it's as if you're attached at the umbilical. But with the baby, you're going to want some more steel around you. And then there's the car seat and all that kid stuff you have to carry around. What do you think about an SUV?"

"I think they guzzle gas."

"Then how about a nice, conservative, ultra safe Volvo?"

"To be honest, I wouldn't know a Volvo from a vase. The only vehicle I really paid attention to was my Honda. And I *know* I need a new car. It's just..." She shrugged. "I just never thought of myself as a one-night or one-year-stand kind of car person. The car I took home was the one I just kind of planned to keep forever."

"I don't think it quite works that way with cars today, shortie."

Well, she got him laughing, but that didn't completely erase the tension shadowing his mood. When they parked at the mall, she balked at immediately hitting the stores.

"There's a food court here. Could we stop for a little snack?"

"Sure," he said.

She figured he'd be hungry. He was a man, after all. They always needed feeding every two hours. And because she remembered his mentioning a fondness for Chinese food, she picked that concession.

Every teenager in the county seemed to be wandering the mall. From the size of their packages, it looked as if the girls were prom dress shopping, and the boys were simply doing whatever it took to be near the girls. Moms hustled around with babies and strollers and kids just let loose from school. Guys hung by the bookstore. The noise level near the food court was near deafening...except at their table.

She sampled Nick's sweet-and-sour chicken, and some of the potstickers, and some of the shrimp fried rice and War Sui Gui and the other two dishes she couldn't recognize. It was odd, how she could hear Nick in spite of the noise. Odd, how she saw only him. Odd, how even arguing with him was better than not having the chance to be with him.

He asked about her dad. About whether her dad was still sounding depressed, about whether Luther had made any sounds about finding a place of his own. Then he asked about Russell—although he expressed no surprise that her cousin seemed to have undergone a major mood transplant and was barely hanging around her place, much less moping. Then he asked about her sister, and her friend Merry. Then came questions about the baby. Had she thought about wanting to stay in the duplex she was living in, or did she want to move to another place? Did she have someone hired to do the yard for the summer?

"If you don't quit it," she said finally, "I'm going to send you to a time-out. I mean it, Nick. You're completely out of control."

"Say what?"

"Quit being so darn nice. You're aggravating the devil out of me. You're also coming across as if I needed a full-time supervisor."

He put down his fork. "Luce, I never meant to insult you—"

"I know, I know. But pregnancy isn't a disease. And every conversation we have doesn't have to be dominated by *my* life. What about yours?"

"What about it?"

"Has Orson let up? Stopped pushing you to marry me?"

Nick pushed another dish toward her. A noodle concoction with a ton of vegetables. She had to give it to him; he was definitely a sharer. "Orson isn't a problem. Don't worry about it."

"I *am* worried. You're in an even tighter corner than me."

"Hardly," Nick said wryly.

She cocked her head. "When do you play?"

"What kind of play?"

"Any kind. You travel a ton, but it always seems connected to Bernard's. Your parents died so young. You went to school and all…but long before you finished school, you were learning the company, making decisions, doing the work from the ground floor up. That woman, Binnie, Sinnie—"

"Linnie," he said dryly.

"I don't doubt you've found time for *that* kind of play. Only in the four years I've been around the company, no woman ever showed up at your side. Not that you'd automatically have brought a woman to work with you. But I'd have thought, if you were tight with someone, that you'd have wanted to show them around the place, share that part of your life—"

"And your point is?"

"My point is, that of the two of us, I thought I was supposed to be the prissy, uptight, overly fussy workaholic. But now I'm not so sure. You've got the looks, the clothes, the car, the whole appearance of being the wild bachelor. But I can't seem to ever catch you taking time to let down your hair."

He folded his arms and scowled at her. "Why am I getting the impression that you never intended to shop?"

"Because you're a bright man. Of course, we're not going to shop, Nick. Why in God's name would I drag you through a maternity clothes department? I *do* need some new clothes, since almost nothing I own seems to fit any more. But I'll get around to that kind of shopping when I have time."

"You don't even want to look at cribs and baby stuff?"

She hesitated. "I don't mind doing that. It's up to you. For me, the question is more...how do you find it easier to talk? When you're walking and moving around, or when you're sitting still?"

"We've *been* talking," he said suspiciously.

"Not tough talk." She got up, deciding that walking around was probably the best way to motivate more discussion from him. Heaven knew he'd leveled all the food, so he couldn't still be hungry. And because he was male, looking at high chairs and cribs should scare him good—which meant he'd be more inclined to reveal things he wouldn't normally let slip out.

They hiked the length of the mall, until they came to Mauer's—the classic anchor store. Lucy steered him past men and women's wear and up the escalator. Although she'd never been near the kids' section before, she knew Mauer's. She and her mom had never missed a Mauer sale if they could help it.

"Whoa," Nick said, and pretended to gasp for breath. Possibly she'd been galloping at racehorse speeds, but she couldn't help it. The shopping gene came from her mother's side. Still, she truly had only one serious thing on her mind. "Slow down," he begged again. "What is this tough stuff you want to talk about?"

"I just think we need to get down to the nitty gritty. We tried when we first talked about the pregnancy. But we know each other better now. Some things have become clearer. Some murkier. And I need an honest answer to an honest question."

"Which is?"

Mauer's organized the baby gear section by decorating a half-dozen mini-nurseries. Right by the circus setup, she turned around to face him. "What do you want from me over the next few months, Nick?"

He frowned, studying her face. Again, people milled all over the place. Kids chased up and down the aisles, flanked by harassed-looking moms. A baby cried somewhere. But she only saw his face, only heard his voice.

"I don't know how to answer that, except—" He took a breath. "I want this pregnancy to go the best it can for you. I don't want you to feel alone. I don't want you to feel pressured by anyone—my grandfather, your parents, anyone. I just want you to do what you think is right for yourself and this child."

Well, the damn man. She was hardly going to cry in the middle of the store, but she almost wished she could go back to the time when she'd had an immature crush on him. Instead, he kept *doing* things. Things that made it impossible not to love him.

"Hell," he muttered with alarm at her expression. "Don't get all mushy on me."

"I'm not. I'm the least mushy person you'll ever know. There's just dust in here." She swiped at her nose. "Anyway. I have another hard question. And that is…what do *you* need from this situation? To make it work out for you in a positive way?"

He stuck his hands in his pockets, and they started ambling past the rest of the displays. The circus theme obviously didn't catch his interest because he walked on by. The cartoon nursery didn't seem to fire his jets, either. He hovered by the nursery decorated in rainbow colors for a moment…or maybe it just took him that long to come through with an answer. "Lucy—I just don't see that my needs figure in the equation. Not now. *Now,* the whole thing has to be about you and the baby. Because the baby's the most vulnerable one in this situation. And your health, your life, is totally affected. I'm just…secondary."

She ambled past the Disney display, then past the teddy bear décor. "Come on. That sounds too darn noble."

"I'm not noble. I'm trying to be practical. It's just one of those life truths—the woman is more affected by a pregnancy than the man. You have a lot of people making demands on you. As well as a job that's challenging. So…what I see that my role is—especially in these coming months—is to get debris out of your way. Clear the path for you. Whenever I can."

"Go further than that. Do you want to be part of the baby's life?"

"Yes."

"You're sure?" She held her breath.

"I wasn't so sure when you first told me you were pregnant. I mean, it was a knee-jerk response to say I'd be an active father—because that was the only right thing to say. But now…" Again he met her eyes. His were dark and evocative and deeper than a lake at midnight. "Now I actually mean it. I never stopped missing my parents, my dad. It was one of the best relationships of my life. And I'd like to be a dad like that, guess I always envisioned having a pack of kids. This isn't how I thought it would happen. But it doesn't change my feelings. I've always loved kids. In fact, half the time I think I like kids a ton more than I like adults."

"That's a major ditto."

He chuckled, and then followed her into a nursery section decorated with baby animals. Puppies and kittens and ducklings snuggled together on the wallpaper. A mobile of kittens danced above the white crib. A lamp was shaped like a snoozing puppy. "We've got some things straight that some couples never do," Nick said. "Financially, the baby's taken care of—no worries there. You and I also live in the same area, so it's easy for both of us to spend time with the baby, to share whatever needs to be shared. And we're not enemies. I can't imagine us ever being enemies. In fact, as far as I can tell, we seem to get on better than most married couples."

She crouched down to touch the puppy rug under the crib—the rug was big and soft and shaped just like a bassett hound. But she glanced at Nick. "Ditto on that, too."

"You want tough talk? I'll add a tough factor to this."

"What?"

Now it was his turn to poke around the puppies and kittens. He opened the drawers of a baby changing table, secured with miniature fuzzy chicks and ducklings. Later it occurred to her that he might have been making a point of not looking at her directly. "Right from the start, Lucy, you said that you didn't want to be married. Or that you didn't want to marry me. And I keep thinking about that. That there's no reason in hell we have to make marriage part of this equation. Ever. I think everyone agrees that a kid ideally needs two parents…but we can be active parents without being married. There's no guarantee being married has any relationship at all to whether people are good parents or not. So if you start feeling pressured by anyone, I want you to come to me. We're in this together. We'll protect each other."

She opened her mouth and then closed it. Instead of talking, she sank into the white rocker with the comforting arms and the soft kitten cushion. There was a lump in her throat. A growing lump. If it got any bigger, it was going to be the size of Alaska.

She'd known he didn't love her. Known that he would likely never considered her as a lover if she hadn't thrown herself at him. But they'd been building this odd, special relationship over weeks now.

They'd made such wonderful love, and they seemed to figure out ways to talk to each other. He'd shown caring and perception and sensitivity, and darn it, he just seemed to *accept* her. Even when she was hurling. Even when she was boring him comatose when she ranted on about cacao growing. He also happened to be the most fabulous lover she'd ever dreamed of and more.

The bottom line was that she fiercely, terribly, totally wanted a marriage with Nicholas Bernard.

But not, of course, if he didn't love her.

That lump in her throat not only grew, but seemed to develop thick, sharp barbs. They'd made a deal. No, it wasn't a deal written in stone, but they'd both agreed on the basics—she was having the baby, he was supporting her choice and marriage wasn't on the agenda. She was the only one who wanted to change the deal. Spending all this time together, she'd gotten the wild idea that just possibly a serious, lasting love might grow between them.

Now, that dream cracked wider than a windshield in a collision. It was nothing he'd said, at least not exactly. It was that everything he said, every single time, addressed his responsibility toward her. Possibly he'd even marry her, if she pressed. God knew, he'd done everything but turn cartwheels to fulfill anything she'd asked or even hinted she needed.

Ironically, that was precisely why she never wanted him to know how much her feelings had changed. She didn't want him to marry her—or be with her—out of obligation or responsibility.

"Hey, what's wrong?" Nick suddenly crouched down. His knuckles gently poked under her chin so he could see her face. "You feeling sick?"

"No, honestly."

"Because if you're sick, don't be shy about telling me. We'll get out of here—"

"I'm not sick. I just—"

His dark eyes widened with alarm. "Are you *crying?* Luce, are you in some kind of pain—"

"No. I promise, no." She swallowed, or tried. And then tried again.

He suddenly jerked around, as if desperate to find something to divert her attention. "Hey…this is the one you want, isn't it?" He motioned to the nursery setup. "The puppies and the kittens. The rug and crib and all. The minute you looked at it, I should have guessed it'd be the one you'd pick out."

She fiercely wanted to be diverted, so that made it easy to go along. "You're right. I have to admit it was my favorite from the start—"

"And I like it, too. So let's buy it."

"Wait! No!" Good grief, he was already pulling out his credit card. "Nick, I don't have room for a bunch of nursery furniture in my house yet. I haven't even found the right time to tell my family about the baby. Until then—"

"That's no sweat. We'll have the furniture shipped to my place. And that goes for anything else either of us starts buying or collecting. Why not? I've got rattling room in my house."

"Okay," she said and won a smile. He leaned up and kissed her brow.

"That's my girl," he said.

But she wasn't. He'd kissed her with all the affection he'd show a sister. She didn't doubt, for even a second, that he liked her...or even felt the kind of loving affection he'd have for a sister.

But she wanted to be his girl. His girlfriend, his lover, his mate. Yet for all they'd been through together, she seemed trapped in the role of burden and responsibility to him. Occasionally they seemed to generate enough chemistry to jumpstart a rocket, but come morning, Nick seemed to remember his responsibilities to her, and they went back to the kindly friendship thing again.

Lucy could taste the kind of love she wanted from Nick. The kind of love she wanted for him.

But she had to stop believing it would ever happen.

CHAPTER FOURTEEN

LUCY DROVE HOME that night, initially feeling more
blue than a hot saxophone in New Orleans. But the
more she mentally replayed her discussion with
Nick, the more her attitude suffered a major setback.

She had to get her mind off herself. Her needs.
Her feelings for him. Everything wasn't about her,
for Pete's sake.

Nick had been doing everything—including
standing on his head—to be there for her. The closer
they became, though, the more she discovered that
he could darn well use someone in his corner, too.
Not just because of his rift with Orson. But because
there just didn't seem to be anyone.

It was almost seven when she pulled into her
drive. The temperature was still lushly warm, kids
outside playing kickball in the streets. Trees were all
leaf-covered out now; spring flowers busting full out
and early summer scents starting to saturate the
neighborhood.

The evening soothed her soul. She grabbed her

purse, then pulled two packages out of the backseat. Once she'd left Nick, she'd stopped by an inexpensive store on the way home and picked up two pair of maternity pants. Nothing fancy, just jeans she could wear to work. She plucked the mail from the box, then juggled her purse and bags as she went up the walk, feeling beat—but not bad. Just reflective. The day had been tumultuously full; she was definitely ready for some feet-up down time.

She pushed open the door and started to call out, "I'm home, Dad,"…when her jaw dropped instead.

Two suitcases blocked the entrance by the front door, looking dropped there like flopped puppies. A shirtsleeve stuck out of one case, a sock out of another. Grocery bags half-filled with assorted debris tracked further into the hall, making it almost impossible to negotiate a trail.

"Dad?"

Noise was coming from somewhere. Not the kitchen, not the spare room. The bathroom?

"Dad?" She stumbled past all the junk, worry climbing her pulse faster than a fireman up a ladder. "What's going on? What's wrong?"

Her dad barreled out of the bathroom, carrying his dop kit—unzipped, bandages and spare blades and tweezers and heaven knows what—all spilling from it as he jogged toward the front door. "You're home! I didn't know when you were finally going to get home tonight, Lucy! I'm leaving."

"Leaving." She tested the sound of the word—it wasn't unfamiliar in her vocabulary, but she'd stopped believing she would ever hear it coming from her father. At least not in the next century. If that soon. "Leaving," she repeated.

"That woman!" Luther thundered, and then disappeared back into the spare room. He emerged again carrying a single sock, blue, which he tossed on the growing heap of spare belongings in the hall.

"What woman?"

"Greta! *That* woman," he repeated, and then stuttered to a stop again. Two magazines were hurled on top of the growing pile. Then the round container of poker chips, which, of course, immediately spilled.

Lucy crouched down, starting to scoop them up. What a mess. "All right, Dad. Just *stop*. Tell me what's going on. What about Greta?"

To her knowledge, Greta had come twice—the first, for a marathon spring cleaning, and then on one other occasion. Nick had arranged it, which Lucy knew. And though she'd appreciated the help, she felt uncomfortable with him paying for her housecleaning needs, which she'd mentioned to him one time…but they'd been both so busy, the subject just never came up again. If Greta had been there a third time, Lucy hadn't heard of it before now.

"I'm moving out," her father said wildly. "I'm not staying here another day."

"Well, of course you can do that if you want to,

Dad…but could you stop for a second and fill me in about what's going on?"

"She came on to me, that's what! That's the fill in the blank! That woman—and at my age!"

Lucy blinked. She stopped scooping up poker chips and sank back against the wall. When her dad emerged from the spare room this time, he wasn't wearing a shirt. He reclaimed one of the shirts he'd thrown in one of the grocery bags.

"She made a pass at you?" Lucy repeated.

"She did. I've never been so mortified in my entire life. She said, if I was leaving my wife, then I was free, right? That sex always made a man feel better. That she was very, very good at sex."

Lucy sucked in her lip to keep from laughing.

"It's *not* funny, Lucy. I didn't even know what to say. She talks in that broken English, you know? All that yah, yah, yah stuff. She came in this afternoon, as if she were checking on me. I admit there was a little mess in the kitchen—because I'd just made lunch. You know I've been trying to clean up more. I don't want to be any trouble—"

"I know, Dad."

"She said I was living like a bum. Like someone who expected maid service all the time. As if she knows anything about me! That woman doesn't know me from *Adam*."

"I see," Lucy said gravely.

"I explain how depressed I've been. And that's

when she started up. Sex is a good cure for depression, she informs me. And if that's all I needed to give me a good kick in the butt, she'll help me out." Her father clawed at his scalp, but then seemed to remember that he didn't have hair up there. Not anymore. He gestured. "She's over six feet tall, for Pete's sake. Built like a battleship. I could hardly fend her off."

"Oh?"

"I just can't stay here any longer. I've been here too long already. And she could come back any time. That's how she's been from the start. You never know when she's going to walk in. When she's going to find a mess. When she's going to start yelling at you. But her making a pass…that was the *end*, Lucy."

He hurled the front door open and started carrying things. At this rate, he'd be doing it until midnight, because he was carrying one poker chip and one grocery bag at a time. Lucy trailed after him, carrying a bit herself. Between the two of them huffing and puffing, his car trunk quickly filled up.

At some point he suddenly whipped around. "And how was your day, dear?" he asked.

Any other time—*any* other time—she'd have burst out laughing. Her dad's stress wasn't funny, but the longer she studied him, the more she saw the high color in his cheeks. The high energy. For damn sure he wouldn't agree, but Lucy had the sneaky suspicion that Greta's pass had been the best, the most motivating, thing that had happened to her dad in a long time.

"My day was fine," she said. "Now. Where are you going from here?"

Again he glanced at her, at first blankly, as if that problem had never occurred to him. "I don't know. Later tonight, I suspect I'll stay at a motel. Or with a friend. I'm not sure. But right this minute, I'm driving to your mother's."

He bent down to give her a kiss. "I love you, sweetheart. But I do think you should fire that woman. Not that I'm staying, anyway. She could come back. I just can't be in your house right now."

"Okay, sweetie." She patted him on the back as he slid into the car seat.

"Worry about me, okay?"

"You know I will." She waved him off, thinking that every parent in the universe told their kids *not* to worry about them. Her parents wanted her to worry. They liked her to worry.

When she walked back inside the house, it was quiet—for the first time in months. Completely quiet. *Clean* and quiet. It was *her* place again.

Thoughtfully she made a glass of fresh iced tea and sat on the back porch, breathing in the spring night, absorbing everything that had happened today. She wondered if Nick had put Greta up to seducing her dad—or pretending to seduce her dad. It was like Nick. Not to pull a manipulative trick, no matter how well-meaning—but very like him to find a way to get her father to budge.

It was past time her dad had figured out his life and left hers. She just hadn't been able to force it. But Nick had. She'd seen him do something similar at Bernard's a dozen times—face a problem square-on, find a way to make the problem turn into an opportunity, a way to make a situation better instead of worse.

It seemed to Lucy that he'd coached her about the pregnancy with the same philosophical attitude. Neither had planned the baby, but now both needed to be motivated to create something special and wonderful for this child, for their lives.

She thought of his face when she'd kissed him that afternoon.

She thought of the puppy-and-kitten wallpaper.

She thought of his eyes, his voice, the way he'd studied her expression so intensely, when he'd said, "There's no reason we have to be married. Ever."

And then she glanced at her watch. More than an hour had passed since her father had left. She got up, went in the house and searched for her cell phone. The thing always seemed to move to a new, secret location when she wasn't looking. This time it had walked into the bathroom. She dialed her mom.

"Hey, darling, how are you?" Her mother sounded peppy and breathless, as if she'd been caught on the run.

"Just great. I need to tell you something."

"Great, what's new?"

"If Dad isn't there yet, he's on his way."

"Here?"

"Yes. There. And when he gets there... Mom, I need to have lunch with both of you. This weekend, if we can all agree on a time. How about Sunday at 1:00. Milliker's."

"Honey..." Eve's voice took on a patient note. "I know you're upset about the divorce, but—"

"No, honestly, this isn't about the divorce. There's just something I need to discuss with both of you."

"I know you better than that, sweetheart. You want to interfere. You want to bring us back together. I understand. You're worried about us. And I realize it has to be traumatic for you to have your parents talking about divorce after all this time—"

"Mom. 1:00. Sunday. Milliker's. Both of you."

She didn't hang up on her mom—couldn't imagine doing that in a million years—but she quietly put down the receiver. Otherwise, the conversation could conceivably spin in circles indefinitely. Her mother was intent on doing the same thing her dad had just done. Assume Lucy wanted to talk about them. Assume Lucy was worried about their lives.

Restlessly Lucy threw in a load of wash, wiped up a counter that didn't need wiping, sorted through mail without seeing it. For weeks it had seemed so crazy that she hadn't told her family about the pregnancy before this. But she'd wanted to. She just hadn't want to blurt it out. She'd wanted to find a quiet moment that wasn't fully occupied with their crises and that moment never seemed to exist.

For no particular reason, she found herself standing in the living room, staring at the picture of the eagle soaring over the water.

She had the crazy feeling there was an answer in that picture. An answer to what she was doing wrong in her life. To who she really was. To who she wanted to be. To what was holding her back.

If she could just grasp it.

MILLIKER'S WAS WILDLY CROWDED on Sunday. She should have remembered it was a favorite haunt for the after-church crowd. She showed up before both her parents, which was just as well since there was a slow line. The sun was dazzling bright—which certainly wasn't unusual in Minnesota—but the temperature had soared almost to eighty before noon.

That didn't happen. Not this early in the season. Lucy straightened the collar on her yellow cotton sweater and glanced down to make sure her pants looked okay. The ugly elastic insert at the waist had appalled her when she first bought the new pants. But man, they felt so comfortable after being restricted by her regular clothes. And the insert didn't show, thank heavens. So far, even if she was starting to feel like a swelling blimp, no one but Nick had noticed any change in her figure.

Abruptly she saw her mother walking past the glass windows in front. Almost as quickly she recognized her father parking across the street, just getting out of his car. So they'd come separately. Both were church-cleaned up and wearing smiles stiffer than pokers.

Her mother walked in first, found her near the head of the line, and immediately kissed her cheek. She glanced at the crowd. "I understand you want to talk, dear, but we could have done this almost anywhere quieter than here."

Then came her dad, who also kissed her cheek. Neither parent looked at the other. Both said a brisk hello and nothing else to each other. Lucy felt like the white center of an Oreo, being squished by the dark weight of their awkward stiffness.

Once seated, her mother ordered a grapefruit and coffee. Her dad opted for a bagel and cream cheese with orange juice. Lucy went for a three-egg double-cheese omelet, a side dish of blueberry pancakes with whipped cream, milk and a couple of orange muffins. Her parents looked at her askance.

"I'm a little extra hungry, I guess," she said.

"You could feed a third-world country with that order," her mother said.

"I care about world hunger. But right at this minute, I'm awfully motivated to care about my own," she said wryly.

"Well, all right, let's get this over with," her

mother said firmly. "Your father and I saw an attorney two weeks ago Thursday. Which you know. I filed separation papers. At this point, what we're both supposed to be doing is putting our assets down on paper."

Her father said, just as briskly, "Your mother's theory is that we'll save each other money if we get all the paperwork done before seeing the attorney again. If we agree on how to separate everything, a divorce won't cost so much."

"Except that your father hasn't come through with a single list so far."

"Because one of us doesn't want a divorce. And I can't believe things have gone so far that you won't even consider talking to me—"

"I've talked to you for thirty years. Talking never changed a darn thing."

"Then maybe you could talk to me in a different way. Because I honestly don't get it, why you're so unhappy—"

"You can't stop me from getting a divorce, Luther. The only thing you can do is make the whole thing cost a ton more money than it has to, and make the whole process messier and uglier than either of us want it to b—"

"I'm pregnant," Lucy said. By that time the waitress had served the food—thank God. She'd been starting to feel weak. She dove right in.

Her parents shut up for the first time in twenty-eight years—or at least in her memory. But their silence didn't last long.

"Who's the man?" her father barked.

Her mother jumped in. "It doesn't matter who the man is, Luther. All that matters is whether she's all right and healthy." To her, "At your age, you didn't think about birth control? What were you thinking?"

Even if she'd wanted to immediately answer, her father interrupted again. "Eve, leave her alone. Lucy, we'll be there for you no matter what. But about this man—are the two of you thinking of getting married? What's going to happen with your job, your work?"

Then her mother again. "As if her work mattered, Luther, when something this critical in life is happening to her. Who's the father?"

Then her father. "I just asked who the father was, and you snapped my head off."

When Lucy had appeased the first round of hunger—half the omelet was gone—she said, "I didn't plan this. Which is a disgrace and a half at my age, I know. But over these past weeks, I've come to believe that I really want the baby, want to be a mom. And that I can cope. Actually, I don't want to just *cope*. I want to be either a good parent or nothing…"

She was prepared to go on, but it seemed both her parents were over the first shock and building up a more serious head of steam. They didn't know anyone important was in her life. She couldn't possibly have gone back to seeing Eugene again, had she? If not him, who? Her father had been right there, didn't know of anyone she was seeing regularly. Was her insurance going to cover the cost of delivery? Who was her doctor?

The doctor subject was a catastrophe. Like all families, theirs had certain conversational topics that erupted in immediate all-out war. For the Fitzhenry family, the sticky topic was doctors. Luther immediately listed the only acceptable ob/gyns from his frame of reference. Eve countered with the list of ob/gyns that passed the doctors' wives test—and doctors' wives were a mighty fussy group.

The doctor Lucy had chosen wasn't on anyone's list.

She finished the omelet, the pancakes, the first muffin. She thought she was fairly full, until the waitress carried a tray past the table with desserts for other customer. She saw a lemon meringue pie that almost made her drool.

"Lucy!" Tears brimmed in her mother's eyes. "I can't believe you didn't tell me before this, darling. We could have talked—"

"You could have talked to *me*," Luther said plaintively. "I've been right there. You know I'd never have judged you. That I'd do anything for you, sweetheart."

"What are we going to tell people," her mother said suddenly. "Have you told Ginger already? Anyone else in the family?"

"Eve, we don't care what anyone else thinks. It's not their business. This is about *Lucy*."

"I'm trying to think what I saved in the attic. I've got a trunk of things from both you and Ginger. I know I saved the high chair…"

For a brief moment both parents seemed temporarily out of breath, so Lucy grabbed her one opportunity to slip in. "That's why I wanted to meet with you together today—rather than having to discuss all the same things twice. Also so neither of you would have your feelings hurt by my telling one of you before the other. The baby's due around Thanksgiving. I'm feeling great."

Both seemed to hear her, but then that was that.

"Clothes!" Eve said. "We've got to go shopping for maternity clothes! They've got such cute styles today, nothing like when I was pregnant."

"You still haven't told us who the father is, Lucy."

"You've told them at work?"

Halfway through the piece of double-cherry pie— she'd changed her mind about the meringue—she felt an odd sensation in her stomach. A fluttering. Not like a stomachache or a cramp. Not like a tickle. Not like an itch. The sensation was completely different than anything she'd felt before.

She lifted a forkfull of cherry pie toward her mouth, but then stopped. There it was again. Just the barest, softest sensation. As if, on the inside, she was being brushed with butterfly wings.

The baby.

She'd actually felt the baby.

Who knew it was real? Who knew all the rest of everything hadn't been high drama and stress and life complications? How could she have known that none of that stuff mattered at all, even remotely?

"What's wrong?" her mother asked.

"Nothing, Mom. I just need a quick trip to the bathroom." But she didn't zoom for the bathroom, although truth to tell, she had to pee. Instead, though, she hiked outside, into the warm spring air, into the sunshine, and dialed her cell phone as fast as she could push the buttons.

Nick didn't answer. Maybe he was on one of his zillion foreign trips. Or maybe he was doing something for Orson. Or maybe he was just out and about, busy.

When his voice mail came on, she blurted the short message. "I felt it, Nick. Really felt it. The baby. That's all. I just…wanted you to know."

Stupid, she thought immediately, wishing she could take it back, wishing she hadn't left any message. Yes, they were allied on the baby. But that didn't mean he wanted to be close. Not this kind of close. Not the kind of close where he cared about hearing the emotional, personal details of the pregnancy.

He didn't love her. She had to get that through her thick head and accept it.

* * *

ON HER WAY HOME from brunch, she stopped at a nursery to pick up a flat of double impatiens. At home, she quickly changed clothes, grabbed a spade and towel to kneel on, and then spent an hour outside with the sun baking her back. When she was finished, the flowers made a riot of cheerful colors on both sides of her front door.

She tromped inside with dirty knees and fingers, tired and content, only to notice the message light blinking on her answering machine.

"I was gone. Sorry I missed the call. So…what'd the baby feel like? Was this a nice kick or a nudge? You think we've got a boy or a girl on our hands?"

That was it, the whole message. It tugged at her tummy more than the butterfly flutter had. She washed her hands, gulped down a whole glass of chilled lemon tea, then damnation, just couldn't resist punching his number.

Again, she reached his voice mail. Again, she told herself not to leave a message…but if she didn't, wouldn't he think that she never received his? So she just spilled out, "The kick was just a gentle thing. It was just so amazing. To feel…life. I think it's a boy. Does it matter to you?"

She'd barely clicked off her cell phone before it rang.

But it wasn't Nick. It was Merry, who wanted to know if she had time for a movie.

Life had been so jam-packed that she hadn't done a girls' night out in forever—she also felt badly about neglecting her friend. They talked on the phone often enough, but that wasn't the same thing as face-to-face conversations. So Lucy cleaned up, locked up, and grabbed the keys to her car.

They met halfway to Mankato and stopped at Panera Bread for dinner. Their intention was to hit the sappiest chick flick they could find after that, only instead, they ended up talking. Merry claimed she'd set up a major physical at Mayo to settle the bipolar question once and for all. And since Merry was spilling personal beans, Lucy confessed about the pregnancy.

She'd wanted to tell her friend before, but Merry's life had been in such a crisis that somehow she never seemed to work it in. Now, though, it felt like such a relief to tell a friend, nonfamily, someone who would support her wholesale. And Merry did support her wholeheartedly. She just couldn't seem to resist throwing in a couple side opinions.

"You think it was an accident that you ended up sleeping together," Merry said. "But I don't. Maybe it was meant to be."

"I stopped believing in 'meant to bes' when I was sixteen," Lucy said wryly.

"Come on. I'm not just talking about a fairy tale. Don't you think nature sets us up to be attracted to the people we're supposed to be attracted to? Maybe nature wanted Nick to be the father of your baby."

"Then maybe nature should have let me in on that little secret. Because I'm not used to losing my head. And if I'd had a clue there was any chance I was going to, I'd have been prepared with birth control."

"But that's the point." To Merry, this was logic. "You overthink everything. You overworry everything. Nature knew that. So nature set you up with the ideal man for you to have a baby with and overruled your common sense."

Lucy set down her fork, even though she'd picked the two most luscious desserts on the menu. "To begin with, there is no ideal man for anyone. And to end with, he's not an ideal man for me. All I've done is goof up his life. And mine. By being irresponsible and thoughtless. And it's scaring the hell out of me. Those are not good qualities to bring to a baby."

"You're a complete idiot," Merry informed her. "You'll be the most terrific, devoted, loving mother in the entire universe."

"You're just biased because we've been friends forever. And besides that, you're not thinking well because you were taking that goofy drug." Lucy peered at her. "You're not still seeing that guy who conned you into believing you were bipolar, are you?"

"Well…I *have* to see him. We're working pretty closely together."

"But you're not going *out* with him, are you?"

That was the last chance Lucy had to talk about

Nick or the baby, because the next hour was devoted to Merry's life. They didn't get around to leaving the restaurant until well after dark, and that was the first Lucy realized there was a message on her cell. She climbed into her car before clicking it on.

"Don't care if it's a boy or a girl, but confess we've got a ton of males in my family now. Would be nice to have a girl. Does it matter to you?"

She told herself that she'd try to reach him one more time, but that was it, enough of this phone tag. But when she punched in his number, just like before, she got nothing but his voice mail. She almost hung up, but then, in the darkness of the car, she closed her eyes and leaned her head back and somehow found herself sharing more. "I honestly don't care if it's a boy or a girl. But sometimes...often, I guess I have to admit...I clench up. That I'm not bringing enough character, enough strength, enough maturity to be a mom. At least not a good one. I can't seem to be sure, to get sure."

It was such a stupid message that she could have kicked herself for sending it. She'd been around people she loved and cared about all day—people where sharing her insecurities and fears should have been natural. Only she tried. Her family never seemed to hear her, and her friend typically and affectionately dismissed her concerns. It wasn't as if she wanted anyone giving her blindly supportive attagirls—or for anyone else to solve her problems, either.

She just wanted someone she could be honest with.

On the drive home, she coiled herself into a good, tight, nasty emotional knot. Fretting her failings. Fretting the future. Fretting the untenable relationship she had with Nick—including spilling stuff on his head he undoubtedly didn't want to hear.

When push came down to shove, it seemed as if she hadn't done a single thing right since the Night of the Chocolate.

Her mood sunk lower and lower, until a well pit would have seemed high. She'd never be a crier or a whiner, but by the time she turned onto her street, she was snuffling hard and her eyes were stinging.

To add insult to injury, when she pulled in her drive, she saw another car. A sleek black one. Nick's.

And he seemed to be sitting on her front porch, in the dark, waiting to see her.

CHAPTER FIFTEEN

NICK COULDN'T PRECISELY EXPLAIN why he'd leapt in the car and sped over to her place. He'd been gone all day. First, he'd had to attend a school concert where Gretchen had a flute solo, and after that he'd been stuck at a Sunday afternoon dinner gig at an aunt's.

Initially the phone tag with Lucy had struck his sense of humor. It was only as the messages piled up that he recognized that Lucy's tone changed with each call. Initially she'd started out clearly ecstatic about feeling the baby move. In the next message, she'd sounded more subdued, a little stressed. By the last call, he could barely hear her whispered voice.

That was when he'd started worrying like hell.

Now he saw her step out of her cranky old rust heap and thought *whoa*. Panic put a serious boogie in his pulse. Lucy was the one of the most upbeat people he'd ever known. She never lost it, not in front of others. She was always the cheerleader, the comforter, the one who steered people past their funks.

But right now—even in the dark—he could see her eyes glistening. She was walking with her arms wrapped around her middle. And he could hear the choke of a sound coming out of her throat.

He surged toward her, thinking damn it, he was going to have kill anybody who'd hurt her. "Hey. *Hey.* What's wrong?"

"Nick?" Another choke. And now he was close enough to see the tears welling up and spilling over. "Good heavens, what are you doing here?"

"Forget me. What's going on? For God's sake, don't *do* that. Are you sick? Did something happen?"

"No, sheesh, stop worrying. It's nothing. I'm just having a blubber fest. A major nasty mood." She ducked her head and fumbled in her purse for her house key. She couldn't find it, fumbled some more.

"*Something* had to bring this on. Just tell me. Somebody hurt you? Somebody give you a hard time?"

"Honestly, nothing's going on here but an embarrassing meltdown. Pregnant women are supposed to have regular melt downs. It says so in all the books. I'll be over it in two shakes." She bent her head again for another key search. No key emerged. A bubble of a sob came out like the sound of a heart breaking.

"Luce. You're killing me here." He grabbed her purse and started rifling through it. In a second flat, he had the key, had the door open, had his hand on her arm. "Come on. Talk to me. Tell me something, anything. I'm not leaving until you do."

"Nick, somehow I'm giving you the wrong impression. There's no crisis or anything. I'm just feeling low. I started thinking what a mess I'd made of everything and it just...got to me."

"You haven't made a mess of anything."

"Yeah. I have. You and your grandfather were always wonderful close until I got in this picture. Now you two are at odds, because of me. And I'm tying up your place all the time, and now we're going to clutter it up with baby furniture—making it awkward for you to pursue any other relationships, or even to live your regular life. I just feel to blame. I used to think I was a decent person..."

"You *are* a decent person." Inside, she'd left no lights on. Yet even in the pitch black, he could smell fresh lilacs and daffodils, and all he could think was what was he supposed to do now? "Look. Something must have happened to bring this all on—"

"Yeah. Me. I brought it all on when I jumped you that night. I swear I never planned it ahead of time. But you know I was joking about blaming Bliss, right? I really know it wasn't the chocolate. I've really known all along what's responsible."

"What?"

"Some big hole in my character, that's what. Some irresponsible, selfish..." She seemed to be just kind of flinging herself back and forth from one doorway to the next, not aiming anywhere, just letting loose one of those scary sobs every gulp or two.

He turned on lights, then more lights, looked frantically around, then ran into the bathroom and brought back the roll of toilet paper. "Blow," he said.

She did, clearing her nose with a force that would have done a trumpet proud. "I don't have any excuse. I'm just so sorry, Nick."

"Would you cut it out?"

"How am I supposed to cut it out? I'm *responsible.* And ever since then, everything else has fallen apart, too. I used to think I hadn't weaned myself from my parents, that I was immature—but no. They never weaned themselves from *me.* My cousin was still trying to get me to nurture him, shelter him, just like I always did. Only it wasn't helping. My friends tend to depend on me. It all adds up to my being some kind of sick enabler."

"Lucy, you're not."

"Worse yet, it's just scaring the wits out of me, because I don't want to be that kind of mother."

"What kind of mother?"

"A screwed-up kind of mother." She waved her hands in the air again, as if the phrase and hand gesture said it all. She blew her nose again—a big blow. Then hiccupped once.

And then she made this sound…Nick had the horrifying intuition that she was going to melt into another puddle of tears. So he grabbed her. It wasn't his intention to kiss her.

It was just his intention to shut her up. To make her stop crying. To get her attention. Whatever it took.

"You keep blaming yourself for everything, Luce. But you think I didn't want to sleep with you? That I wasn't attracted to you? That it was on just your side?"

"Huh?" she said.

He yanked her into his arms and kissed her. His lips sank against hers and stayed glued there.

Almost immediately his heart stopped pounding and his pulse stopped racing. God. There was nothing more frightening than a crying woman. And that was a thousand times worse because it had been *Lucy* crying. Lucy, who never got overemotional and just wasn't the type to pull scary things on a guy if she could possibly help it. Seeing tears in her eyes— he just couldn't stand it.

Only...

Only suddenly his heart was hammering again.

Suddenly his pulse was rocketing.

Not in terror of her crying this time, but in terror that she'd stopped. Slower now, his arms twined around her, trapping her softly to him, snugly. Slowly that first shut-her-up kiss gentled.

Suddenly every sense in his body seemed to tune up, like a Stradivarius finally unlocked from its case. She didn't play him the way other women had played him. She didn't even know his chords to pull. Hell, he wasn't even sure if she knew what plucked her own chords.

But until then, he didn't know how much skill and finesse were vastly overrated. Emotion was a whole different world, and what eclipsed his whole being right then was how she just...gave. The more he kissed her, the more she laid herself bare for him.

And when she kissed him back, he felt skinned down to some naked level. It shook him. He was used to feeling in control, always. Only it was unnerving for Luce to do just that—to give him control, all the control and power over her that he could possibly want. And all without doing anything but giving...of her infinitely soft skin. Her winsome mouth. The texture of her fingers rifling through his hair, the wary soft sounds she so unwillingly let loose. He could feel her nipples, tight and hot, through his shirt. He could feel her wanting.

He could feel his own.

With his eyes closed, he couldn't remember exactly where they were. Still, he kissed her for more long, long moments before opening his eyes a slit. The hall.

"Lucy—?"

"Hmm?"

"We're going to your room."

"Hmm."

He interpreted that as another sound of approval,

and started moving them. From the archway to the living room, he caught a glance at the eagle picture. Moonlight gleamed on the eagle, on her white hearth. Lucy's phone rang. She didn't stop kissing him. She didn't loosen her arms around his neck. They back-walked the few feet down the hall, past the bathroom, made the turn toward her room without killing themselves, then finally across the threshold into the purple pen.

He admitted feeling a little wary in here. Even in the dark, there was a wild mix of girl smells and girl colors and textures that looked breakable, crushable. Her bedroom was just a universe different from his austere, cool, quiet navy-blue.

That stuff didn't scare him, though. It was sensing that Lucy fiercely kept a secret in that bedroom of hers. Everyone saw her as a hardworking, practical, no-hesitation-about-getting-her hands-dirty kind of sturdy woman. And she was. But beneath that surface was the soft side. The pure girl side. The lavender and frills side. The vulnerable side.

The sexiest woman on the planet side.

He kissed her again. Kissed her as if he'd needed her all his life. As if he'd been lonely his whole life. And maybe both those things were true, because she kissed him back with all the wild, sweet yearning of a woman who recognized her mate.

They peeled off clothes, tumbled on her bed. He knew what ignited her now, and God knew, she knew what ignited him. They climbed toward Everest with the same intensity, fighting to give each other pleasure, desperate to have each other.

It wasn't wild, hot sex. Nick had had wild, hot sex. That was…magic. That was wild, hot sex with another ingredient. Lucy.

When it was over, they were both slick with sweat, and almost laughing as they sank against the pillows, struggling for breath. She touched his cheek, started to say something…and then didn't.

He realized moments later that she'd fallen asleep. His eyes stayed open as he cuddled her naked body against him, stroking her, then pulling up the sheet so she didn't get a chill and stroking her all over again.

Gradually he sobered. The rash, rapt explosion of ecstasy faded into something quieter…and more disquieting. Under the covers, he felt her swelling breasts, the rounded curve of her tummy—all the signs that her pregnancy was getting more pronounced every day. An instinct of protectiveness surged through him.

So did guilt.

He had no business making love to her again— no right to complicate a situation that was already touchy and fragile.

He'd sworn to do the right thing by her. Maybe his grandfather's code of honor wasn't the same as his, but Nick believed just as strongly that honor mattered. That when someone more vulnerable than you was in trouble, you stepped up.

Lucy had feelings for him. He'd known that forever—but he also knew that a powerful sexual attraction always complicated a relationship. He'd been trying to be there for her, be the one person in her life who didn't create or cause her more stress. Everyone seemed to want something from Lucy. He wanted to be the one person who gave something to her—instead of being another taker.

He understood Lucy was willing—totally. But damn, he'd been *trying* to put her needs before his. To not add complications to her life right now. And it seemed he'd screwed that up yet again by losing his head, and his heart, in Lucy's arms.

LESS THAN TWO WEEKS LATER, Lucy was in her office at work, grumbling about the amount of paperwork that seemed to triple every day, when the alarm light suddenly flashed on the far wall.

It wasn't the security system, which she could easily have ignored. These days there were zillions of security people already running around, so it was mighty unlikely anyone needed her to add to the crowd. But this particular light flashed in the new Bliss greenhouses when something was going wrong—water or temperature or some other critical factor.

She took off down the hall, yelling Reiko's name

at the same time. Reiko stepped out of the restroom, caught a glance at Lucy's face. They both went running, punching codes to get through different security setups, then running some more. Outside, it was an ornery, stormy day, spitting rain, then growling thunder. It wasn't so gloomy dark that they couldn't see, but the light was grayish-dim in the greenhouses.

Still, at a glance Lucy saw the water rivering down the aisles. "Has to be a blowout in the trickle, and a pretty darn big one," she yelled to Reiko—a waste of breath. They both knew what the water meant, and both went jogging up and down the aisles, looking for the blowout.

Greger showed up almost as fast as the women. The right amount of water was critical for the young trees, and the ideal way of delivering it was trickle irrigation. Blowouts happened. Just life. Even the most expensive system on the planet wasn't perfect. But the baby trees couldn't take a real flooding; they were still too vulnerable, so the blowout needed to be immediately fixed and patched...and then any standing water or mud swiftly suctioned out. No standing water was allowed. Not in Lucy's cacao forest.

"You stay clear. I'll find it," Greger said.

"No. You just turn off the water—all the water."

"You do that. I'll do the messy work—"

"Greger! Do it my way!" She loved him, she really did, but who knew if Greger knew how to fix and

patch irrigation hose? Not that it took rocket science. But even if he knew how, he wouldn't do it the way she'd do it. And since her way was the only right way, she pushed up her sleeves and crawled in.

"I found it, Reiko!" she called out in a matter of minutes.

"You need new hose? Tape? What?"

As soon as supplies were gathered, Reiko got right in the mud with Lucy. Greger almost had a nervous breakdown—for Greger. For a short time there was a lot of hollering. Naturally she and Reiko got quickly soaked and muddy, but it wasn't as if they were hurt. It took a mess to clean up the mess.

And that was when the intercom buzzed. Fritz's voice boomed over the loud speaker. "Lucy—you need to head up to the big house. They're having some kind of big meeting. And they need you. Pronto."

"I can't go right now," she responded.

"Lucy. It's the *boss.*'

Boss, schmosh. She hadn't forgotten waking up that morning after making love with Nick. He'd been very nice. Very kind. Cosseted her as if she were elderly, maiden aunt who couldn't take care of herself. She got it, she got it—that she'd undoubtedly freaked him out by having a crying fit all over him the day before.

But there'd been no kisses that morning, no references to their making love. Obviously he didn't want to risk igniting any more chemistry, and even though days had passed, that hurt was still fresh as a blow.

They'd talked several times since. It was always the same. He was funny and kind and affectionate. But he steered physically clear from her as if determined not to risk even accidental touches. And she'd had it. Had it with mooning over him, with hoping he'd love her, with feeling this fragile *hurt* all the time.

So she'd set new goals. She was going to be good friends with him—and good parents with him—if it killed her. But more than that, no. So she was hardly going to chase off to the big house because Orson and Nick were there. Both of them could use a telephone, couldn't they? And more to the point, all they wanted to do was talk business.

The intercom burst on again ten minutes later. Nick's voice was unmistakable. "Greger. Carry her up here."

"Oh, for Pete's sake," she muttered, but by then the leak was fixed, and Reiko was on track to test the rest of the lines. When she climbed down from the growing area, though, Greger dramatically put a hand over his eyes.

He didn't have to speak to convey the message that she looked like something a gorilla would throw out of the jungle. "So why don't you just go up there for me, ask the guys what they want, and then let me know," she suggested.

"Because Mr. and Mr. Bernard asked for you."

"Yeah, but they hired me to do a job. And this is the job. I'm worthless around marketing and numbers and all that junk. Everybody knows it. They don't really want me, they just probably think they need to include me in nonsense like that. Wasting a great day like this on a meeting is ridiculous."

"Yah? I'll meet you in front. Five minutes."

Five minutes gave her enough time to scrub her face and hands, slap on some lip gloss and change to shoes that weren't crusted in mud—but that was it. Darn it, it was supposed to be a straight workday. It wasn't a day she was supposed to be clean. It wasn't a day anyone was supposed to see her outside the lab, and her theory on managing all the new staff was that she couldn't expect them to dig down and do the gut work if she wasn't willing to.

"Better," Greger said when she slid into the front seat of the company Jeep.

"They'll never let me in the house. Even through the back door."

"Yah, they will."

He let her off at the front door, where Baby and Boo Boo greeted her as if they hadn't seen her in a decade. Great Dane slobber was probably less debilitating than, say, Newfoundland slobber, but dog kisses in general didn't appreciably make her appearance look more corporate. Neither did the tummy.

Just because she'd bought maternity pants didn't mean she intended to suddenly fill them out. But over the last ten days her abdomen had turned into a stunning potbelly. It was kind of weird because she didn't look exactly pregnant. She just looked more as if she were a lazy, indulgent beer drinker, and her grime-crusted jeans and ANYTHING FOR CHOCOLATE T-shirt didn't add any promise of respectability.

She hiked through the long, elegant hall, feeling her defensiveness bristle up. She'd told the staff last week about the pregnancy. The crew was still watching over her with ridiculous protectiveness—but mostly the news was old news now. Work had been going like a house afire.

The five new greenhouses were complete. Extra staff had been hired: a good number of grunts but also two new horticulturists, and another kid interning, going for his degree in botany. The first two houses were completely filled with new seedlings and the grafting work for those was finished. More trees were due in by the end of next month, allowing for staggered plantings. In the meantime, another batch of criollos in the base Bliss greenhouse were close to harvest.

She'd been running like a chicken with her head cut off—and loving every single minute of it. No one could prove that she'd been avoiding Nick. She'd even convinced herself that she couldn't have fit in any more heart-to-heart talks with him even if she'd wanted. And she didn't want. She'd had enough pining after the man to last her until hell froze over.

Abruptly, though, she heard the sound of voices—not emanating from Orson's favorite sunroom, but the library. She slowed down and edged through the doorway.

The library had ten-foot-tall doors with a transom, and inside, two floors of books with a ladder on wheels to reach the tomes on the top shelf. It was a book-lover's Shangri-La. A center-stone fireplace heated the room on cold winter days. Otherwise the room smelled like old books and fresh lemon oil. The guys were gathered around a big burl oak table, and at a glance, damnation, she could see they were all suits.

Her eyes met Nick's—she didn't *mean* to look at him, but it was like a magnet around iron filings. She *had* to look. Just to make sure he was okay…and naturally, he was more than okay. He looked like a *GQ* ad in his navy suit, his hair just long enough so he didn't look *too* put together, his white shirt stark and striking next to his golden skin. He looked tired, though. Worrisomely tired. But she had to move her eyes away and attend to business. Orson spotted her and stood up to extend a greeting.

She knew most of the guys. Pete Neilson was the numbers man from the main plant. Ray Floord was another mainstay of the business, and one she'd made a personal friend of—he was, after all, responsible for production on the truffle line. Orson introduced her to three others. She nodded to the rest she knew. Clint was sitting at the far end, by Nick— it was odd to see him at any Bernard business meeting, but he was as suited up and serious as the rest of them.

"Sit down, Lucy, sit down," Orson urged her.

She scooted quickly into the red leather chair by the door, the only free seat. Nick was almost out of her line of vision, which helped. She still had no idea why she was here and Orson lost no time in filling her in.

"We've had a leak on Bliss," he told her, and passed on a cut-out newspaper article from the *Journal*.

She skimmed it quickly. The section was on trading news, affecting the tea and sugar exchange. An insider speculated that there was a major secret at Bernard's, a private company with big earning potential. A good company to watch, because if the secret proved out, they could well run a stock option…or seek capital investment for major growth via some other venue. Something was brewing there, for sure.

Most of the lingo was Greek to Lucy, but she got the gist. "How on earth did this guy know? How could anyone know what we've been doing?" she asked.

"Some secrets are impossible to keep for long," Nick said.

Orson agreed. "We've had a lot of building going up on the premises. Ordered volume of supplies we never did before. The rumors were going to start sooner or later."

"But we're not ready—" she said with a gulp.

"And we won't be ready for a good long time yet," Nick said calmly. "But since the cat's out of the bag, it makes the most sense to turn that into an advantage. We've got the problem, so let's find a way to capitalize on it."

"Okay," she said hesitantly, still unsure where the group was going with this, or what her participation would be.

"Our thought," Orson said, "was to stage a little unveiling. A sample of Bliss to selected markets. To stir interest and awareness. The point is to get ahead of the curve. To do it on our timetable. In a way we control."

Clint hadn't said a word so far, Lucy noticed. He was just sitting there in that stiff gray suit. But he was scribbling ten for six on a legal pad. Involved.

Nick picked up the conversation. "So the goal, Lucy, is to produce a prototype Bliss product…to be available around Thanksgiving. That timing would hit the pre-Christmas crowd, when chocolate's a common purchase. To wow the chocolate world with what we're doing."

"So you want a Bliss truffle, or something on that par," she said.

"Exactly. We want it in an exceptionally terrific

package, but we'll put marketing on that. What we're thinking is…two or three pieces in a package. No more. Very limited amounts, to be determined later. We're thinking of charging one hundred dollars for three pieces."

"Say what?"

"There's two theories on marketing new product. One is to give free samples—which, in theory, we don't object to. But another thought is to make it expensive. Make it desired, make it harder to find, harder to get. Make the price say this is nothing ordinary but something rare and valuable. We all think, for Bliss, that's the best approach."

She didn't disagree. It was just going to take a second to get her mind around spending a hundred bucks for three pieces of chocolate.

Then that second passed. All she had to do was remember the taste of Bliss. God knew, any chocolate was better than no chocolate, but serious chocolate was like serious sex. Sex, before Nick, had seemed wonderful enough. But sex, after Nick, had probably ruined her for all other men. The metaphor worked perfectly for Bliss.

Of course she'd have other chocolate in her life again. Wouldn't she? She hadn't raided the truffles in her glove box in a while, but that was only because she had the key to the Bliss vault.

Yet she suddenly pictured a friend handing her a candy bar—a plain old candy bar—and her turning it down. Even a chocoholic had her lines in the sand. What seemed like ecstasy six months ago just wasn't the same anymore.

"Lucy? Are you still with us?" Orson asked.

"Yes, sir. I was just considering the ideas you're all bringing up."

"Well, our question for you, is whether you'll have enough Bliss at that time to put into product. We'll have Helmut, our chef from the plant, work directly with you. And marketing. But we can't do this—can't even try taking this to the next step—until we get some figures from you on how much Bliss we could have available at that time."

"Okay. Let me study it. When do you need to know this?"

"ASAP. Next Friday?"

She shook her head. "I don't need that long. I just need a few solid hours to work up a study. I should be able to give you something on paper by Monday, latest."

"That sounds terrific."

They released her from their business powwow. She found herself flying down the hall and leaping down the steps, feeling euphoria build in her blood like a heady drug.

The unveiling of Bliss—this was it. The beginning of it. The dream they'd been working on for so long was becoming real, becoming solid, was really going to happen.

Greger was waiting for her, and had already opened the door to the Jeep for her to pop in. They were halfway back to the lab when a small detail hit her brain. Thanksgiving. They wanted the prototype Bliss by Thanksgiving.

That was when the baby was due.

CHAPTER SIXTEEN

NICK STOOD at his living room window, watching for Lucy's car, feeling more rattled than a caged bear.

He'd blown it with her. He wasn't sure how, but like any other male, he didn't need a blue print to realize he was in the doghouse. Possibly a very serious doghouse. Luce been extremely busy for the last three weeks. So had he. But that didn't explain her suddenly treating him like the mangiest hound in the pound. It couldn't possibly be anything he'd said, because he'd only said nice things. Kind, careful things. Sensitive things.

Well, maybe not *sensitive* things. How the hell did he know what a sensitive thing was, anyway? But for damn sure, he'd been trying to be good to her. The harder he tried, the more she turned on the frost.

He figured at first it was just a mood—or pregnancy hormones—but the problem was getting worse instead of better. Eventually he'd pinpointed her change of attitude to the last night they'd slept together. Maybe she felt he'd taken advantage? Or she just didn't want to be close that way?

Probably because he felt guilty as hell, he was wary of confronting her.

So he hadn't.

He'd just conspired to find another way to get her to his place.

Finally, he spotted her car pulling up his drive. Clint suddenly seemed to be standing beside him. "You hear that sound?"

"You mean the sick sound that she thinks is a viable car engine?"

"Yeah." Clint winced when she cut the engine. "That car is one sick puppy. Guessing it's got a rod going. And the carburetor's wheezing. You can't pay her enough to buy a decent car?"

Nick sighed. "When's the last time you tried to tell Orson he was wrong about something?"

"That's not funny."

"Well, multiply that problem tenfold for Lucy. Ain't nobody gonna budge her into buying a new car until she's good and ready."

Lucy popped in the back door, and then blinked, a little startled to find both guys standing there, as if primed to pounce the minute she showed up. Nick just took in her appearance. Her hair had grown, had turned a paler blond from time in the sun. Freckles dotted her sunburned nose and cheeks. She was wearing sandals, a sundress, earrings that looked like silly, cheerful sunflowers.

"I love conspiracies," she said by way of greeting.

That quickly, Nick watched his brother relax. It was as if she'd found just the right thing to say to make Clint feel he could be honest and easy with her. "It's not really a conspiracy," he said with a chuckle. "It's just that I really wanted to brainstorm some ideas about Bliss. And I knew Gretchen was going to a movie with a friend, so I had an hour or so free."

"And more to the point, Orson wouldn't have to know," Lucy teased him.

Again, Nick watched his brother's tension level ease. Clint didn't know it, couldn't know it, but Lucy was just doing her usual magic. In any gathering, she plucked the wallflowers from the wall, honed in on the nervous ones, found a way to smooth waters. "My grandfather and I don't seem to communicate real well," Clint admitted.

"Working with family always seems to be extra tough," she said sympathetically. She set her purse on the counter in the kitchen, then lifted a finger. "You two look really ready to talk—and I am, too, but just give me a second to pee first. I'd be more polite about it, but my reality these days is that I'm likely to run to the john about every twenty minutes."

"You want a drink?" Nick asked.

"Of course I want a drink. That'll make the problem even worse," she said wryly.

"Lemonade or iced tea?"

"Oh God. Lemonade. A tall one." She wagged her

finger again. "Don't you two dare start the meeting without me."

She dashed into the bathroom, but found them less than five minutes later. Nick had set up outside, with legal pads, pens, drinks. It was shady on the flagstone patio, with a wrought-iron table and cushioned lounges. It was one of those lazy summer afternoons, golden, lazy, still.

All three of them took chairs, and Clint picked up the ball from the start. "I just really want to be involved in the unveiling of Bliss. Behind the scenes. But part of it. I just… Hell, it's exciting."

"You bet."

Clint hesitated. "It'd probably be best if my grandfather didn't know I was behind any kind of idea. I don't need or want credit for anything. He doesn't ever have to know I had anything to say. I just wanted in on some brainstorming."

Finally, Nick saw Lucy relax, too. She'd agreed to come over, when he told her Clint wanted to talk about Bliss, but she'd still been stiff about it. Now, though, she obviously saw a role to fill—the nurturing she did best. His big, brawny brother, who could look tougher than a Hells Angel on a big Harley, was melting under Lucy's warm smiles just like everyone else.

And once Clint warmed up, he barreled on non-stop. "Most of the time, when you're marketing something, you put the product's positive features up front. You know what I mean. If it's a pretty thing you're trying to sell, you push the pretty concept. You focus on the positive, whatever it is. Never on the negative."

"Right."

"But with Bliss...I wonder if it wouldn't be a good idea to try a different twist."

Lucy propped a foot on the chaise, uncorked a pen tip with her mouth and balanced a legal pad on her knee. "Like what?"

"Like...it'd seem the obvious thing to sell Bliss as the best chocolate that's ever been made. Which it damn well *is*. But other chocolatiers have gone that route, said those words. So I think we should try something else."

"Like...?" Lucy repeated.

"Like that Bliss is dangerous."

"Dangerous..." Lucy stopped writing. Looked at him.

"I've got this picture in my head, of an ad made up of short, fast snapshots. A picture of a kid skydiving. Then a picture of an elderly couple white-water rafting. Then a young woman climbing K-2. I'm saying, snapshots of people who because of their age or appearance, would seem to be doing something exceptionally risky for them. Something dangerous. Then one last snapshot, just showing a single piece of Bliss."

"Oh God, oh God, this is good, Clint. I love it!"

"If there has to be some written copy, then adding something like…don't even take the first bite unless you're up for some danger."

Nick added, "Not for the shy or safe. Bliss is more dangerous than anything you ever dreamed of."

"Oh God, oh God," Lucy said again. "You two are so smart. This is terrific. Perfect for Bliss."

Neither were half as brilliant as Lucy made out, but Clint thrived under her praise until he was almost talking nonstop, ping-ponging ideas off the two of them faster than lightning. It was fun, not work. Nick hadn't heard his brother let loose with a big old belly laugh since he could remember, yet all of them were laughing as they stormed through a creative fest of ideas.

When they finally wound down, Lucy made another trek to the bathroom. Nick took the empty glasses into the kitchen, and made a point of waiting for her.

When she came back out and saw him, she hesitated for a moment, but after all their invigorating talking, she couldn't seem to hold her stiffness with him, at least not right then. "Why doesn't he do that with Orson?" she asked.

Nick knew she meant Clint. "He never loosens up with our gramps. Always brings an attitude. So does Orson, for that matter."

"He's so hungry to be part of Bernard's."

"I know." He added, "You really helped him, Luce."

"I wanted to." She smiled at him—the way she hadn't smiled at him in long, long days now.

He wanted to capture that smile, kiss it, kiss her, so badly it felt like a sore clawing inside him. She was so…Lucy. There was so much love in her. So much giving. She nurtured everyone, found a way to make everyone around her feel good about themselves. She didn't even see how special she was.

"Well…" When he didn't immediately say something else, she turned toward the door.

"I know I did something to hurt your feelings," he blurted out. "I'm sorry."

"No, you didn't. Nothing to be sorry about." There went the poker up her spine.

And there went panic zinging up his pulse. "You're angry at me because of making love that last time," he said.

"Why would I be angry because of that? Neither one of us said no." But she wasn't looking at him.

"But neither of us planned it. And I shouldn't have pushed."

"You didn't."

Well, no, he hadn't *exactly* pushed her. He'd just started kissing her to stop her from crying, and Armageddon sort of erupted from there. But she was chilling faster than an iceberg in the Arctic, so obviously trying to talk about that night wasn't helping. He switched gears.

"We've both been beyond busy. I haven't had a chance to ask you how the last doctor visit went."

"Fine."

Her voice was crisper than lettuce, but he tried again. "At some point you have birthing classes, right? I've been reading. I understand you need a coach—"

"Nick," she said quietly, firmly. "I don't need anything from you. You've done enough. You don't need to feel obligated to do a single other thing."

"I don't feel *obligated*—"

She interrupted. "Look. You've been great. I'm sure you don't intend this—but the problem with your being so responsible is that it makes me feel like a burden. I swear, I don't need a caretaker."

Her voice might have been gentle, but he still heard the door slam on his ego. Pretty damn obvious, she didn't want to be anywhere around him.

She surged outside and started talking to Clint. He took another second, using the excuse of dealing with the tray of glasses, but truthfully he just needed a second to get his breath back.

He'd not only lost her as a lover. He seemed to have lost her as a friend.

It was hard to imagine feeling worse, but he pulled himself together, ambled back outside. Clint was standing, getting ready to leave, just as Lucy was. But the two of them were talking like old pals.

"Okay," Clint was saying. "After work on Tuesday is a good time for me, too."

"What are you two talking about?" Nick asked.

"Lucy finds car shopping as much fun as measles," Clint said.

"You've got that right."

"So I'm going to take her. I'll bring Gretch, so the two of them can talk the color and comfort stuff, make sure she gets a girl car. But I can look under the hood for her, do that part of the job." And to Lucy, "Don't worry. We'll get this done."

"Thanks, Clint," Lucy said warmly. "I've been dreading doing this like you can't imagine."

"A lot easier when you share it with someone else."

Once they both drove off, Nick stood there, feeling stunned. She'd fought him tooth and nail on helping her buy a new car, yet was willing to let Clint do it. Clint, but not him...as if he'd suddenly turned into the lowest worm in the swamp.

Worse yet, he felt like a worm. Somehow he'd hurt her. He *had* to have hurt her. Badly. It was the only explanation for her shutting him out so completely.

It seemed like an impossible problem—how to win back a woman he'd never had.

More painful yet was that he didn't know how to even start.

BEFORE CLIMBING OUT of her audaciously red Volvo, Lucy leaned over and popped the glove compartment. Some people undoubtedly wouldn't consider her new car to be either an audacious color nor a wicked sort of wild car. Truthfully, she was getting teased right and left for her sedate choice. Others, of course, knew nothing. The glove compartment was spacious enough to hold twice the truffles her old car did.

Today was one of those days when she needed those truffles and she needed them *now*.

When both cheeks were stuffed, she opened the car door and braced for the blast of sultry August heat. Typical of this entirely ghastly day, the temperature was hot enough to fry sweat.

Like she didn't have enough to do, she'd had to leave a precious work day for a doctor appointment. It was the six-month check. Which was fine—she wasn't about to miss a checkup on the baby—but the instant she heard the baby was thriving, she relaxed. And then started getting antsy and annoyed.

The doctor claimed she hadn't gained enough weight—which was ridiculous. She was eating more than any five men put together. The doc kept asking questions about her plans, whether she wanted the baby's father as her coach, or did she want him to talk with the father about what to expect in the labor and delivery.

Lucy slammed the door on her way into the lab. Yeah, she wanted Nick for a coach, but there wasn't a way in the universe she was going to ask him. The doctor visit had only infected the sliver in her heart. Nick already felt responsible for her…and it was the one feeling she *didn't* want from him.

She was no dependent slug, dagnabbit. She'd gain

more weight, if the doctor wanted her to. And by damn, she'd be calm and happy for the baby's sake if it killed her.

"Hey, Luce. How'd the checkup go?" Reiko paused in the doorway, appeased after Lucy gave her a thumbs up and kept jogging on. "The kids are waiting for you!"

"I know, I know…"

Two bodies were waiting for her in the lab. She reminded herself that her life was going absolutely fabulous and that she was happier than she'd ever been—with only that one exception. It seemed one of those days when her mind dwelled on Nick, no matter how hard she tried. She firmed up a smile and glued it there.

"Baker, Nancy…you two ready to boogie?"

"You bet, Lucy!"

"Okay. Let's set up…." She blew a strand of hair from her face and dug in. The Bliss project was, of course, exploding. All systems were go. The greenhouses were full, extra staff and security all hired and onboard.

Lucy was just extra conscious that gigantic risks were on the table, too. They needed quantities of Bliss available for the unveiling of the initial product on Thanksgiving which meant that the initial product had to come from the original Bliss trees. After four years, those first experimental trees were in their prime production, but they needed to pour out output for that first introduction into the market-place…and the output had to be perfect.

Lucy had been fighting with the chief chocolatier at the main plant for several weeks on recipes. They still hadn't agreed on the final product, primarily be-cause Almondo refused to admit she was right.

And this afternoon, Bernard's two newest horti-culturalists needed a lesson on roasting. She'd been elected to give it to them, because no one knew the procedure as well as she did. Or so she'd told every-one, and no one—but no one—was wasting time ar-guing with her lately.

Barker and Nancy were both fresh from college. Nancy was a tall six-two and skinny as a stick. Barker had a basset hound's face and a pudgy frame, but he was sharp. They both were. She liked them both. And as it was time to work with a new batch of Bliss beans, it was also the ideal time to expose them to the roasting process.

"The thing is," she explained, "you two are used to thinking about the growing side of things. As it should be. That's your primary job. But if you don't understand what happens to the bean after that, then you'll never get the whole picture of what it takes to create a quality chocolate."

She checked once in a while to make sure their eyes weren't glazing over—it's not as if she didn't know she had a tiny tendency to rant on forever. And every few minutes, Greger's face showed up in the doorway. The third time he motioned to her—as in giving her an unspoken order to sit down.

She did. Until he was out of sight.

"We roast the bean for two reasons, and both are important. Roasting develops the flavor and aroma. And secondly, the roasting process make it easier for us to get the husk off the nib…"

When Reiko paused in the doorway a little later and pointed the royal finger, Lucy again sat down. Until she was out of sight.

The newbies were doing most of the work; Lucy just couldn't possibly take a complete back seat. They seemed to realize that she couldn't help feeling protective of her baby, because they both treated the beans with appropriate awe and respect.

"Roasting is probably the most critical part of the process, because too much or too little ruins everything. Too much will destroy the natural flavor of the bean and make it bitter. Too little makes it hard to remove the husk. And different kinds of beans need entirely different roasting temperatures. For Bliss…"

The intercom clicked on. "Hey, Luce." Fritz's voice came through. "You've got a visitor in your office."

"Who?"

"I believe it's your father."

"What?"

She couldn't leave the novices—or Bliss—at that instant, but she paged Reiko and Greger to take over for her. Once they arrived, she hustled—holding her tummy, because it wasn't easy to run with her burgeoning stomach these days—down the hall to her office.

Her dad was sitting in the side chair, hunched over, his head in his hands.

"Hey, Dad." She swooped down on him for a hug and kiss, worried to death when she saw his red eyes.

"I just came from the lawyer with your mother."

"What happened? Tell me."

"She…slapped me." Luther could barely get the words out.

Lucy tried to hunch down next to him—but that position wasn't possible—so she yanked out her own desk chair and wheeled it next to her dad. Her mom, of course, couldn't have slapped her father. Her mother had never even spanked Ginger or her when they were kids, and God knew, they'd done things to drive even a saint of a mother insane.

"You know the craziest thing, Lucy?" Her father lifted his hands in a helpless gesture.

"What?"

"She's the one who wanted the divorce all this time. I've been fighting it every step of the way. I love her. She's the one who doesn't love me anymore. Or that's what I thought. And then today, out of the blue…well, we were going over all the assets and all. I told her she could have anything she wanted. Everything she wanted. And she got all mad. I mean furious."

"I don't understand," Lucy said gently, and then reached behind her swiftly, to pour a fresh glass of water for her dad. He gulped it down like he'd been dying.

"She said she'd never wanted a divorce. I said *what?* And she said, if I gave a damn, I could have stopped this all along from the very beginning. And I said, Eve, I don't know what you want me to do. And that's when she just got all upset and kind of…slugged me."

"Slugged?"

"Well…slapped."

"Slapped?"

"I'm telling you, she *pushed* me, Lucy! I'm not making it up!"

"Okay, okay." She soothed, patted, hugged…but somewhere in her heart, she realized that she'd tried the soothing, patting, hugging thing from the beginning of this crisis with her parents. It hadn't helped her dad. Or her mom.

All her life, she'd wanted kindness to work. She was willing to give kindness a zillion chances more than anyone else did. But sometimes, as miserable as it made her, it seemed the only choice was straight old blunt honesty.

"Dad…you want to be married because being married solves some things for you. But Mom doesn't want to be a convenience. She doesn't want a marriage because it makes life easier for you—or because it makes life easier for her."

"I don't get what you mean," her father said wearily.

"Mom wants you to like being with her. And if you don't actually enjoy being with her, then she wants out."

"But of course I like being with her!"

Lucy shook her head. "Then you'd damn well better find a way to show her. Fast."

"You mean like a present?"

She could almost see the wheels turning in her dad's mind. "No," she said firmly. "You don't get off that easily, Dad. Diamonds won't solve this."

"Then *what?*"

At that exact moment—as if her pulse was suddenly exposed to an electric charge—she sensed Nick. His coat jacket was open, his face ruddy as if he'd been running. He paused in the doorway, stopped dead, and saw immediately that she was having a major personal crisis going on with her dad. If he needed her for something, he didn't let on, only made a gesture to let her know he was leaving, would catch up with her later.

"Like what?" her father repeated. "If you don't think I should give her a present—"

"Presents are nice, Dad. But they're cheap in comparison with giving her time. You need to show her that you *want* to be with her. You need to do that by spending time with her. Listening to her. Enjoying her company."

Her father fell silent, as if intensely trying to take in what she was saying.

Lucy said, "Dad. You need to get this. It isn't a game. You can't just devote a weekend to her and then go back to the way you were. Or think everything's suddenly all fixed. Because the thing is, it has to be true. You either have to really, honestly, enjoy being with her—and Mom has to be enjoy being with you—or you two really shouldn't be married anyway."

"You mean that's all your mother wants? That's all this whole crisis has been about? That's *all?*"

"That's all?" Lucy echoed. "Dad. It's everything. Love isn't about diamonds. It's about finding someone who makes you feel good about yourself. Who you can trust. Who you can share things you can't share with anyone else. Who you can…giggle with."

"Giggle," Luther echoed.

She said, "Can you still laugh with my mother?"

He said slowly, "We used to laugh all the time. Sometimes at the silliest things."

"Yeah. That's it. What you need to find again. What you need to show her. Either love her for real, Dad, or let her go."

Her dad left a short time after that. It was the craziest thing, because he seemed to feel better, and yet she felt tears threatening in her eyes.

Still, she had no time to cater to herself. She pulled herself together, and headed out—both to check on the Bliss roasting project—and to find Nick.

The roasting project had gone fabulously, but Nick was no longer around—not in any of the labs or greenhouses or offices. No one knew why he'd stopped by. Greger just mentioned that he'd seen Nick head back to his car a short time earlier.

When she sat down in the lab with Barker and Nancy again, the baby suddenly kicked, hard and exuberantly. She loved those secret baby kicks, yet this time, she touched her tummy and felt a fierce sense of loss and loneliness.

She had no reason to think Nick had stopped by just to see her—God knew she hadn't invited casual catch-ups with him in quite a while now. But damn. Her heart seemed to hold onto a little hope, no matter how hard she'd tried to turn herself into a full-time realist.

Lucy could be tough when she had to be. With her dad. With her work. With her life. And heaven knew, with herself.

So why was it so impossibly hard to stop loving that damn man?

CHAPTER SEVENTEEN

NICK SNATCHED the instruction sheet and read it for the dozenth time...then looked at the bowl full of screws and nails and washers on the floor. The instructions lied. Either that, or the manufacturer had neglected to put in the parts they claimed. Nothing worked the way it was supposed to. The piece of furniture was cockeyed and squee-jawed and a puff of wind would likely blow the whole thing apart.

Worse yet, he'd been working on this for hours. Actually, he'd been working on this multiple construction project for days—every spare hour he could beg, borrow, or steal. But this was the first time he could see the light at the end of the tunnel.

There was a chance he was going to get this done. A slim chance, but definitely a chance.

Nick figured he had only a slim chance this was going to work with Lucy, but the dynamic was the same. At least it *was* a chance. And he was sure as hell running out of time.

Heat poured in the windows. Itchy, restless heat.

Early September wasn't supposed to be this hot, yet sweat trickled down Nick's neck, under his arms, making him antsy.

Or maybe that was nerves.

Nothing was better between him and Luce. Except for the five days he'd spent in Tokyo for Bernard's, he'd seen her almost every day. She was nice. He was nice. She was helpful. He was helpful.

If they got any damn friendlier, he was gonna lose his mind. You'd think they'd never made love. You'd think they could win a prize for The Ideal Working Relationship. She didn't seem to want him any more. Hell, she didn't seem to even remember wanting him.

Where he felt sicker and lonesomer and more lost without her after every damn day.

Nick picked up a hammer and a new construction part, feeling his blood pressure zoom again, trying to remember the last time he'd laughed. But that memory didn't help him, because—wouldn't you know it?—it involved Lucy.

It *had* been funny, though. Orson had called in the middle of the afternoon. Baby was in heat, and Orson had brought in a fine Great Dane to mate with her. Whatever happened between the two dogs didn't seem to be love, because Orson was frantic. Baby had somehow gotten over the seven foot fence, leaving her would-be lover frustrated and alone.

Nick could relate all too well with the male Great

Dane. But at the time, the stress in his grandfather's voice had been the issue. He hightailed it out of the office, unfortunately wearing a suit and good shoes. Orson and Madris and the house staff were all outside, all trying to corner Baby—who was normally the most obedient dog in the universe—but not when she was in heat.

The problem for Baby, as everyone swiftly figured out, was a male marauding dog. A mutt. Uglier than sin, collarless, scruffy. So everyone was screaming and yelling, trying to catch Baby before she mated with the loser, trying to scare off the loser mutt, and nothing anyone was doing was working. Orson put in a call to the lab to get Lucy.

Baby fiercely loved Lucy. They all thought there was a chance Lucy could get the dog to come. So Lucy jogged out of the lab and charged into the fray.

The entire Bernard operation didn't come to a halt that afternoon, but close to it. He'd been the one to catch Baby. He'd taken a flying leap over a bush and tackled her. She'd seemed to remember that she loved him. Stretched out on top of him full length and lapped his face affectionately. His Italian gray suit was ruined. He'd lost a shoe. And Lucy started laughing...

He still remembered it. That sound, like music. That sound, like the one thing that could always lift his heart from any pit. That sound, like the joy he'd always felt when he was with her, that easy laughter, that spirit of fun.

When everyone returned to work—the lovelorn marauder shipped off, Baby returned to her protective pen. Orson had stood next to him for several minutes. There'd been a smile on the old man's face that finally faded.

Out of the blue he said quietly, "I've missed you, Nick."

"I've been right here."

"I mean…I've missed being close. Missed talking to you. Being with you, the way we were before."

Nick hadn't known what to say. "I never blamed you for being angry with me. I've been just as angry with myself."

"And I admit, I *was* angry." But then Orson motioned toward the lab, clearly meaning the direction Lucy had gone. "But every since, every time I see you two together, I realize I should never have opened my mouth. I shouldn't have doubted your character. I *know* what a good man you are, son. I was wrong."

Nick was speechless. He never remembered Orson offering an apology to anyone. When he lifted an arm, his grandfather immediately stepped into a shoulder-patting hug. Nick felt the fragility in the old man's bones, the comfort of being able to show caring again. No matter how rigid Orson could be sometimes, Nick fiercely loved him.

Orson pulled back after a moment, seemed to have one more thing to say. "There's no question that she's in love with you, Nick. Or why. I just wish I had a magic wand to make it right for the two of you." His grandfather had squeezed his shoulder, then ambled away.

Nick still remembered that moment, still remembered the relief he felt to have the rift healed between them...yet he was also startled at his grandfather's certainty that Lucy loved him. He'd believed just the opposite. Yet his grandfather must have seen something for him to say those words.

And if there was something to see, Nick kept thinking that there was something to fight for. So he'd started concocting a plan—a plan to win Lucy. To woo Lucy. To reach Lucy in a way he'd failed to before.

It wasn't a great plan—but once he got it in his head, he went at full-bore—and finally came together tonight.

Two o'clock in the morning, Nick sat back and surveyed his handiwork. His hands had cuts; his knees were bruised and he was whipped to beat the band. But the preparation was finally done.

Now, all he had to do was risk his heart.

Dawn rose on a dew-drenched September morning. Nick still had a mountain to put together at the last minute, but at work, he cleared his desks. Cancelled appointments. Turned off phones and pagers. He also brought Greger into the plan, so only life-threatening interruptions could get through.

Finally, at four in the afternoon, he showed up at

the lab. Naturally, when he was so anxious to find her he could hardly think, she wasn't in her office—or in any of the other nice, clean, air conditioned offices. The general lab was chock-full of staff working on various experiments and projects, ditto for the private labs after that.

Knowing Lucy, he told himself that she was probably somewhere knee-deep in mud. But his nerves were strung tighter than razor wire by the time he'd stalked in and out of three of the greenhouses and still not found her. By complete accident he finally uncovered her—actually, almost ran smack into her—charging out of a door. A restroom door.

"Nick!" she said, surprise in her voice and a flush immediately blooming on her cheeks. "I didn't know you were coming over today. What's up?"

Everything, he wanted to say, yet the look of her went straight to his head. Her tummy had blown up to about the size of a basketball now. She was wearing typically practical clothes, a red top over blue pants, a cheerful flag scarf pulling back her hair. She was still galloping around, but her full speed now had a hint of a flat-footed waddle to it.

No woman had ever struck him as sexier or more alluring. The flyaway hair and broken nails and swaybacked posture…damn. He just wanted to kidnap her, hide her away where no other men could see her. Just him.

"Nick?"

He frowned. "Lucy…I know it isn't the end of the work day. But can you manage to get away? I have something critical to tell you. About Bliss. But not here—I'd like to get off-site to talk."

"Of course." She bought into his premise with no hesitation at all, just shot him an immediate worried look. "Give me two shakes to leave word with Reiko and tell Greger that I'm leaving."

He nodded gravely. "I'll be waiting for you at the door."

It was so easy he almost felt guilty. All he'd had to say was Bliss, and Lucy never raised a single objection, didn't protest or waste time asking questions. She piled into his car without even asking where they were going. She obviously didn't care.

And that was so typical of her, he thought. When something was her responsibility or her problem, she never ducked out—even if she had to risk being with someone who'd hurt her. Someone who'd trampled her fragile heart. Someone who'd been damn stupid about how to treat her.

Someone like himself.

When his Lotus took the last turn, she glanced at him. Obviously she realized they were headed to his house now.

"It'll be totally quiet at my place. And I realize we left your car at work, but that isn't that hard to take care of. What a great choice of vehicles, by the way—"

"I've been teased right and left for picking a fuddy-duddy old-lady car," she said wryly.

"Are you kidding? That Volvo wagon is a beauty."

She slid him a sideways glance. "To be honest, I think so, too."

When he saw the new car—the one Clint had helped her buy, instead of him—Nick had had an instant, painful revelation. He'd grown up thinking of himself as basically cool, primarily because fast-lane women and people in general seemed to treat him that way. It had taken knowing Lucy to realize that he was staid in his ways. Old-fashioned, if not downright archaic, in his values. A fuddy-duddy extraordinaire—and a far, far worse one than she could ever be.

But right then, he wasn't about to dwell on anything related to himself. He swung in the drive. "What I need to talk to you about—what I need to show you—is in the far back room on the west side."

"West?"

"Left," he qualified, thinking he should have known directional words weren't her strong point. They weren't his, either, even if he'd never admit it in public.

Once he unlocked the door, she glanced at him again, as if waiting for more directives—drinks first, a clue to what was happening, anything? But no, he just motioned her with a quiet, grave expression to head on in.

It was possible she'd seen the far west room before. She'd been in the house alone several times, had probably explored all she wanted to. And certainly there was nothing special about that specific room. He just usually kept the door closed—no point in getting rooms dusty that he wasn't using.

She hesitated again, obviously building up a good head of curiosity now, but when he motioned she readily opened the door to the west room and stepped in. After that, there was silence. A lot of silence. Maybe three long, long minutes of complete and total silence.

When she finally spoke, her voice had a haunted whisper in it. "I thought you said this was about Bliss." She turned to face him, with cheeks suddenly gone pale and lips she had to press together to stop from trembling.

"It is," he assured her, and then stepped in himself.

Since Lucy could usually talk the ear off a magpie, he took her initial silence as a good omen. At least, he wanted to think so. When a man had sweated blood, guts and pride on something, he needed to know it was appreciated by someone who mattered to him.

The damn puppy wallpaper—well, a guy didn't quit just because something was confoundingly impossible, but for damn sure, he was never doing wallpaper again. Ever. The north wall was still a wee bit slanted. The crib was no longer rickety, though. In fact, it was sturdy as steel, and the torturously complicated mobile with the dancing baby animals no longer fell apart when you turned it on.

The changing table was another thing that had to be put together. In point of fact, he'd had to personally put it together three times. The basset hound rug just took throwing on the floor. Ditto for the cushion on the white rocker. Since he didn't really know what babies needed beyond all the furniture stuff, he'd bought diapers. And since diapers seem to come in fifty-seven size varieties, he'd filled up the closet with boxes of them. After that, he really didn't know if there was anything left to do. He sure hoped not.

"Nick…" Lucy said, but then stopped talking again.

"Come in. Sit down. On the floor," he coaxed her, and to speed things up a bit, he pushed off his shoes and sat down himself.

He'd laid the yellow carpet himself. He wasn't sure if yellow was okay for a nursery or not, but it was the softest, thickest carpet in the store, so that was how he'd chosen it. And in the middle of the floor space, he'd spread out a navy-blue sheet—the only color sheet he'd found in his linen closet, which certainly didn't lend itself to formal tablecloths.

In the middle of the sheet was a picnic basket. Inside was a cooler, with iced shrimp and raspberry tea, and a miniheater for the asparagus tips and carrots with almonds and egg rolls and cheddar mashed potatoes and prime rib and chicken Florentine. Planning dinner had been a little tricky. He'd known she'd be hungry; he just didn't know for what. Dessert, though, was easy.

Seven chilled cups revealed various selections of her favorite food group. One bowl held double chocolate-dipped cherries, and then came the cup of chocolate cinnamon Tuiles. Then a chocolate tiramisu tart. Down deeper was an extra large piece of a chocolate orange Marquise—bigger than the rest, because he was positive she'd really, really like it. And the last dish was a specialty in Brussels, called a Queen of Sheba cake, made with some liqueur—surely that bit of alcohol wouldn't hurt her? As long as it was baked in?—and roasted almonds and creamed butter and egg whites, and of course, the best chocolate saved for last. Bliss.

It took another few moments before Nick realized this wasn't going the way he'd hoped. She was supposed to be happy. Delighted. Surprised. Instead, she knelt down and just kept looking, then looking some more. She examined every one of those dessert cups, one at a time, and suddenly her eyes met his again.

He damn near panicked. Her eyes were welling. And she still wasn't talking.

"Take it easy, take it easy," he said rapidly. "This is not a hairy deal. This is nothing to get upset about. I just figured you'd want to eat. So that it'd naturally work out easiest if you weren't hungry when we started to talk—"

"Nick," she said. But she'd already said his name twice and then stopped up like a dam yet again.

"This is the thing." He started spilling fast—as fast as he could get the words out. He'd anticipated all kinds of responses from her when she saw the done-up nursery, but not *tears*. God. Anything but tears. "Do you remember the day your dad was in your office? Because I heard you talking to him. You were explaining to him how he was screwing up with your mom."

"You mean—a few weeks ago?"

He nodded, and then plowed on. "You were trying to tell your dad why he'd lost your mom. Your dad was more than willing to give her diamonds and presents. Couldn't wait to do that kind of thing, in fact. I understood that completely, because it was such guy thinking. But you..."

"I what?" she prodded him when he didn't immediately complete the thought.

"You explained to him that your mom didn't want *stuff*. No matter how expensive. Your mother needed to know that he *liked* being with her. She needed to feel listened to. She wanted him to enjoy her company—and for her to be able to enjoy being with him the same way. It just struck me like a thunderbolt. I couldn't stop thinking about it."

Lucy took a long straggly breath. "And that relates

to all this…" She motioned around the nursery. "How?"

"Because it made me think. It made me realize how much I'd been trying to give you *stuff*. I thought that was what you wanted. I thought that'd show you that I cared about you." It seemed his turn to take a long straggly breath. "But I hadn't really thought about it, Luce. About how much I like being with you. How much I really just plain like your company. I mean, that doesn't sound very romantic, does it? That I like to hear your ideas. That I like arguing with you. That I like listening to you rant on and on…about anything in hell you want to rant on about…because you're so damn much fun to be with when you're excited and high on life. You make me high. Hell. Just knowing I'm going to be with you lifts me up, even when I think we're going to be fighting, for Pete's sake."

She opened her mouth, but he was afraid to let her respond right then. He hadn't gotten the things said that had to be. And damn, this was hard. "I *know* you don't want to marry me, Luce. I know you don't seem to care about me that way. And I know you were really put out that last night we made love—"

"I wasn't—"

"Yeah, you were. Because you barely talked to me after that." He waved a hand, indicating that issue was irrelevant. God knew it had torn up his heart at the time, but now his heart and soul both were on the line. And her eyes were still all filled up. He had to boogie here. "Unfortunately, by the time you really seemed to want to cut us off, I realized how completely I'd fallen."

"Fallen…in love?"

"Oh, yeah. In love. Totally. With you." He tried to say it blithely, so she wouldn't realize a sudden sharp word would probably kill him right then. "But I didn't understand…until you talked to your dad…about the reasons I'd fallen so deeply. About the *whys* and *hows*. Lucy, we belong together."

Her lips parted, but he shushed her.

"Just hear me out, okay? I'd just never understood before…that some of the hugest things in life can be the simplest. As simple as a heartbeat and the sun coming up in the morning. But it *is* simple, Luce. I'd rather be with you than anyone else on the planet. I'd rather listen to you. And argue with you. And work with you. Than anyone else. Luce, I'd rather be *bored* by you. Than anyone else."

Now, he stopped looking at her. He wasn't a fragile kind of guy. Never had been, never would be, but damn. This was risking everything. And that's what had to be, his exposing his whole heart to her. But climbing K-2 couldn't be half this terrifying.

"I don't want to be with any other woman, ever," he said huskily. "It's not because of the baby, even remotely. It's only about you and me. It's about wanting to have a picnic on the floor with you. And if a man has to suffer shopping, then I only want to suffer it with you. If we see Mount Fuji or Tahiti, I went to see it with you. If you're sick, I only want you to be sick with me. And when I need to talk something out, or brainstorm, or just think through a problem, you're the one, Lucy. You're always the one. And then there's sex—"

He raised both hands to beg her for just another minute not to argue with him. "For a long time, forever, I thought sex was sex."

"It's not?" she asked.

"No. With you, it's magic." He took a deep breath. "Lucy?"

"What?"

"I told you the truth about the reason I wanted to bring you here. I needed to talk to you about a critical thing related to Bliss. This is it. You're my bliss."

Okay. He had to look up then, to see what her reaction was, to see if there was rejection in her face, or if she was thinking or if she was annoyed or what. A guy could only hold his breath for so long before dying.

She took one long, slow look...and then she jumped him.

The picnic basket went skittering. One of her sandals went flying. That tummy of hers was big enough to knock over a whale, even when she was being gentle, and she wasn't being all that gentle right then. Not with him.

"It just occurred to me…you're not eating," he realized suddenly.

"Oh, I'm hungry. You can take that to the bank. But not for food." Her slim hands framed his face, held him still, took a long, hard, hot kiss. So long, so hard, that he wasn't dead positive she was even considering letting him up for air. Ever. Eventually, though, she lifted her head, with eyes suddenly blazing. "Why didn't you ever let on that you loved me?"

"I thought I did."

"Well, you didn't, you dolt. I thought you were being nice. I thought you felt responsible. That's exactly what killed me after that last time we made love. You woke up the next morning and were all about whether I felt like hurling. Whether I needed to be spoon-fed breakfast. My sexy lover was gone. You were back to being my caretaker. Damn it, Nick, you broke my heart."

"I was trying to be *nice,*" he said, aggrieved.

"You *were.* Only I thought the only reason you were so good to me was because you felt obligated. I was a burden you felt responsible for. I could hardly tell you I was crazy in love with you, Nick, when I was the one who'd gotten us into trouble to begin with!"

"Maybe in the next life, this is going to be funny. Because I thought I couldn't tell you how hard I'd fallen, for the same reason. I thought you felt responsibility toward me. You kept trying to make the situation easier for me. I didn't have a clue you felt love. Not *that* kind of love."

"But, Nick, for heaven's sake. I slept with you. I jumped you. I sure as Pete didn't do that because I felt responsible."

"Yeah, well, I slept with you. And the last two times, I jumped you. And believe me, there was nothing remotely related to responsibility on my mind."

The way she was lying on top of him, his lungs tended to be crushed. It was an uncomfortable position for a man to live out the rest of his natural life, but the idea still soothed him. She was so close. For the first time in weeks, he had his hands on her. The feel of her skin, the scent of her hair, her silk-soft lips—the look of her went to his head like a burst of joy. Luce couldn't fib worth beans, and the look in her huge blue eyes was unquestionably, intensely loving.

"I love you, Nick. And the truth is…I'm not sure I did when I jumped you that night. I was wildly attracted. Painfully attracted. Still am," she said in a fierce whisper. "But I didn't know you well enough then to really love you."

"You don't have to say anything—"

"I don't want to talk, either. We've got years to talk. But I just need you to know, want you to know, that I'm not still in love with an image of a hero. I'm in love with the man, Nick. With you. I never saw who you were before. You're lonely, the way I am.

You take care of others, the way I do. You're so used to taking responsibility that it's tough to let down your hair. But I hope you'll find that you can, with me. Always, with me."

And then she closed her eyes and ducked down. She kissed him—really kissed him that time—in that wicked, amoral, immoral, wild way of hers. The whole world saw Lucy as the girl next door, but Nick knew, intimately well, how she could make a guy feel helpless and hot and sucked right under a spell that was bigger than him.

It took a third kiss before the last trace of anxiety whooshed away in a slow, lazy sigh. He finally believed it. That she was home with him, for good.

That *they* were home. And home free together. Just the three of them.

Talk about bliss…

EPILOGUE

LUCY PUT A HAND on her tummy—until she caught her husband glancing at her from the far side of the podium. Immediately she dropped her hand and put on her most radiant smile.

The smile was certainly real. She was just having a tiny problem with labor pains.

The baby had waited this long, so surely the darling was willing to wait for just another couple hours.

It was the day after Thanksgiving—the day a small, fancy package of Bliss had been hand-couriered to selected people around the world. Since the news was out, Orson and Nick had determined that a press conference was in order. The group had assembled on the steps of the big house.

A few crystals of snow danced in the air. Orson, Nick and Clint stood together for the first time in years. Lucy had been given a seat, possibly because her tummy was now the size of a walrus and standing for more than three seconds was downright tricky. The select handful of press didn't seem to mind coming out in the cold. Lucy's guys were all suits, so they had to be on the cool side, but she was swaddled from head to foot in down. Gretchen was sitting beside her, and on the steps near Gretchen's feet, Boo Boo was sprawled next to an extremely pregnant Baby.

Orson took first shot at the podium, introduced himself—as if the audience didn't know who he was—and then, quite quickly, turned the mike over to Nick. So typically, Nick said something brilliant and scintillating and wonderful, but then, my God but sometimes her husband could be aggravating.

He lifted a hand in her direction and introduced her, as if she had any kind of real responsibility for Bliss. Equally embarrassing was that he told the press that his wife had a surprise for all of them. That was true. But she'd never wanted credit for the idea.

Getting out of the chair almost took a forklift, but she managed to waddle over to the podium. Nick knew, darn it, he *knew* she couldn't easily shut up when the subject was Bliss, but she did her best to keep it brief.

"What we're announcing is the most revolutionary event that's ever happened in the chocolate world. Chocolate goes back three thousand years to the Olmec people…and yes, this was long before the Aztecs, contrary to traditional belief. The Olmecs were one of the earliest Mesoamerican cultures. We know this for sure because historical linguists managed to identify one of their common vocabulary words—cacao. But what the Olmecs discovered is nothing compared to what Bernard's are going expose you to with Bliss."

When she was done, one of the press in the front row piped up, "Aw, come on. But no matter how good this Bliss is, it can't possibly be all that different from other great chocolates!"

Lucy smiled. Her back ached so bad that she could barely walk—even with one hand holding her spine. She hadn't seen her feet in the last month. Had been having labor pains since six that morning.

But nothing in the universe could have stopped her from carrying a tray down to the front row. One by one, the press were allowed to choose a single truffle from the sterling tray. They were small, one-bite truffles. One bite, Lucy knew, was all it was going to take.

The dozen reporters—who were normally incapable of shutting up, and certainly incapable of telling a story without adding a sensational, scandalous slant, fell completely silent.

Lucy glanced back at Nick, who immediately winked at her. "You go, girl," he mouthed.

But she couldn't. The awed silence of the group was certainly reward for all the months and years of hard work. But she already knew that was going to happen.

Bernard's had more than a winner in Bliss. They had the future of chocolate.

But just then, she felt a spiny fist clench her tummy in two.

Granted, she was four days overdue. And she'd guessed this morning that the start of these labor pains was the real thing. Still, everyone knew first babies took forever and she'd desperately not wanted to miss this press conference. It was just…the other little twinges tended to be annoying.

This one almost brought her to her knees.

Nick, being Nick, seemed to immediately sense she was in trouble. He pelted off the podium faster than a racehorse at the Derby.

"I'm fine," she promised him. "There's no reason to hustle to the hospital. It'll be forever. And look at them, Nick. They're drooling. They're in love with Bliss. It's so wonderful. It's…" Yikes. Another crippling pain took her.

Next thing she knew, Clint had herded off the press; Nick had taken off to get the car and Lucy was installed with Orson in the warm front hall.

When another labor pain tore out all of her insides, she started to feel a little testy. "I don't know why we got married when we're never having sex again," she told Orson.

"Maybe that was a little more than I needed to know, sweetheart."

"You have no idea how impossible your grandson is. He has to have his toast buttered right to the edges."

"I'll be darned. That's what he says about you."

"He wakes up in the morning totally alert. God forbid anyone should try to sleep in for two minutes."

"Hmm. He was just mentioning that you're up at the crack of dawn, rain or shine, even on Sundays."

"It's not *me* who's fussy, Orson. It's *him*."

"Uh-huh." Orson shot another worried glance at the window, then came back down beside her.

"Orson?"

"What, dear?"

"You're not worried about us, are you? Because I love him more than my life. And he loves me. It was always my fault. The pregnancy. Not his. I really don't want you ever thinking it was his. But he is so wonderful. I never imagined being this happy—or that marriage could be this splendiforously magical. Although I have to admit, at this specific moment..."

There it was. Another wave of a pain, coming with the speed of a tidal wave.

Orson, who hadn't been listening to her, said, "Damn it. Maybe we should have called an ambulance."

A joke, Lucy thought. Nick would never trust an ambulance. Not with her and the baby. And less than a second later, he shot through the front door and immediately scooped her up. It was no small feat, scooping her up now that she weighed several million pounds—at least temporarily. But at the moment, she forgot Orson, forgot the dogs, even forgot Bliss.

She was in Nick's arms, looking up at his dark, loving eyes, feeling the fast, rough brush of a kiss before he handed her into the front seat of the car. That kiss shouldn't have made her think of eagles, but it did.

The lone eagle winging across the water alone—the picture they both owned, both loved—had always been her Nick. His loneliness had reached her the same, exact way that hers had reached him.

Her lover was so like her.

But neither were lonely any more.

And an hour and sixteen minutes later, they had a dark-haired, dark-eyed beauty of a son. Their first.

But not their last.

* * * * *

Jennifer Greene will be back with another fabulous book for HQN soon. In the meantime, don't miss her Silhouette Desire, THE SOON-TO-BE-DISINHERITED WIFE, available in June 2006.